超簡單
英文文法速成

◎ 實踐大學應用外語學系專任副教授 李普生 著 ◎

書泉出版社 印行

序 (Preface)

　　如果說文法是一門生動活潑的學門，絕對沒有人會相信；規則繁特例多，觀念抽象解說難懂。多少人原本想要學好英文但卻因文法的阻撓而興趣大失信心大損！但是，文法就如雞肋：食之無味棄之可惜。

　　如同古人所說：無規矩不成方圓。做事要有計畫，做人要講道理；學好英文就得從掌握熟悉並善用文法開始。近日有不少專家學者主張，學英文時文法不重要。如果今天講的是學「英語」，編者絕對舉雙手說贊成，因為語言使用首在溝通，只要意思能夠傳達出去，過份拘泥在文法對語言的使用實在只有百害而無一益。但若今天所專注的是「英文」的學習，那文法，不論喜歡與否，它都是重要而不可或缺的基本入門知識！既然文法不可免，何不用一種輕鬆的心情，透過簡明扼要的敘述和淺顯易懂的例句說明來徹底且一勞永逸地解決它？這就是本書編寫時所抱持的態度。

　　本書從名詞出發，在對代名詞和動詞的說明後，討論主動詞之間數的一致；接著進入與動詞相關的各種應用，然後形容詞和副詞等修飾語的使用，再進入與句意雖無直接關聯但卻能影響句意詮釋的冠詞和介系詞，最後全書以基本句型做結束。編者以為這種編輯順序最能將各種詞類彼此的關係和影響表現無遺。在每個章節中，「定義」將基本說明首先帶出，「重點」則告訴讀者在本章節中應該要有的觀念和認知，「用法」則分門別類將可能有的應用列舉出來並配合與文字說明順序一致的例句加以佐證；每個章節後並提供「實用測驗」幫助讀者對先前的討論做驗收。

如同做任何事一樣，成功之道無他唯勤而已；要能確實掌握文法，就必須花時間下功夫勤背誦多練習。只有讓自己能先在腦海裡有英文文法規則，才能在日常口語表達文字說明閱讀聆聽中找到可以依循的道理規則，才能確實了解句意文義並學會應用表達。

　　願以上述「笨鳥雖慢飛但終能飛」的傻勁與所有有志學會學好英文的人共勉之！

李普生

目錄 (Contents)

序 001

第一章　名詞 001

第二章　代名詞 033

第三章　動詞 063

第四章　主詞與動詞間數的一致 093

第五章　時態 103

第六章　助動詞 123

第七章　語態 137

第八章　語氣 151

第九章　不定詞 165

第十章　動名詞 181

第十一章　分詞 197

第十二章　形容詞 209

第十三章　副詞 ·· 241

第十四章　介系詞 ·· 263

第十五章　連接詞 ·· 283

第十六章　冠詞 ·· 299

第十七章　子句，句子及基本句型 ·· 311

1 名詞 (Nouns)

用來形容人事物地方或抽象觀念的字詞。不論任何語言,名詞幾乎是所有人所學到的第一種詞。

■ **本章重點**

- 名詞的用法
- 名詞的種類
- 名詞的數
- 名詞的格
- 名詞的性別

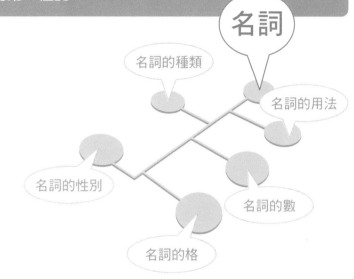

● **名詞的用法:** 名詞的功用是用來充當句子的主詞、直接受詞、間接受詞、主詞補語、受詞補語,以及主詞同位語。

名詞當主詞	**Jack** has been working for the ABC Company for ten years. Jack 已在 ABC 公司工作達十年。
名詞當受詞	Jack told **Mary** that he would be late for dinner this morning. Jack 今早告訴 Mary 他晚餐時會遲到。
名詞當直接受詞,當間接受詞	Jack gave a **bracelet** to **Mary** as her birthday present. Jack 送 Mary 一支手鐲當生日禮物。
名詞片語當主詞補語	Jack is **a diligent worker**. Jack 是位勤勉的工作者。

名詞片語當受詞補語	Jack picked John **his teammate**. Jack選John當他的隊友。
名詞片語當主詞同位語	Jack, **an experienced worker**, has been with our firm for ten years. Jack，一名經驗老到的工作者，已在我們公司十年之久。

● 名詞的種類

1. 可數名詞

◆ 普通名詞：表示同類的人、地方、動植物及事物，所共有的名稱。

例 a boy、an orange、the bird、this city、those tigers、some books、many flowers...。

1 單數普通名詞前需加冠詞a、an、the；若名詞前用所有格（如：my、your、his、her、our、their、John's...）或指示代名詞（如：this、that、these、those）或不定代名詞（如：one、each、every、some、any、which...）修飾時，則可不必再加冠詞。

▶He is **a** smart **boy**.
他是一位精明的男孩。

▶I met **a beggar** on my way to work this morning.
我今早在上班路上遇到一名乞丐。

▶**John's bag** is heavier than mine.
John的袋子比我的袋子重。

▶**Which book** do you like better?
你比較喜歡哪本書？

2 複數普通名詞後需加 -s或 -es或 -ies，前面不可加冠詞；若為限定用法則可加定冠詞the。

▶Boys are usually taller and bigger than girls in size.
一般而言，男孩比女孩體型來得大。

▶The boys who are playing baseball are my students.
在打棒球的男孩是我的學生。

3 「冠詞 + 單數普通名詞」與複數名詞同樣可用來代替同類的全體。

▶A computer is a useful tool in searching for information.
= The computer is a useful tool in searching for information.
= Computers are useful tools in searching for information.
電腦在搜尋資料時是個有用的工具。

➕例外 若man指全人類或全體男人，woman指全體女人時，前面不加冠詞。

▶Man is the lord of creation.
人類是創造之王。

▶Man is usually stronger than woman physically.
男人在身體上較女人來得更強壯。

4 「The +單數普通名詞」有時可當抽象名詞使用。

▶The pen（=literary influence，文字影響）is mightier than the sword（= military power，武力）.
文比武強。

▶What is learned in the cradle（搖籃）（=infancy） is carried to the grave（墳墓）（=death）.
幼時所學至死不忘。

5 普通名詞當作專有名詞用時，通常指家族或親屬關係，其字首需大寫。

▶Father will leave for Hong Kong tomorrow.
我父親明天將去香港。

▶Tiger belongs to the Cat family.
老虎屬貓科。

6 普通名詞當作物質名詞用時，不需加冠詞，意思指構成該
名詞的物質。

▶ Do you like to eat **fish**?
你喜歡吃魚嗎？

7 有些普通名詞若用來表示功用而非具體存在的事物體時，
尤其在介詞片語中，則不需加冠詞。

▶ The wounded man was sent to **hospital** immediately.
傷者立即被送醫。

▶ The wounded man was sent to the **hospital** immediately.
傷者被立即送到這家醫院。

類似

at school（上課）、at home（在家）、at table（用餐）、
by train or bus（搭火車或公車）、give ear to=listen to（傾
聽）、on foot（步行）、hand in hand（攜手）…。

◆ 集合名詞：是生物或事物的集合體的名稱；可視為成員總
和，但習慣上被視為一個整體。

例 family、class、fleet、committee、audience、crowd、crew、par-
ty、army...。

1 集合名詞也有單複數之分。

▶ There are three **families** living in this building.
這棟建築物中有三戶人家。

▶ He was born in a large **family**.
他來自一個大家庭。

2 有些集合名詞當句子的主詞，其意在強調整個集合體，應
視為單數，故取單數形動詞；若該集合名詞是強調組成該
集合體的各個份子時，雖為單數形但需用複數形動詞。

▶My **family is** a large one.
我的家庭是個大家庭。

▶My **family are** all well.
我的家人都安好。

3 「people」當「人」的意思時，除限定用法外，否則不需加冠詞，也不可加 "s"，其後接複數形動詞；若作「民族」解釋時，視為普通名詞，可有單複數形，且單數形時亦可加冠詞。

▶The streets were crowded with **people**.
街上擠滿了人。

▶**The people** living in this street are to vote for him.
住在這條街上的人都將會把票投給他。

▶The Chinese are **an** industrious **people**.
中國人是個勤勉的民族。

▶There are many **peoples** in Asia.
在亞洲有很多不同的民族。

4 有些集合名詞無複數形，但當複數用。

▶The **police are** searching for the murderer.
警察正在搜尋謀殺犯。

▶**Mankind are** intelligent animals.
人類是有智慧的動物。

🔖類似

clergy（神職人員）、gentry（上流人士）、jury（陪審團）、the Chinese、the Japanese、the French、cattle、poultry（家禽）、the public（公眾）、the majority of...。

5 意思上為集合名詞的物質名詞，只可用單數形，取單數動詞，不能用冠詞來修飾。若需修飾，要用a piece of、an article of、an item of、much、little或a little等數量詞來表示其量。

▶Chairs and desks are **all furniture**.
桌椅都是家具。

▶There is **little furniture** except an old piano in the room.
屋內除了一架舊鋼琴外幾乎沒有任何家具。

▶**A** bed is a useful **piece of** furniture.
床是件有用的家具。

> **類似**
>
> 類似名詞有food、clothing（衣物、衣類）、produce（農產品）、game（獵物、野味）、merchandise（商品、貨物）、machinery（機器）…。

2. 不可數名詞

◆ 專有名詞：用來表示特定的人、地或事物所專用的名稱。

1 歷史文件、機構組織、宗教派別以及它們的聖蹟史書等也屬於專有名詞。此類名詞的第一個字母需大寫，一般不加冠詞，也沒複數形。

例 John、Shakespeare...、Taiwan、New York...、The Bible...。

> **類似**
>
> 一年的十二個月（January, February...），一星期的七天（Monday, Tuesday...）要大寫，但一年的四季（spring, summer...）則不要。天體的名稱如：Mars（火星）、Venus（金星）等要大寫，但earth, sun與moon則不需。

2 有些專有名詞如：河流、海灣、海峽、海（洋）、船名、群島、半島、山脈、公共建築物、新聞雜誌或刊物、沙漠、條約、國家全名等前需加定冠詞the。

例 the Yellow River（黃河）、the Taiwan Strait（臺灣海峽）、the China Sea（中國海）、the Pacific Ocean（太平洋）、the Queen Mary（瑪麗皇后號）、the Philippines（菲律賓群島）、the Alps（阿爾卑斯山）、the White House（白宮）、the Ministry of Education（教育部）、the Reader's Digest（讀者文摘）、the China Times（中國時報）、the Sahara Desert（撒哈拉沙漠）、the Treaty of Paris（巴黎和約）、the Republic of China...。

➕例外 孤山孤島不需加 the，例：Mt. Ali、Formosa。

3 有些語文的名稱之後有 "language"時則要加 "the"。

▶Many foreigners say that **the Chinese language** is hard to learn.
很多外國人說中文很難學。

▶Chinese is my native language.
中文是我的母語。

4 有些人名的專有名詞前若附有表示特質的形容詞時，其前要加冠詞。

▶the dauntless Sun Yat Sen.
不屈不撓的孫中山。

▶the ambitious Caesar.
野心勃勃的凱撒。

5 專有名詞轉為普通名詞時，第一個字母仍需大寫，但前可加冠詞且可當複數用。

▶He wishes to become **an Edison**
他希望能變成像愛迪生般的發明家。

▶There are **many Edisons** in our class.
我們班上有許多發明家。

▶He is **the Edison** of the age.

他是當今偉大的發明家。

▶There are **a Monet** and **two Millets** in the art museum.

美術館中有一幅莫內和兩幅米勒的畫。

◆ 物質名詞：用來表示製成物品的物質名稱。

例 材料：cotton、silk、cloth、paper、stone...。

食物：meat、fish、bread、sugar、butter...。

液體、氣體：water、ice、ink、oil、air、gas（煤氣）、smoke、wind...。

金屬：gold、silver、iron、lead（鉛）、copper（銅）、tin（錫）...。

化學元素：oxygen（氧）、hydrogen（氫）、nitrogen（氮）...。

1 物質名詞前不加冠詞，沒複數形，但限定用法時前可加冠詞。

▶**Water** is very important in our life.

水在我們生活中非常重要。

▶I had **a lot of** water after the 10-mile run.

在十英哩路跑後我喝了很多水。

▶**The** water in that bottle tastes funny.

那瓶中的水嚐起來怪怪的。

2 物質名詞可用表示數量的形容詞來修飾。

▶Is there **any water** left in the bottle?

瓶中還有任何水嗎？

▶**A great deal of money** was spent on this project.

這個計畫花了很多錢。

🔖 類似

類似形容詞有a cup of、a bottle of、a spoonful of（一匙）、a piece of、a sheet of（一張）、a loaf of（一條）、a cake of（一塊）、a pound of、a gallon of（一加侖）、a yard of（一碼）、a foot of（一呎）...。

（其他數量修飾語請參看本章最後的「補充」1）

3 物質名詞也可當普通名詞用。

▶ It's a good **wine**.
這是好酒。

▶ There **are various wines** at that store.
那店裡有不同種類的酒。

▶ Iron is **a** useful **metal**.
鐵是種有用的金屬。

▶ There was **a** heavy **rain** last night.
昨晚下了場大雨。

▶ I saw **a light** in the distance.
我看到遠方的一道光。

◆ 抽象名詞：表示性質、動作、狀態或學科、疾病等無法接觸或感觸的名稱。

例 性質：honesty、kindness、wisdom、diligence...。

動作：success、failure、movement、action...。

狀態：manhood、friendship、neighborhood...。

疾病、學科：literature、physics、influenza、measles、can-
cer...。

1 抽象名詞一般用法不能用複數；除了限定用法時前可加定冠詞the外，其餘皆不可把冠詞置於其前。

▶ **Health** is better than **wealth**.
健康勝過財富。

▶ That **time** is **money** is true.
時間就是金錢是真的。

▶ **The poor** envy the comfort of the rich.
窮人羨慕富人的舒適。

2 抽象名詞轉用作普通名詞時，有複數形，其前亦可置不定冠詞。抽象名詞在下列情形下可轉用作普通名詞。

表示據該抽象名詞特質的人、事、物。

▶The woman was **a beauty** when she was young.

這婦人年輕時是位美女。

▶Humility is one of **his beauties**.

謙恭是他的美德之一。

表示具有該抽象名詞特質的行為。

▶He has done me **many kindnesses**.

他幫我很多忙。

▶Would you do me **a kindness**?

能幫我個忙嗎？

表示特質的種類。

▶Patience is **a virtue**.

忍耐是種美德。

▶Not having enough fresh water is **a hardship**.

沒有足夠的飲用水是件苦事。

（其他用法請參看本章最後的「補充」2）

3 抽象名詞的慣用語

抽象名詞 + itself	= very + 形容詞
all + 抽象名詞	

▶He is **kindness itself**.

= He is **all kindness**.

= He is **very kind**.

他很仁慈。

🔹類似

all cruelty = cruelty itself = very cruel（很殘忍）

all patience = patience itself = very patient（很有耐心）

all hospitality = hospitality itself = very hospital（很好客）

4 of + 抽象名詞 = 形容詞

of + great + 抽象名詞= very + 形容詞

of + no + 抽象名詞 = not + 形容詞

▶He is a man **of ability.**

= He is an **able** man.

他是個有能力的人。

▶It is **of no use** feeling sorry for what had already happened.

= It is **useless** to feel sorry for what had already heppened.

= It is **not useful** to feel sorry for what had already happened.

對過往的事感傷是於事無補的。

🎵 類似

of ability = able（有能力的）、of experience = experienced（有經驗的）、of value =valuable（有價值的）、of beauty = beautiful、of learning = learned（有學問的）、of courage = courageous（有勇氣的）、of wisdom = wise（有智慧的）、of wealth = wealthy、of interest = interest-ing、in length = long、in depth = deep、in width = wide、in height = high。

▶The river is one hundred feet in width.

= The river is one hundred feet wide.

這河有一百呎寬。

▶The retired president was a man of wisdom.

= The retired president was wise.

這位退休的總經理是個智者。

5 with / in / by / on + (great) + 抽象名詞 = (very) + 副詞

▶All students are doing their work **with care** (= carefully).

所有學生都小心地做功課。

▶I met him **by accident** (= accidentally) in the convention yesterday.
我昨天在大會和他不期而遇。

▶I didn't mean to hurt you **on purpose** (= purposely).
我不是故意想傷害你。

▶The girl was flushed **in excitement** (= excitedly).
這女孩因興奮而臉紅。

類似

▶with ease = easily、with diligence = diligently、with patience = patiently、with difficulty = difficultly、with fairness = fairly（相當地）。

▶by chance = by accident = not on purpose = accidentally（偶然地）、by mistake = mistakenly（錯誤地）、by good luck = luckily。

▶in wonder = wonderfully、in amazement = amazedly（吃驚地）、in time = early enough（及時地）、in private = privately、in public = publicly、in triumph = triumphantly（凱旋地）。

▶on time = punctually（準時地）。

6 定冠詞 + 形容詞 = 抽象名詞

▶**The poor** discourages me very much.
= **Poverty** discourages me very much.
貧窮讓我沮喪。

▶**The beautiful** pleases us.
= **Beauty** pleases us.
美麗愉悅吾心。

類似

the rich = wealth、the true = truth、the false = falsehood

定冠詞+形容詞也可能會變成集合名詞：
▶ The rich are not necessarily happier than the poor.
富人未必比窮人更快樂。

7 有些普通名詞在某些情形下被當抽象名詞用。

▶ You didn't use your **head** when you did it.
你做這事時沒用腦子。

▶ He did this to save his **face**.
他做這事是為了保住面子。

（其他用法請參看本章最後的「補充」3）

● **名詞的數**：單數，複數；而變化則有規則及不規則兩種。

1. 單數名詞的基本規則變化

單數名詞變複數名詞，在字尾加-s；若字尾為無聲子音讀成【s】，為有聲子音時讀成【z】。	例 book-books、daughter-daughters、month-months。
若單數名詞字尾為「-s」、「-sh」、「-ch」、「-x」、「-z」時，加es讀成【ɪz】	例 bus-buses、box-boxes、watch-watches。
若單數名詞字尾為「-子音 + o」時，通常加es讀成【z】。	例 hero- heroes、potato-potatoes 但 piano-pianos、photo-photos。
若單數名詞字尾為「-母音 + o」時，只加s讀成【z】。	例 radio-radios、zoo-zoos、bamboo-bamboos、kilo-kilos、tobacco-tobaccos、tempo（速度、拍子）-tempos、solo（獨唱、獨奏）-solos、kimono（和服）-kimonos。

2. 單數名詞較複雜的規則變化

若單數名詞字尾為「-子音＋y」時，把y改為i再加es，但「-母音＋y」時，只加s，發音都讀成【z】。	例 country-countries、lady-ladies、baby-babies、boy-boys、valley-valleys。
但單數名詞字尾為「y」，而其前為「qu」時，仍需把「y」改為「i」再加「-es」。	例 colloquy（對白）-colloquies、soliloquy（獨白）-soliloquies。
單數名詞字尾為「f」或「fe」時，改為ves讀成【vz】。	例 thief-thieves、wife-wives、wolf-wolves。

➕ 例外 ▶belief（信仰、信念）-beliefs、chief-chiefs、roof-roofs、safe（保險箱）-safes。

▶proof（證據、物證）-proofs、gulf（海灣）-gulfs、fife（笛子）-fifes、handkerchief-handkerchiefs。

3. 複合名詞把主要字改為複數形

例 mother-in-law→mothers-in-law、go-between（中間人）→go-be-tweens、forget-me-not（勿忘我）→forget-me-nots、passer-by→passers-by、step-son→step-sons、washer-man→washer-men（洗衣工人）…。

有些複合字變複數時，每個字都要改為複數形。	例 man-servant→men-ser-vants、woman-student→women-students。

4. 數字、文字、字母或記號的複數加「-'s」或「-s」

例 6→6s / 6's
90→90s / 90's
+→+'s（加號）

six→sixes

four→fours

?（問號）→?'s

B→Bs／B's

M.P.→M.P.s／M.P.'s

-（減號、負號）→-'s (minus signs)

but→buts／but's

that→thats／that's

但

No (number).→Nos.

Rd (road).→Rds.

yr.→yrs.

hr.→hrs.

apt.（apartment）→apts.

dept.（department）→depts.

+例外 ▶ l.（line）→ll.（lines）

▶ P.（page）→PP.（pages）

▶ adj.→adjj

▶ ft.（foot）→ft.（feet）

▶ in.（inch）→in.（inches）

5. 有些名詞改成複數時是採用不規則的變化

例 man-men、woman-women、tooth-teeth、foot-feet、mouse-mice、ox-oxen、goose-geese、child-children、louse（蝨子）-lice、Englishman-Englishmen、Frenchman-Frenchmen、gentleman-gentlemen、Mr.-Messrs。

6. 有些名詞單複數同形

例 sheep、deer、Chinese、Japanese、Portuguese、Swiss、gross、swine、aircraft、corps（軍團）、fish、meat、rice...。

7. 有些名詞則是複數形單數義

例 falls（瀑布）、series（叢書、聯賽）、measles（麻疹）、shambles（屠宰場、流血事件）、summons（傳票）、lens（透鏡、水晶體）、bellows（風箱）、amends（賠償）、cross-roads（十字路口）、news...。

8. 有些名詞則是複數形複數義

例 scissors、riches（財富）、pants、remains（殘骸）、savings（儲蓄）、dregs（殘渣）、tongs（火鉗）、arms（武器）、pincers（鑷子）、annals（年鑑）...。

9. 有些名詞單複數形各有不同意義

例 color / colors（顏色 / 旗幟）、custom / customs（習俗 / 海關）、compass / compasses（羅盤 / 圓規）、effect / effects（效果 / 動產）、glass / glasses（玻璃 / 眼鏡）、letter / letters（字母 / 文學）、manner / manners（方法 / 禮貌）、number / numbers（數字 / 算數）、order / orders（命令、訂單 / 宗教、社團）、part / parts（部分 / 零件）、force / forces（力量、勢力 / 軍隊）、good / goods（利益、好處 / 商品、貨物）、look / looks（觀看 / 容貌）、advice / advices（忠告 / 消息）、honor / honors（名譽 / 優等）、work / works（作品 / 工廠）、spirit / spirits（心境 / 烈酒）、air / airs（曲調 / 裝腔作勢）...。

10. 有些名詞則有兩種複數形且每種複數形的意義皆不同

例 brother-bothers / brethren（同道、同好）、antenna-antennas（天線）/ antennae（觸鬚）、cloth-cloths（布）/ clothes（衣服）、foot-feet / foot（步兵）、genius-geniuses（天才）/ genii（精靈）、horse-horses / horse（騎兵）、index-indexes（索引）/ indices（指標）、medium-mediums（媒介物）/ media（媒體）、penny-pennies（一分錢）/ pence（便士）...。

11. 有些名詞則會有不同於一般複數變化的複數形

例 analysis-analyses、axis（軸心）-axes、basis-bases（基礎、基本原理）、crisis-crises（危機）、ellipsis（省略法）-ellipses、emphasis-emphases（重要性）、parenthesis（括弧）-parentheses、thesis-theses（論文、主題）、alumnus（男校友）-alumni、alumna（女校友）-alumnae、focus-foci（焦點、中心）、nucleus（核心、細胞核）-nuclei / nucleuses、stimulus-stimuli（刺激）、formula-formulae（公式、配方）、bacterium（細菌）-bacteria、datum-data（資料）、medium-media（媒介、媒體）、appendix（附錄、盲腸）-appendices、phenomenon-phenomena（現象）、bureau（五斗櫃、辦公室）-bureaux、madame（女士）-mesdames…。

12. 複數的數詞與名詞連成一個複合字時，該名詞需用單數形

▶He is a ten-year-old boy.

= The boy is ten years old.

他是一個十歲大的男孩。

▶This is a ten-story building.

= The building is ten stories high.

這是棟十層高的建築。

13. 數詞之後的字，如：dozen、score、hundred、thousand、million等數量詞時，不可加「s」；但這些字若表示不定數量而且其後接著「of」的片語時，則要加「s」

▶Can you lend me ten thousand dollars?

你能借我一萬元嗎？

▶There are thousands of people in this auditorium.

在禮堂中有數以千計的人。

14. 表示自某年起至某年止之中的各年代的名詞要用複數形

▶He stayed in the U.S. when he was in his **teens**.
他十幾歲時待過美國。

▶They married when they were in their **twenties**.
他們在二十幾歲時結的婚。

● **名詞的格：** 名詞因在句中的位置和關係，可分三種格：主格、
受格和所有格。

1. 主格：句中擔任主詞、主詞補語、主詞同位語或稱呼語

主詞	**John** is the most diligent intern in the office. John是所有實習生中最勤奮的。
主詞補語	The most diligent intern in the office is **John**. 最勤奮的實習生是John。
主詞同位語	My cousin、**John**、visited me at work yesterday. 我的表（堂）兄弟John昨天來我上班的地方拜訪我。
稱呼語	**Boys**、be kind to others. 孩子們，待人要仁慈。

2. 受格：在句中擔任動詞或介詞的受詞、受詞補語或受詞同位語

動詞的受詞	I **know the boy** standing at the door. 我認得站在門口的男孩。
介詞的受詞	He likes to play **with Mary**. 他喜歡和Mary一起玩。
受詞補語	We call **him Peter**. 我們叫他Peter。
受詞同位語	I met **Mr. Smith, the principal**. 我遇見校長Mr. Smith。

> 🎧 小提醒

> 名詞的拼法不會因主格或受格在外觀上有任何改變；
> 相形之下，代名詞則會因主格、受格或所有格而在拼法
> 上有所不同。
>
> ▶John loves Mary; he loves her so much.
> 　John愛Mary；他愛她。

3. 所有格：在句中擔任形容詞用來修飾名詞。有生命的名詞在字尾加「's」或「'」即成名詞的所有格

▶ **Tom's** father is a popular musician.
　Tom的父親是位音樂家。

▶ That is my **brother's** dictionary.
　這是我兄弟的字典。

1 無生命的東西，僅能用of片語形成所有格。

▶ The name **of the game** is to win.
　贏得勝利就是遊戲規則。

▶ The people **of this country** are all hard-working people.
　這個國家的人民都是辛勤工作的人。

2 「's」的發音與複數字尾的發音相同。若為無聲子音【k、p、t、f、θ】，「's」發為【s】；若為有聲子音或母音，「's」發為【z】；前有【s、z、tʃ、ʃ、dʒ】時，「's」發為【ɪz】。

例 Philip's、cat's、Ruth's、king's、girl's、Betty's、prince's、boss's、George's...。

3 複數名詞字尾有s時，只加上「'」。

例 a girls' school、birds' nests。
若複數名詞字尾沒有s，仍要加「's」。
women's club、children's hospital。

4 有些專有名詞的字尾剛好有「s」，此時變成所有格要加「'」
或「's」皆可；但也有些只能加「'」。

例 Keats' poems / Keats's poem（濟慈的詩）、Mr. Jones's children /
Mr. Jones's children（瓊斯先生的小孩）、Jesus'、Socrates' works
（蘇格拉底的作品）、Moses' teachings（摩西的教誨）…。

5 "sake"此字之前的名詞字尾沒有發【s】音則加上「's」；若前
字字尾有發【s】音，則只加上「'」。

例 for pity's sake（發發慈悲）、for God's sake（看在老天份
上）…。
for convenience' sake (=for the sake of convenience)（方便起
見）…。
for goodness' / goodness sake（行行好）、for conscience'（良知）
/ conscience sake…。

6 複合名詞、名詞片語中的所有格，在最後一個字加「's」。

例 my brother-in-law's bicycle、somebody else's hat…。

7 由and所連接兩個以上的名詞共有一物或數物時，只在最後一
個名詞字尾加「's」；各有其物或數物時，每個名詞字尾都要
加「's」；共同所有物後接單數形動詞，個別所有物後接複數
形動詞。

▶Jack and Mary's school is located on the top of the mountain.
John和Mary的學校座落在山頂。

▶Jack's and Mary's schools are located on the opposite sides of the
mountain.
John的學校和Mary的學校在山的兩邊。

8 若所有格所修飾的名詞為house、store、shop、hospital…時，名
詞通常可省略。

▶I met him at my uncle's (house).
我在我叔叔（伯伯）家遇到他。

▶My father is now in the barber's (shop).
我父親現在在理髮店。

▶I have a toothache, and have to go to the dentist's (clinic / office).
我牙疼，我必須去牙醫診所。

9 雙重所有格：所有格不能與下列形容詞如：a、an、this、that、these、those、another、some、any、no、which、what同時放在同一個名詞之前；若必須，則以「a, an, this... + 名詞 + of + 所有格名詞」的句型表示。

▶I met a friend of mine.
我遇到我的一個朋友。

▶Any friend of my daughter's is welcome here.
歡迎我女兒的任何朋友來這。

▶That watch of my brother's is of famous brand.
我兄弟的手錶是名牌。

10 所有格的功用

表所有者	the boy's watch、my father's book...。
表發明者、編著者	Edison's phonograph、Shakespeare's plays...。
表用途目的	a girls' school = a school for girls 女子學校 a children's hospital = a hospital for children 兒童醫院
所有格 + 名詞 = 主詞 + 動詞的關係	He is sure of his son's success. = He is sure that his son will succeed. 他確認他的兒子會成功。 He insisted on Tom's punishment. = He insisted that Tom should be punished. 他堅持Tom該被處罰。

所有格＋名詞＝動詞＋受詞的關係	They came to that boy's rescue. = They came to rescue that boy. 他們來救那男孩。 I am surprised at John's passing the entrance exam.＝ I am surprised that John has passed the entrance exam. 我對John通過入學考試感到驚訝。

11 下列名詞雖為無生命，但可用「's」或「'」形成所有格。

時間	a day's work（一天的工作）、two weeks' pay（兩週的薪資）、today's paper...。
距離	a mile's walk、a stone's throw（近處）...。
重量	a pound's weight、five tons' cargo...。
價值	ten dollars' worth...。
擬人化名詞	the sun's ray（陽光）、the earth's surface（地球表面）、the ocean's roar（海洋的怒吼）、Heaven's will（上天的意旨）、fortune's smile（幸運之神的眷顧）、Nature's work（大自然的傑作）…。
慣用語	He came to his journey's end. 他已到了人生的盡頭。 When he heard the news, he was at his wit's end. 他聽到消息後束手無策。

🔗 類似

at one's fingers' ends（精通）、out of harm's way（安然無恙）、to one's heart's content（盡興的）、at arm's length（伸手可及之處）、at one's wit's end（智窮計盡）、by a hair's breath（千鈞一髮）、at a stone's throw（一箭之遙）、at the sword's points（劍拔弩張）、a wolf in sheep's skin（偽善者）、in one's mind's eye（想像中）、a bird's eye-view（鳥瞰）…。

● **名詞的性別：**可分為陽性、陰性、通性和無性等四種。

陽性（**masculine**）	father、man、boy、he。
陰性（**feminine**）	mother、woman、girl、she。
通性（**common**）	student、child、teacher、parent。
無性（**neuter**）	desk、stone、pencil、tree、building。

1. 陰陽兩性用不同的字來表示

例 father-mother、uncle-aunt、brother-sister、gentleman-lady、sir-madam、king-queen、widower（鰥夫）-widow、monk-nun、ox / bull-cow、dog-bitch、cock-hen、drake（公鴨）-duck、horse-mare、lad（少年）-lass（少女）、bridegroom（新郎）-bride...。

2. 在名詞前或後加上一個字來區分陰陽

例 boy friend-girl friend、peacock（孔雀）-peahen、male cousin-female cousin、he-goat-she-goat、landlord（房東）-landlady、bull-calf（小公牛）-cow-calf、man-servant（男僕）-maid-servant...。

3. 在陽性名詞字尾加「ess」，或稍加變化再加「ess」

例 lion-lioness、count（男伯爵）-countess、host（男主人）-hostess、author-authoress、actor-actress、tiger-tigress、governor-governess（女家庭教師）、heir（男繼承人）-heiress、poet（男詩人）-poetess、emperor-empress...。

4. 陽性名詞均用he、him代替，陰性名詞均用she、her代替，通性名詞可用he、him或she、her代替，無性名詞用it、its代替

▶ My **uncle** called my mother to ask her when she would visit **him** in Taichung.
　我舅舅打電話問我母親何時她會到臺中探視他。

▶ Every **boy** has **his** own book.
　每個男孩都有自己的書。

▶ I bought a **pen** and gave **it** to my friend.
　我買了支筆並把它給我朋友。

▶ **Children** depend on **their** parents for living.
　小孩依賴他們的父母維生。

5. 「infant」、「baby」、「child」可用he或she代替，但「infant」與「baby」通常以it代替較普遍

▶ The **baby** cries when **it** is hungry.
　小嬰兒餓了就會哭。

▶ The **child** lost **his** way in the crowd.
　這小孩在人群中迷路了。

6. 國家或都市的名稱通常視為陰性，多以she、her代替，但也會有用it、its代替的用法

▶ **China** is proud of **her** long history.
　中國以她悠久歷史為傲。

▶ **Finland** is famous for **its** / **her** numerous lakes.
　芬蘭以她無數的湖泊著稱。

7. 船、飛機、火車等交通工具通常視為陰性

▶ The **ship** was on **her** maiden voyage.
　這艘船在她首航中。

8. 擬人化名詞的性別雖多屬無性，但在詩歌散文戲劇童話中

(A)凡具「強而有力」，「偉大」，「恐怖」等特質的名詞，習慣視為陽性。	the sun、war、death、summer、winter、mountain、time、wind、anger。
(B)凡具有「柔弱」，「優美」，「善良」，「溫和」等特質的名詞，習慣視為陰性。	the moon、peace、hope、the earth、nature、spring、autumn、night、liberty、fortune、virtue（美德）、mercy。

▶ The **sun** is shining in all **his** glory.

陽光勁力四射。

▶ The **moon** hid **her** face behind the clouds.

月亮躲在雲後。

■ 補充

1. 單位修飾語

an army of soldiers / beggars / officials　一隊士兵 / 一群乞丐 / 一批官員

an attack of fever　發燒

a band of musicians　一團樂手

a bar of chocolate　一塊巧克力

a batch of cakes / letters / recruits　一爐蛋糕 / 一批信 / 一批新兵

a bench of judges / examiners　一席法官 / 考官評審

a bevy of bees / ladies　一群蜜蜂 / 女士

a blade of glass　一片玻璃

a blade of grass　一片草地

a block of ice　一大片冰

a board of directors　董事

a bottle of milk　一瓶牛奶

a bowl of rice　一碗飯

a brood of chickens　一窩小雞

a bucket of water　一桶水

a bunch of keys / rascals　一串鑰匙 / 一群流氓

a bundle of straw　一束乾草

a burst of cry　一陣大哭

a cake of soap　一塊肥皂

a choir of singers　一隊歌手

a cloud of horsemen　一隊騎兵

a cluster of flowers / bees / spectators　一束花 / 一群蜜蜂 / 一群旁觀者

a congregation of prayers　一群祈禱者

a crew of sailors　一船水手

a crowd of pupils　一群學生

a cup of tea　一杯茶

a cut of meat　一塊肉

a display of arms　一場武力展示

a drop of water　一滴水

an ear of corn　一穗玉米

a field of cattle / workmen　遍地的牛群 / 工人

a flash of lightening　一道閃電

a flight of stairs　一層樓梯

a flock of birds / sheep　一群鳥 / 羊

a fit of temper　一陣脾氣

a galaxy of beauties　一群引人注意的美女

a gang of thieves　一群賊

a glass of water　一杯水

a grain of salt　一撮鹽

a group of people　一群人

a grove of trees　一小片樹叢

a herd of cattle / elephants / deer　一群牛 / 一群大象 / 一群鹿

an item of news　一則新聞

a litter of puppies　一窩小狗

a loaf of bread　一個麵包

a lump of sugar　一塊方糖

a mob of protestors / demonstrators　一群示威者

a pack of cigarettes / lies / wolves　一包香菸 / 一堆謊言 / 一群狼

a pair of glasses / shoes / trousers　一副眼鏡 / 一雙鞋 / 一條褲子

a party of guests　一群賓客

a peal of thunder　一聲響雷

a piece of advice　一個忠告

a ray of light　一道光

a roast of meat　一塊烤肉

a sack of earth　一袋泥土

a school of fish　一群魚

a sea of clouds　一片雲海

a sheet of paper　一張紙

a slice of bacon　一塊培根肉

a speck of ink　一點墨水

a stack of wood / corn　一堆木頭 / 玉米

a staff of teachers　一群老師

a stick of chalk　一根粉筆

a string of pearls / beads　一串（珍）珠

a strip of land　一片狹長的土地

a swarm of ants / bees / people　一窩螞蟻 / 蜜蜂 / 人

a team of players / experts　一組球員 / 專家

a troop of soldiers　一隊士兵

a troupe of actors / dancers　一組演員 / 舞者

2. 有些抽象名詞可將抽象觀念具體化，用來表示具有該抽象特質的人或物

beauty-a beauty　美人

curiosity-a curiosity　古玩

character-a character　角色

justice-a justice　法官

production-a production　產品 / 戲劇製作

business-a business　商店

3. 有些可數名詞可以用來代表抽象觀念

at table　吃飯

at school　在校上課

at college　上大學

at sea　在海上

after class　下課後

after school　放學後

go to bed　上床

go to school　上學

go to college　上大學

go to camp　去露營

go to hospital　去醫院

go to prison　進監獄

go to market　上市場

go to church　做禮拜

go to sea　出海

in bed　臥床不起

in school　上學

in prison　蹲監獄

in class　上課

on holiday　渡假

■ 實用測驗

1. I met her at the _____.

   ① the grocer's　② grocer's　③ grocer　④ The grocer

2. He likes to eat _____.

   ① fishes and beefs　② boiling eggs　③ frozen meat　④ fried potatos

3. It isn't John's; it belongs to _____.

   ① a friend's of his　② a friend of him　③ his friend's　④ a friend of his

4. You can sew the _____ together by hand.

   ① two pieces of clothes　② two pieces of cloth　③ two pairs of clothes

   ④ two pairs of cloth

5. The police _____ on the track of the suspect.

   ① is　② are　③ am　④ was

6. All my family _____ businessmen.

   ① are　② is　③ am　④ do

7. I was born on a _____ of _____ , a nice _____ day.

　　① Friday、March、Spring　② friday、march、spring　③ Friday、March、spring　④ Friday、march、spring

8. I need a _____ of toothpaste.

　　① cake　② piece　③ tube　④ bottle

9. He bought three _____ of furniture last night.

　　① articles　② bundles　③ armful　④ bowls

10. The teacher drew a diagram with _____ .

　　① a chalk　② a fleet of chalk　③ a dozen of chalks　④ a piece of chalk

11. Your plan is _____ .

　　① use　② with useless　③ of no useful　④ of no use

12. He gave me some _____ .

　　① informations　② clothings　③ advice　④ funs

13. He is only small potatoes; that is, he is a man _____ .

　　① on importance　② of ability　③ of no importance　④ of some abilities

14. Man : men =

　　① Mother-in-law : mother-in-laws

　　② Phenomenon : phenomenons

　　③ Milk : milks

　　④ Editor-in-chief : editors-in-chief

15. Have you read _____ yet?

　　① the paper of today　② the paper of today's　③ today's paper　④ today paper

■ 試題解析

1. ① 名詞（人）'s + (house、store、shop ...)。

2. ③ fish、beef為物質名詞，沒有複數；boiling egg：正在沸騰的蛋；frozen meat：冷凍的肉；potato的複數應為potatoes。

3. ④ a friend of his。

4. ① cloth為物質名詞。

5. ② The police後皆複數形動詞。

6. ① family作「家人」為複數，若作「家庭」則為單數。

7. ③ 週及月份需用大寫，季節則不需要。

8. ③「一條牙膏」。

9. ① 家具的計算單位是a piece of... 或an article of...。

10. ④ chalk為物質名詞不可數；計算時要加單位a piece of...。

11. ④ of no use = useless。

12. ③ information、clothing、advice及fun都是不可數。

13. ③ of no importance = unimportant; small potato：「小人物、瑣事」。

14. ④ 岳母的複數是mothers-in-law；phenomenon的複數為phenomena；milk是物質名詞沒有複數；主編的複數是editors-in-chief。

15. ③ 度量衡、時間、價值單位的名詞，所有格是…'s。

筆記頁

代名詞 (Pronouns)

代名詞是用來代替名詞或名詞相當語（noun equivalents），以避免兩者在句中重複使用。

■ **本章重點**

- 人稱代名詞
- 指示代名詞
- 不定代名詞
- 疑問代名詞
- 關係代名詞

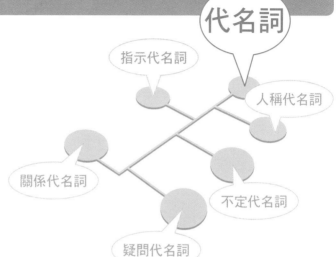

- **人稱代名詞：**用來代替特定的人、事、物，並會因為人稱、數量、性別和格而改變形式。

		主格	所有格	受格
第一人稱 （泛指說話者）	單數	I	my	me
	複數	we	our	us
第二人稱 （泛指說話的對象）	單數	you	your	you
	複數	you	your	you

		主格	所有格	受格
第三人稱 （泛指談及的對象）	單數	he	his	him
		she	her	her
		it	its	it
	複數	they	their	them

🔊 小提醒

its（它的）；it's = it is（它是）

▶I saw a cat yesterday; **its** color is black.
　我昨天看到一隻貓，牠的顏色是黑的。

▶I saw a cat yesterdayl; **it is** my friend's cat.
　我昨天看到一隻貓，牠是我朋友的貓。

1. 人稱代名詞格位的用法

1 主格：當句子的主詞及分詞構句中主詞及主詞補語。

▶**She** knew what she wanted.

（代名詞she當主詞）她知道她要什麼。

▶She having come early, we were not ready.

（代名詞she當分詞構句having come early的主詞）她來早了而我們還沒準備妥當。

▶It is I that am wrong.

（代名詞I是虛主詞it的補語）是我錯了。

2 受格：當動詞及介詞的受詞及受詞補語。

▶I met her in the party last night.

（代名詞her當動詞met的受詞）我昨晚在聚會中看到她。

▶We are very fond of him.

（代名詞him當介詞of的受詞）我們很喜歡他。

▶ At first, I thought her him.

（代名詞him當受詞her的補語）我一開始把她想成他。

✦比較 I thought it to be him.

him用來代替it，所以用受格當受詞補語。

I thought (that) it was he.

he用來代替it，所以用主格當主詞補語。

It was thought to be he.

he用來代替it，所以用主格。

I like him better than you.

= I like him better than I like you.

you為受格，當動詞like的受詞。

I like him better than you (do).

= I like him better than you like him.

he為主格，當動詞like的主詞。

3 所有格：充當句中修飾語。

▶ This is my book, not yours (=your book).
這是我的書不是你的書。

▶ The children all have their homework ready.
孩子們都把家庭作業準備好。

2. 人稱代名詞的排列順序

單數	$2^{nd} + 3^{rd} + 1^{st}$
複數	$1^{st} + 2^{nd} + 3^{rd}$

▶ You, he and I are attending the same school.
你、我和他都上同樣的學校。

▶ We, you and they are all taking the same class.
我們、你們和他們都在同一班。

3. "we"、"you"、"they"用來泛指一般人

▶ Whenever **you** see a bee, **you** will find it working.
只要看到蜜蜂，就會看到牠在工作。

▶ **We** should be kind to the poor.
對窮人要仁慈。

▶ **They** say the harvest is good this year.
大家說今年收成好。

4.「it」代替特定的單數普通名詞，「one」代替不特定的單數普通名詞

▶ Have you **the book** I gave you? Yes, I have **it**.
你有我給你的書嗎？是的，我有。

▶ Have you **a book**? Yes, I have **one**.
你有書嗎？是的，我有。

5. 特定的物質名詞用「it」代替；特定的複數普通名詞用「they」代替；不特定的物質及複數普通名詞用「some」代替；抽象名詞用「it」代替

▶ Do you like **the coffee**? Yes, I like **it**.
你喜歡這咖啡嗎？是的，我喜歡它。

▶ Have you read **the books** I lent you? Yes, I have read **them**.
你讀了我借給你的書嗎？是的，我已經讀完它們了。

▶ He wanted **some water**, so I gave him **some**.
他要些水，所以我就給他一些。

▶ He can speak **Spanish**, but I have never heard him speak **it**.
他能說西班牙文，但我從沒聽他說過。

6. 陽性單數名詞用「he」代替；陰性單數名詞用「she」代替；動物或無性的單數名詞用「it」代替；複數名詞用「they」代替

▶ The **girl** has a red rose in **her** hand.
這女孩手上有枝紅玫瑰。

▶ The **horse** broke **its** legs.
這馬跌斷了牠的腿。

▶ The **baby** cries when **it** is hungry.
嬰兒餓了就會哭。

▶ **Children** enjoy **their** time on the beach.
孩子們享受在海邊的時光。

7. 所有格代名詞（所有格＋名詞，如：mine、ours、yours、his、hers、theirs）之後不可再接名詞

▶ Your parents were present at the PTA, **mine** (my parents) were not.
你的雙親出席家長觀摩會，我爸媽卻沒有。

▶ His pen is not as good as **yours**.
他的筆沒你的筆來的好。

8. a, an, this, that, any, some, no, several, these, those, such,...etc. 不得和人稱代名詞的所有格（my, your, his, her, our, their）並用，若必須連用，要用雙重所有格表示

▶ He is a friend of mine.
= He is one of my friends.
他是我的一個朋友。

▶ I like that hat of hers.
= I like her hat.
我喜歡她的那頂帽子。

9. 反身代名詞（myself / ourselves, yourself / yourselves, himself / herself / itself / themselves）的用法

1 表示行為者自己承受自己所做的動作。

▶ Jenny killed **herself** last night.
　 Jenny昨晚自殺了。

▶ He is talking to **himself** now.
　 他現在在自言自語。

2 用以加強語氣。

▶ I **myself** did it for you.
　 我自己為你做的。

▶ You told me the news **yourself**.
　 你自己告訴我的。

3 某些動詞，如：amuse（娛樂、消遣）、apply（應用）、absent
（缺席）、avail（利用）、devote（致力於）、seat、dress、
pride（以⋯為榮）、behave（表現）等的受詞常是反身受詞。

▶ The children amused **themselves** all afternoon.
　 這些小孩一下午都自己找樂子。

▶ Mary absented **herself** from work yesterday.
　 Mary昨天缺席了。

▶ He availed **himself** of the opportunity to speak to her.
　 他找機會和她說話。

4 反身代名詞相關的慣用語。

例 by oneself = alone（獨自）、for oneself（為自己）、of oneself
（自行）、beside oneslef（發瘋）、enjoy oneself（玩得愉快）、
seat oneself = sit（坐下）、absent oneself from = be absent from
（缺席）、dress oneself in（穿著）、devote oneself to（致力
於）、help oneself to（自行取用）、pride oneself on = be proud
of = take pride in（以⋯為榮）、come to oneself（甦醒）、make
oneself at home（不用客氣）。

● **指示代名詞**：this / these、that / those。

1. 「this」和「these」指較近的人或物；「that」和「those」指較遠的人或物

▶ **This** is my book and **that** is yours.
這是我的書，那是你的書。

▶ Who is **this** speaking? **This** is John speaking.
請問是哪位？這是John。

▶ Please pick up **these** things instead of those.
請拿這些而不是那些。

2. 「this」和「that」可代替前面已說的句子或子句，可用and / but連接

▶ He always gets up early. **This** makes him do much work in the morning.= He always gets up early, **and this** makes him do much work in the morning.
他總是早起，而他早起讓他能在早上做好很多事。

▶ He will give his vote to me, **but that** is not enough.
他會把票投給我，但他投票給我還不夠。

3. 「that」和「those」代替前面已說過的名詞，以免重複

▶ The climate of Japan is not so mild as **that** of Taiwan.
日本的氣候不如臺灣的氣候溫和。

▶ The days in summer are longer than **those** in winter.
夏天的白晝長過冬天的白天。

4. this (these) = the latter = the other（表示「後者」）；that (those) = the former = the one（表示「前者」）

▶ Health is above wealth, **this** (=wealth) does not give us so much happiness as **that** (=health).

健康重於財富；後者帶來的快樂不如前者。

▶Dogs are more faithful animals than cats, **these** (=cats) attach themselves to places, and **those** (=dogs) to persons.
狗是比貓還死忠的動物；貓戀家狗戀人。

 小提醒

此種用法多以事物或動物為主。

5. 「this」和「that」可用來代替接下來要說的事

▶Let me tell you **this**: I have not got any news for you.
讓我告訴你：我沒有任何事要告訴你。

6. 「those」=「those people」；「that which」=「what」

▶**Those** who are idle can't succeed.
呆滯不前的人無法成功。

▶**That which** is good is not beautiful.
= **What** is good is not beautiful.
漂亮的東西未必是好東西。

7. 「this」和「that」也可用來當副詞用，表示程度或範圍

▶I can not walk **that** far.
（那麼遠）

▶Can you start at five? No, I can't start **that** early.
（那麼早）

▶The table is about **this** wide.
（如此寬）

8. 「such」作代名詞用時指「如此的人或事物」

▶He is a child, and must be treated as **such**.
他是個孩子，應該以對待孩子的方法對待他。

▶Such is life.
這就是過日子。

● **不定代名詞**：指不定數量的人或物。常見的不定代名詞有：all、another、any、anybody、anyone、anything、each、everybody、everyone、everything、few、many、nobody、none、one、several、some、somebody、someone。

1.「one」（複數為ones；所有格為one's）表示一般的人或物

▶One often fails to see one's faults.
人常會無法看到自己的錯誤。

▶One who works hard will succeed.
努力工作的人終會成功。

1 若one前面如有any、some、no、each、every時，其後代名詞應用he、his、him、himself。

▶Everyone must do his best in whatever he does.
每個人在任何事上都要盡他最大的努力。

▶Anyone must do to the best of his ability to save the country.
每個人都要盡力來救國家。

▶One of the boys left his homework on the bus.
一個男孩把他的作業忘在巴士上。

2 one代替前面所說過的單數普通名詞，避免重複。

▶Do you have a blue pen? Yes, I have one.
你有藍筆嗎？我有一枝。

▶I can't find my hat, I want to buy a new one.
我找不到我的帽子，我要再買一頂。

◆比較 I can't find the hat I bought yesterday, I don't know where I put it.
我找不到我昨天買的帽子，我不知道我把它放到哪了。

3 no one及nobody通常取單數動詞。

▶ **No one likes** to play with Jack because he is too selfish.
因為Jack太過自私，所以沒人喜歡和他玩在一起。

4 none是one和ones的否定，可表示單數或複數，但最近趨勢多以複數為主。

▶ **None** of the boys **are** interested in dolls.
沒有任何男孩對洋娃娃感興趣。

▶ **None have** made the mistake in these questions.
沒人在這些問題上犯錯。

◆比較 No one knows the answer.
沒有人知道答案。

5 none可放在「too」或「the +比較級」之前，意思為「毫不」、「一點也不」。

▶ He did the work **none too** well.
他這事做得一點也不好。

▶ He has faults, **none the less**, he is the best student in the class.
儘管他有錯，他依然是班上最好的學生。

2. 兩者取其一時，另一個用「the other」，複數為「the others」；兩者以上取其一，其餘中任一個用another

▶ I have two close friends, **one** is at home, and **the other** is in America.
我有兩個朋友，一個在本地一個在美國。

▶ John is here, but **the others** are absent.
John在這裡，但其他的人缺席了。

▶ I don't like this hat, please show me **another**.
我不喜歡這帽子，讓我看看另一頂。

3. 「some」用於肯定句;「any」用於否定句、疑問句、條件句,但some用在疑問句時表示預期肯定的回答;any用在肯定句時表示「任一」的意思

▶ I want some water. Do you have **any**?
我要些水。你有嗎?

▶ If you have any, please pour me **some**.
如果你有水的話倒些給我。（沒有把握對方是否會倒）

▶ Won't you pour me **some** water?（= Please pour me some water.）
你何不倒些水給我?（有把握對方會倒）

▶ You may take **any** of the books.
你可拿這些書裡面的任何一本。

1 not any = no、none

▶ There are **not any** students in the classroom.
= There are **no** students in the classroom.
教室裡連一個學生都沒有。

▶ He has some money with him, but I have **none**.
他身邊有些錢,但我是一點也沒有。

2 not anybody / anything = nobody / nothing

▶ I have **not anything** more to say.
= I have **nothing** more to say.
我沒什麼要說的。

🔊 小提醒

與something, anything, nothing有關的慣用語:
anything but（絕不、並不）、nothing but（=except;只不過）、do nothing but + v.（除…外什麼都不做）、have nothing to do but + v.（只做…）。

▶ She is **anything but** beautiful. = She is ugly.
她很醜。

▶ He is **nothing but** a thief. = He is a thief.
他是個賊。

🔊 小提醒

▶ The boy does **nothing but** play all day.
這男孩整天只是玩。

▶ The boy has **nothing to do but** wait here.
這男孩只好在這等。

4. 兩者選一用「either」；三者以上選一用「any」；兩者皆無用「neither」；三者皆無用「none」

▶ You can take **either** of the two pens.
你可以拿兩枝筆裡的任一枝。

▶ **Neither** of the two girls can come.
兩個女孩都不能來。

▶ **Any** of the students can read it.
學生裡任一個都能讀它。

▶ **None** of them will come on time.
他們裡面沒有一個會準時來。

5. 「both」只能用複數可數名詞，且指兩個，若當主詞用時，其後接複數動詞。both... not或not both表示兩者中的部分否定

▶ **Both** of them are old enough to go to school.
他們兩個都大到足以上學。

▶ **Both** options have been ruled out.
兩種選擇都被排除。

▶ **Both** of the students are **not** diligent.
= **Not both** of the students are diligent.
並非這兩個學生都是勤勉的。（部分否定）

✿比較 Neither of them is diligent.
他們都不勤勉。（完全否定）

6. 「all」代表可數名詞時，若當主詞其後取複數動詞；代表不可數名詞時，若當主詞其後取單數動詞

▶ **All** of them **are** to be here tomorrow.
他們所有人明天都會在這裡。

▶ **All** of his time **was** spent on books.
他所有時間都花在書本上。

▶ **All** that glitters **is** not gold.
並非所有發光的都是黃金。

◆◆比較 「all」的完全否定和部分否定

All of the students are not diligent.

= None of the students are diligent.

沒有一個學生是勤勉的。（完全否定）

Not all of the students are diligent.

= Some of the students are diligent, but some don't.

並非所有的學生都是勤勉的。（部分否定）

🔊 小提醒

與all 相關的片語：at all（全然）、all but（幾乎）、once for all（斷然的）、all in all（最重要的）、with all（雖然）…。

▶ He is **all but** dead.
他幾乎要死了。

▶ She should have told me **once for all**.
她該一次就把話說清楚。

▶ She is **all in all** to her children.
對她孩子而言，她是最重要的。

▶ **With all** the heavy rain, he started his sailing around the world.
雖然下大雨，他依然啟航去環遊世界。

7.「each」和「every」的用法

1 each 注重個別，而every強調全體。

▶ After the explosion, **each** passenger on the bus was questioned by the police.
爆炸發生後，巴士上每位乘客都受到警察詢問。

▶ **Every** passenger (=All passengers) on the bus was questioned by the police after the explosion.
所有巴士乘客在爆炸發生後都受到警察詢問。

2 each可作形容詞和代名詞用，但every只能當形容詞。

▶ **Each** boy received a present.
每個男孩都收到禮物。

▶ **Each of** the boys received a present.
男孩裡面的每一個都收到禮物。

Every one of these books is interesting.（○）

Every of these books is interesting.（×）

3 each用於兩個或兩個以上的每一個；every則用於三個以上的每一個。

each of my hands, each of my parents

every one of my fingers（○），every of my books（×）。因every只可當形容詞，所以絕不會有every of...的用法出現。

4 each other：兩者互相；one another：三者以上互相。

▶ The two men did trust **each other**.
兩人的確相互信任。

▶ Children made fun of **one another**, but they meant no harm.
孩子們互相開玩笑，但他們沒有惡意。

5 否定字not不與each連用；not every則表示部分否定。

▶ **Not every** student walks to school.

= Some students walk to school.
有些學生步行上學。

● **疑問代名詞：**置於句首且第一個字母需大寫，句尾需加問號。

1. who→只能用在人；詢問關係

主格	所有格	受格
who	whose	whom

▶ **Who** is the man over there? He is my uncle.
在那的是誰？他是我叔叔（伯伯）。

▶ **Whose** hat is this? It's John's.
那是誰的帽子？它是John的。

▶ **Whom** are you looking for?
= For whom are you looking for?
你在找誰？

2. which→可用在人、事或物；有選擇的意思

▶ **Which** of those boys is your brother?
你的兄弟是哪個？

▶ **Which** do you want?
你要哪個？

3. what→通常用在事物上；用在人時，是詢問一個人的職業或身分

▶ **What** makes you so sad? Peter broke my glasses.
什麼事讓你如此悲傷？Peter打破了我的眼鏡。

▶ **What** is he? He is a teacher.
他是做什麼的？他是個老師。

4. 由疑問代名詞所引導的間接疑問句,其功能等於名詞子句。

who / which / what + to + v = 名詞子句

▶ Tell me **who** he is.
　告訴我他是誰。

▶ I can't tell you **whose** son she teaches.
　我不能告訴你她教誰的孩子。

▶ I don't know **what** you mean.
　我不知道你的意思是什麼。

🔊 小提醒

(A)"do you think / suppose / guess / imagine / believe / say..."通常要放在疑問代名詞後,回答時不可使用「yes」或「no」。

　▶ Who do you think he is? He is John.
　　你以為他是誰?他是John。

　▶ What do you suppose he will do? I suppose he will review his lessons.
　　你覺得他會做什麼?我想他會複習他的功課。

(B)"Do you know / hear / tell / ask..."要放在疑問代名詞前,要用「yes」或「no」回答。

　▶ Do you know who he is? No, I don't know.
　　你知道他是誰嗎?不,我不知道。

　▶ Did you hear what had happened? Yes, I did.
　　你聽說發生什麼事嗎?是的,我聽說了。

● **關係代名詞：** 一方面做代名詞代表其先行詞，另一方面做從屬連接詞引出從屬子句。

先行詞	主格	所有格	受格
人	who	whose	whom
動物，事物	which	whose of which	which
人、事、物	that	X	that
人、事、物	what	X	what

1. 關係代名詞的用法可分限定及非限定（補述）等兩種

1 限定用法是用以限定修飾先行詞，若省去的話，句意就變得不夠清楚，通常在其前不加逗點（，）。

▶ I want a tour guide **who** must speak Chinese.
我要個能說中文的導遊。

▶ This is the man **whose** house was burnt down last night.
這男人的房子昨晚被燒掉了。

▶ He is the man **whom** I admired the most.
他是我最欽服的人。

2 非限定（補述）用法用來補充說明先行詞，跟先行詞之間用逗點隔開。非限定（補述）用法的關係子句，通常也可改為 "and"、"but"、"as" etc. 所引導的子句。

▶ I met a man, **who** (=and he) showed me the way to the station.
我遇到個人，他告訴我去車站的路。

▶ I will lend you this DVD, **which** (=as it) is interesting.
我會借這片有趣的DVD給你。

◆◆比較 His friend, who is in Japan, will return soon.
他在日本的朋友將很快回來。（只有一個朋友）

His friend who is in Japan will return soon.
他在日本的朋友將很快回來。（不只一個朋友）

2.「who」、「whose」及「whom」只用在先行詞為人時。who做主詞及主詞補語；whose表示所有格，具有形容的功用；whom作動詞或介詞的受詞

▶ This is the girl **who** works in the convenience store.
這是在便利商店工作的女孩。（who當works的主詞）

▶ Is that the girl **whose** brother you teach?
那是兄弟被你教的女孩嗎？（所有格whose修飾brother）

▶ That is the man **whom** we met in the park last night.
那是昨晚我們在公園碰到的男人。（whom當met的受詞）

▶ That is the man **whom** we were looking for a while ago.
那是不久前我們在找的人。（whom當介詞of的受詞）

3.「which」和「whose / of which」（所有格）用於先行詞為人以外的事物；主格與受格同形

▶ He has a dog **which** is faithful to him.
他有隻對他忠實的狗。（which是主格）

▶ There were some reasons **which** he could not see.
有些原因他看不到。（which是see的受詞）

▶ The house in **which** he lives is very large.
他住的房子很大。（which當in的受詞）

4. 所有格的用法

whose + n. = the + n. + of which = of which the + n.

▶ The book whose cover is blue is very interesting.
= The book the cover of which is blue is very interesting.
= The book of which the cover is blue is very interesting.

🔊 小提醒

(A)先行詞若是指人的集合名詞，指集合體用 "which"；如指集合體中份子，則用 "who"。

▶His family, **which** is large, consists of ten persons.
他的家庭是個大家庭，有十個人組成。

▶His family, **who** are all early risers, are healthy.
他的家人都是早起者，他們都健康。

(B)先行詞為人，若指那人的「性質」、「職業」、「地位」時，用 "which"而不用 "who"。

▶He is not the doctor **which** we want him to be.
他不是我們希望他變成的那種醫生。

▶She looked like an actress, **which** she was.
她看起來像女演員，她真是個女演員。

(C)非限定（補述）用法中的which，也可用片語或子句做其先行詞，此時which後用單數動詞。

▶He tried to swim across the river, **which** was impossible.
他試著游過河流，但那是不可能的。

▶She said nothing, **which** made him angry.
她什麼也沒說，這事讓他生氣。

(D)先行詞為年幼的小孩，也用 "which"。

▶They had one child, **which** died in infancy.
他們的孩子幼時就死了。

(E)在非限定（補述）用法時，所有格用 "of which" 較恰當。

▶I found a house, **of which** the windows were all broken.
我發現一間窗戶都破了的房子。

5.「that」用以指人事物，可代替「who」、「which」，不可用在非限定（補述）用法中；當介詞的受詞時，不可把介詞放在其前面

▶ This is the boy **that** (＝ who) lost his watch.
　 這是丟掉手錶的男孩。

▶ Is this the girl **that** (＝ whom) you spoke to?
　 這是和你說話的女孩嗎？

▶ The story **that** (＝ which) he told me is very interesting.
　 他告訴我的故事很有趣。

🔊 小提醒

(A)先行詞有人、事、物時，用that。

　▶ The driver and his car **that** fell into the river belonged to this company.
　　 那一起掉入河裡的人和車屬於這家公司。

　▶ Look at the boy and the dog **that** are crossing the street.
　　 看那在過街的男孩和狗。

(B)先行詞中有形容詞最高級或the only、the very、the same、the first、the last、no、any、every、all等形容詞時，關係代名詞要用that；如先行詞為all時，也要用that。

　▶ He is **the tallest** man that I have ever seen.
　　 他是我見過的人裡最高的。

　▶ He is **the best** tennis player **that** we have ever had in our school.
　　 他是我們學校裡有史以來最好的網球球員。

　▶ Man is **the only** animal **that** can speak.
　　 人是唯一能說話的動物。

　▶ This hat is **the very** thing **that** I want.
　　 這正是我要的東西。

🔊 小提醒

▶ Having my own house is **all that** I want.
有棟自己的房子是我唯一想要的事。

(C)the same後面用that指同一人、事、物，用as代表類似的東西。

▶ This is **the same** watch **that** I lost yesterday.

▶ This is **the same** watch **as** I lost yesterday.

(D)以疑問詞（who, which, what）做先行詞時要用that。

▶ **Who that** has conscience will do such a thing?
哪個有良知的人會做此事？

▶ **Who** is there **that** can help me?
有人能幫我？

(E)加強語氣時

▶ **It is** you not he **that** are to be blamed.
是你不是他該被責備。

▶ **It is** the idle **that** complain they can't find time to read.
只有停滯不前的人才會埋怨找不到時間讀書。

6. 「what」

「what」是屬於複合關係代名詞，它把先行詞包含在內，所以沒有先行詞。

▶ **What** is mine is yours.
我的就是你的。

▶ He saved **what** he had earned.
他把他所賺到的都存起來。

▶ This is just **what** I want.
這正是我要的。

▶ He gave me **what** I wanted.
他給我我要的。

▶I will give you **what** money I have.

= I will give you all the money that I have.

= I will give you as much money as I have.

我會把我所有的錢都給你。

🔊 小提醒

As A is to B, so is C to D.

= C is to D what A is to B.

C與D之間關係就如同A與B之間的關係

▶As water is to fish, so is air to man.

= **What** water is to fish, that is air to man.

= Air is to man what water is to fish.

= Air is to man as water is to fish.

水之於魚如同空氣之於人。

▶Reading is to the mind what food is to the body.

= As food is to the body, so is reading to the mind.

食物與身體的關係就如同閱讀和心靈一般。

---

2 what相關的慣用語

what one is today（今日的成就）

▶My teacher has made me **what I am**.

我的老師造就今天的我。

what one was (used to be)（過去的樣子）

▶She is not **what she was** three years ago.

她已非三年前的樣子。

what is called / what we call / what you call（所謂）

▶He is **what is called** a genius.

他是所謂的天才。

what is / was + 比較級（更…的是）

▶He is a good doctor, and **what is better**, a good scholar.

他是位好醫生，更好的是，他是位好學者。

▶ He lost his money, and **what was worse**, he also lost his wife.
他失去了所有的錢，更糟的是，他也失掉了太太。

what with... and (what with)（半因…半因…）

▶ **What with** teaching, and **what with** writing, I become so busy.
一半因為教書，一半因為寫作，我變的好忙。

7.「as」是指人、事、物的關係代名詞，多用於such、the same、as之後

▶ He is as briliant **as** a painter **as** ever lived.
= He is the most brilliant painter that ever lived.
他是有史以來最才氣煥發的畫家。

▶ This novel is written in **such** easy English **as** beginners can under-stand.
這小說用的是如此簡單的英文，連初學者都能懂。

▶ This is **the same** watch **as** I lost yesterday.
這和我昨天遺失的手錶一個樣。

8.「but」其意思為 "that (or who) ...not"，是個本身含有否定意思的關係代名詞，而其句子中，常含一個如：no、not或few的否定詞

▶ There is **not** a husband **but** loves his wife.
= There is not a husband who doesn't love his wife.
沒有不愛妻子的丈夫。

▶ There is **no** one **but** knows the story.
= There is no one who does not know the story.
沒有不知道這故事的人。

9.「than」當關係代名詞用時，其先行詞必有比較級的形容詞來修飾

▶ Don't give the child **more** money **than** is needed.

別給孩子多過所需的金錢。

▶**Fewer** participants **than** we had expected came to the seminar.
較我們預期來得少的出席者出席了研習會。

10. 關係代名詞的省略：關係代名詞唯有在限定用法中方可省略

關係代名詞在關係子句中當動詞或介詞的受詞時可省略。

▶The CDs (that) I lent you belong to my sister.
我借你的CD是我姊妹的。

▶This is the movie (which) I was telling you about.
這是我那時告訴你的電影。

▶That is not the way (in which) I do it.
這不是我做事的方法。

若當主詞用時，在下列幾種情形中方可省略。

▶There is somebody at the door (who) wants to see you.
門口有人想見你。

▶This is the only one (that) exists.
只有這一個。

■ 觀念測驗

說出下列各句中所出現的代名詞為何：人稱代名詞、指示代名詞、不定代名詞、疑問代名詞或關係代名詞。

1. Jeremy bought a new CD player. He played it nonstop for a week.

2. Yesterday, I worked with each of my brothers.

3. Justin read many of his favorite books over the summer.

4. The dirty clothes are not going to wash themselves today.（髒衣服不會自己洗）

5. Could you distribute these to the students in your class?

6. What to do and how to do it have been bothering Jack ever since he gradurted from college.

■ 實用測驗

1. Mr. Smith really doesn't know _____.
   ① what is the speech about ② what is the speech ③ what the speech is about ④ what about is the speech

2. _____ of the four sons in the Wangs family has gotten married.
   ① None ② No ③ One ④ Some

3. _____ do you think about the new song by Lady Gaga?
   ① How about ② How ③ What ④ What about

4. These T-shirts are expensive. Show me some less expensive _____.
   ① one ② ones ③ T-shirts ④ them

5. Whether I go or not is no business of _____.
   ① yours ② your ③ you ④ yourself

6. Do you know _____?
   ① who is that man ② who that man is ③ that man is who ④ that man is whose

7. It is imperative _____ you should put in all your time and efforts to make that project work.
   ① what ② that ③ which ④ who

8. It is _____ that owe you everything.
   ① mine ② I ③ myself ④ my

9. You go your way and I go _____.

　　① I　② my　③ me　④ mine

10. New cell phones are much more expensive that the used _____.

　　① it　② them　③ one　④ ones

11. I saw him once, and _____ was ten years ago.

　　① it　② one　③ which　④ that

12. Basically, there are two kinds of books, one is books of general interest, _____ is for specific purposes.

　　① other　② another　③ the other　④ others

13. _____ came to see you yesterday.

　　① Her one friend　② Her a friend　③ One friend of her　④ A friend of hers

14. There are ten participants in the seminar, and _____ is trying hard to solve the problem.

　　① every of them　② every one of them　③ each of them　④ each one of them

15. I have to admit that this is probably the best movie _____ I've ever seen.

　　① that　② which　③ of which　④ whom

16. The government has the responsibility to protect _____ people from wars.

　　① its　② it's　③ it　④ itself

17. I see you met my secretary. _____ and I go back many years.

　　① Her　② She　③ Hers　④ we

18. Instead of filling those orders now, take care of _____ tomorrow when you have more time.

　　① them　② they　③ their　④ theirs

19. All of _____ have been invited to the company's cocktail party this Friday evening.

　　① we　② our　③ us　④ ours

20. The idea of new promotion gig wasn't Mary's idea; it's _____.

　　① me　② mine　③ my　④ I

21. Telling somebody that _____ is laid off was a very unpleasant experience.

　　① him　② his　③ he　④ you

22. My notebook has lots of memory; but _____ has more.

① Jack ② Jack's ③ Jacks' ④ Jacks's

23. _____ isn't a good business practice to arrive late for any meeting.

① It ② That ③ This ④ What

24. When _____ grace period is up, you'll have to decide whether to keep this padbook or not.

① it ② it's ③ its ④ their

25. The police were right when _____ advised the bank to install a new security system.

① it ② he ③ she ④ they

■ 試題解析

Ⅰ.觀念測驗

1. He及it均為人稱代名詞。
2. I為人稱代名詞；each為不定代名詞。
3. his為人稱代名詞的所有格。
4. themselves為人稱代名詞的反身受詞形式。
5. you為人稱代名詞主格；thses為指示代名詞；your為人稱代名詞所有格。
6. what為疑問代名詞；it為人稱代名詞；he為人稱代名詞。

Ⅱ.實用測驗

1. ③ 名詞子句的字序：關係代名詞＋主詞＋動詞。
2. ③ none後應接動詞複數形；no為形容詞其後需加所修飾對象；some其後需加動詞複數形。
3. ③ what多問感覺如何；how則多用在問方法或程度，如：
   What do you think of...?
   How do you feel about...?
   How do you like...?
4. ② 以ones代替前面的T-shirts；若仍用T-shirts就會顯得累贅。
5. ① 本題為雙重所有格的用法：no＋名詞＋of＋所有代名詞。
6. ② 解釋同第一題。
7. ② 虛主詞構句：it＋adj. / adv.＋that＋主詞＋動詞。
8. ② 因動詞owe需主詞，所以選主格形式的代名詞。
9. ④ mine＝my＋way；你走你的陽關道，我過我的獨木橋。
10. ④ ones用來代替前面已出現的cell phones。
11. ④ that用來代替先前所出現的句子；若沒有that而用this時，則要選this。
12. ③ 因題目是兩者選一，所以用one..., the other...。
13. ④ 雙重所有格的用法：a＋名詞＋of＋所有代名詞。
14. ② every只可當形容詞用；each雖可當代名詞及形容詞，但只能用在兩者
    如：Each of my parenst is working hard for the family.

15. ① 因句中有形容詞最高級（the best）的出現，其後關係代名詞需選that。

16. ①。

17. ② 因有對等連接詞I的出現，所以要選主格形式。

18. ① 先行名詞為複數（orders），所以要選同為複數形式的代名詞受格形。

19. ③ 當介詞of的受詞。

20. ② mine= my + idea；promotional gig：促銷小手法。

21. ③ 當be動詞is的主詞；說話者通常為第一人稱，聽話者為第二人稱，所談及的對象則為第三人稱。

22. ② Jack's在此處為所有代名詞而非所有格；"This is Jack's book."、"This book is Jack's."兩句中的Jack's功用不同。

23. ① 虛主詞構句；business practice：商業運作、作法。

24. ③ padbook（小筆電）為事物，所有格為its；grace period：試用期，也可說成trial period，若是人的「試用期」則說成probation period。

25. ④ the police為集合名詞，所以代名詞需用複數形。

筆記頁

動詞 (Verbs)

用來表示語句中主詞相關的動作、事件或狀況的詞統稱為動詞。要能了解及物和不及物動詞之分；因反應時間改變而有的現在、過去及未來的規則不規則變化也要特別注意。及物或不及物會決定主動被動語態；動詞的現在過去未來式及現在分詞和過去分詞則會影響時態、語氣和與動詞相關句型的不同使用。

■ **本章重點**

● 動態與靜態動詞

● 動詞的用法

● 不及物與及物動詞

● 規則與不規則動詞

● 容易混淆的動詞

動詞

動詞的用法

動態與靜態動詞

容易混淆的動詞

不及物與及物動詞

規則與不規則動詞

● **動態與靜態動詞**：動詞可因表示動作或存在狀況而分。

1. **動態動詞所表示的動作，其時間可長（如：study、work、play）可短（如：open、shut、knock），它也可以用來表示狀態或位置的改變（如：arrive、come、die、live）**

▶ John has **studied** English for years.
　John研讀英文已有多年。

▶ Someone is **knocking** on the door.
　有人正在敲門。

▶ John's plane **arrives** at Terminal 2 tomorrow morning.
John的飛機明早到達第二號航廈。

2. 靜態動詞主要為表示狀態的動詞，一般不能用在進行式中；若用在進行式中，通常代表意思的改變。感官動詞（如：hear、see、smell、taste、sound）、感覺動詞（如：feel、appear、seem）、感情動詞（如：believe、care、consider），be動詞及have都屬於此類動詞

▶ These strawberries **taste** delicious.
這些草莓嚐起來很鮮美。

▶ It **seems** that John will never come to work on time.
看來John永遠不會準時上班。

▶ I **consider** it rude to interrupt other's speech without asking for permission.
我以為未經允許而打斷他人談話是件粗魯的事。

▶ You **are** being too kind.
你真是仁慈。

▶ They will **have** a meeting tomorrow.
他們明天有個會議。

▶ They are **having** a meeting now.
他們正在開會。

▶ John is **seeing** the sights.
John正在觀光。

▶ He is **seeing** your matter now.
他正在安排你的事。

▶ The manager was **seeing** some guests when I got there.
當我到時，經理正在接見客人。

● **動詞的用法：**通常一個句子中至少一定要有一個主要動詞，但也可能會有兩個或兩個以上，有時也會與助動詞連用來表示不同時態、語態和語氣。

1. 動詞後可以加受詞也可以不加受詞，不加受詞時，可能會接主詞補語；若加受詞，其後也可能有修飾受詞的受詞補語，有時則會有直接及間接受詞。若沒有受詞，通常會用副詞或副詞片語來修飾自己

2. 動詞後有時加形容詞或現在、過去分詞當主詞補語，更會在其後加副詞來修飾自己

▶ John **ate** all the peanut butter.
　John吃了所有的花生醬。（單主詞單受詞）

　= All the peanut butter was eaten by John.（上句的被動語態；翻譯同主動語態）

▶ Lisa **ate** her favorite cake and pastry .
　Lisa吃了她心愛的蛋糕和糕餅。（單動詞複受詞）

▶ John **ate** all the peanut butter and **drank** all the milk.
　John吃了所有的花生醬和喝了所有的牛奶。（複動詞及受詞）

▶ John **works** everyday except Sunday.
　John除了週日外每天工作。（單動詞加副詞）

▶ Lisa always **sings** happily whenever she is taking a shower.
　Lisa淋浴時總是開心地唱歌。（單動詞加副詞子句）

▶ Lisa **sang** her favorite songs cheerfully and danced happily all night.
　Lisa整夜開心地唱歌快樂地跳舞。（複動詞複受詞加副詞）

▶ John **gave** Lisa a watch as her birthday present.
　John送 Lias 一支手錶當生日禮物。（單動詞複受詞）

▶ Tony was **tired** but happy at the same time when he finished his work.
　Tony在完成工作後雖累但很快樂。（雙主詞補語）

▶Tony is **working** on his report now.

Tony正在做他的報告。（現在進行式）

▶Tony has **celebrated** his son's birth and has started saving for his education.

Tony慶祝他兒子的生日並已開始為他的教育存錢。（現在完成式）

● 不及物與及物動詞

1. 不及物動詞：動作因不影響他人而不接受詞

1 若動詞本身意義就相當完整，也就是說，不需要其他的修飾語來說明，稱為完全不及物動詞。英文五大基本句型中的第一種就是由主詞加完全不及物動詞所組成。

$$S（主詞）+ Vi（完全不及物動詞）$$

▶We all need to **breathe**、**eat** and **drink**.

我們都需呼吸、進食和喝水。

▶Flowers **bloom** in the spring.

花在春天開。

▶Mary **smiles** happily.

Mary笑得很快樂。

2 若動詞本身意義不夠完整（例：Jack is.），它需要其他修飾語來幫助它完全地表達句意（例：Jack is happy.），稱為不完全不及物動詞。英文五大基本句型中的第二種就是由主詞加不完全不及物動詞再加主詞補語所組成。

$$S（主詞）+ Vi（不完全不及物動詞）+ 主詞補語$$

▶ I **am** an average **student**.

　我是個普通學生。（名詞當主詞補語）

▶ Mary **is** very **kind**.

　Mary非常仁慈。（形容詞當主詞補語）

▶ John**'s** only goal is **to make enough money**.

　John的目標是賺足夠的錢。（不定詞當主詞補語）

▶ The only hobby Mary has **is collecting coins**.

　Mary唯一的嗜好是蒐集硬幣。（動名詞當主詞補語）

▶ Jack **kept talking** all day yesterday.

　Jack昨天說了一整天的話。（現在分詞當主詞補語）

▶ Mother **was satisfied** with my grades this semester.

　母親對我這學期的成績感到滿意。（過去分詞當主詞補語）

▶ John **is** always **in a good mood**.

　John心情一直很好。（介系詞片語當主詞補語）

🔊 小提醒

　本句型中所用的動詞，有時也稱為連綴、聯繫動詞；此類動詞除了be動詞外還有：keep、lie（在於）、stand（維持現狀）、remain（依然是）、seem、look、appear、become、grow、get、turn、make（讓）、feel、sound、taste、smell。

　▶ Jack **appears** ill.

　　Jack看來生病了。

　▶ Your answers **seemed** way off mark.

　　你的答案似乎錯得離譜。

　▶ Mary has **grown** into a pretty lady.

　　Mary變成漂亮的小姐了。

🔊 小提醒

▶The suggestion **sounds** good to me.
　我覺得這建議聽起來不錯。

▶The offer **remains** valid until next Monday.
　這個提議到下週一前都有效。

2. 及物動詞：有受詞接受其動作的動詞

1 不需補語就能完整地表達意思的稱為完全及物動詞。完全及物
　動詞構成英文五大基本句型的第三種。

S（主詞）+ Vt（完全及物動詞）+ 受詞

▶I **have** a **dream**.
　我有一個夢想。（名詞當受詞）

▶John **hurt himself** in a car accident yesterday.
　John昨天在車禍中受了傷。（反身代名詞當受詞）

▶Mary really **likes reading**.
　Mary的確很喜歡閱讀。（動名詞當受詞）

▶I don't **know where John is**.
　我不知道John在哪裡。（名詞子句當受詞）

▶I don't **understand what he said**.
　我聽不懂他所說的。（名詞子句當受詞）

2 若句中使用授與動詞（如：give、lend、send、write等），其後
　必須接兩個受詞：人（間接受詞）和事物（直接受詞）。英文
　五大基本句型中的第四種就是由授與動詞所構成。

S（主詞）+ Vt（授與動詞）+ O_1（間接受詞）+ O_2（直接受詞）

= S（主詞）+ Vt（授與動詞）+ O_2（直接受詞）+ to / for / of / on + O_1
（間接受詞）

▶ Father told **us a story** every night when we were little.

= Father told **a story to us** every night when we were little.

當我們還小時，爸爸每晚說故事給我們聽。

▶ Mary baked **her husband a cake** on his birthday.

= Mary baked **a cake for her husband** on his birthday.

Mary在她先生生日時為他烤了一個蛋糕。

▶ My teacher wants to ask **me a question**.

= My teacher wants to **ask a question of me**.

我的老師要問我個問題。

▶ John played **his friend a joke** yesterday.

= John played **a joke on his friend** yesterday.

John昨天開了他朋友一個玩笑。

🔊 小提醒

因為直接與間接受詞位置對調所以需使用介系詞。常見的動詞與介系詞關係如下：

	+直接受詞+		+ 間接受詞
give、lend、send、write、bring、hand、pass、deliver、show、teach、tell、sell、pay、owe、do、promise、offer		to	
buy、bring、get、leave、make		for	
ask		for	
play		of	

3 若句中所使用的及物動詞意思不夠完整，所以必須加上受詞補語才能使句意更清楚，此類及物動詞稱為不完全及物動詞。

常見的不完全及物動詞有：choose、elect、make（使…成為）、call（稱呼）、name（命名）、keep、leave（聽任）、find、believe、think（以為）、consider（認為）、take（以為、當做）、know、like、want、wish、see、hear、feel、make（使）、have（使、把）、get（使）、let（讓）等。英文五大基本句型中的第五種就是由此類動詞所構成。

> S（主詞）+ Vt（不完全及物動詞）+ 受詞 + 受詞補語

▶We elected Mr. Ma our president two years ago.
　我們兩年前選馬先生當我們的總統。

▶My parents named me Jack in memory of my grandfather.
　我父母親叫我Jack來紀念我祖父。

◆比較 ▶We called him the King of Rock and Roll.
　　　　我們叫他搖滾樂之王。（受詞補語）

　　　▶He is called the King of Rock and Roll.
　　　　他被稱為搖滾樂之王。（主詞補語）

3.「不及物」當「及物」動詞：有些不及物動詞加上介系詞可以當及物動詞用

▶He **arrived in** Japan last night.
　= He reached Japan last night.
　他昨晚到達日本。

▶I **called on** my high school English teacher the other day.
　= I visited my high school English teacher the other day.
　我那天去拜訪我高中英文老師。

▶I am **looking forward to** my coming vacation.
　= I am expecting my coming vacation.
　我期望我將來臨的假期。

▶Don't **look down upon** the poor only because of their appearances.

= Don't despise the poor only because of their appearances.

別因外表而看不起窮人。

● 規則與不規則動詞

1. 規則動詞：原形動詞＋ed變成過去式及過去分詞；原形動詞 ＋ing成現在分詞及動名詞

原形動詞	過去式	過去分詞	現在分詞
ask	asked	asked	asking
borrow	borrowed	borrowed	borrowing
collect	collected	collected	collecting

◆ 動詞e、ee、ye和ie用法

　1 若動詞字尾是e，直接加d成過去式或過去分詞，但需去e再 加 ing成現在分詞。

原形動詞	過去式	過去分詞	現在分詞
argue	argued	argued	arguing
believe	believed	believed	believing
waste	wasted	wasted	wasting

　2 但若字尾是ee或ye時，直接加ing；字尾是ie時，先將ie改成 y再加ing。

原形動詞	過去式	過去分詞	現在分詞
agree	agreed	agreed	agreeing
dye（染色）	dyed	dyed	dyeing
tie	tied	tied	tying
lie	lied	lied	lying

 比較

原形動詞	過去式	過去分詞	現在分詞
die	died	died	dying
dye	dyed	dyed	dyeing

◆ 動詞字尾是「子音 + y」時，去y加ied。

原形動詞	過去式	過去分詞	現在分詞
bury	buried	buried	burying
cry	cried	cried	crying
try	tried	tried	trying

◆ 動詞字尾是「母音 + y」時，直接加ed。

原形動詞	過去式	過去分詞	現在分詞
enjoy	enjoyed	enjoyed	enjoying
play	played	played	playing
stay	stayed	stayed	staying

◆ 動詞字尾是「短母音 + 子音」時，要重複字尾再加ed / ing。

原形動詞	過去式	過去分詞	現在分詞
beg	begged	begged	begging
can（裝罐）	canned	canned	canning
quit	quitted	quitted	quitting

◆ 若動詞字尾形式同上，但屬雙或多音節字，要重音節在第二音節且第二音節的結構是「子＋母＋子」時，才可適用本規定。

原形動詞	過去式	過去分詞	現在分詞
admit	admitted	admitted	admitting
control	controlled	controlled	controlling
occur	occurred	occurred	occurring

> 小提醒
>
> (A)visit雖是雙音節字，但只能改成visited、visited、visiting是因為它的重音節落在第一音節。
> (B)英文中有一個字picnic雖屬規則動詞，但要特別小心它的變化picnicked、picnicked、picnicking。
> (C)ed的讀音：無聲子音後讀成【t】，有聲子音後讀成【d】，t及d後讀成【id】。

2. 不規則動詞

◆ A-B-B型

原形動詞	過去式	過去分詞	現在分詞
say	said	said	saying
sell	sold	sold	selling

原形動詞	過去式	過去分詞	現在分詞
catch	caught	caught	catching
hear	heard	heard	hearing
build	built	built	building
sit	sat	sat	sitting
feel	felt	felt	feeling
meet	met	met	meeting
lead	led	led	leading
dig	dug	dug	digging
sting	stung	stung	stinging
find	found	found	finding

◆ A-B-A型

原形動詞	過去式	過去分詞	現在分詞
run	ran	run	running
come	came	come	coming

◆ A-B-C型

原形動詞	過去式	過去分詞	現在分詞
sing	sang	sung	singing
speak	spoke	spoken	speaking
bite	bit	bitten	biting
bear	bore	born	bearing
rise	rose	risen	rising

原形動詞	過去式	過去分詞	現在分詞
take	took	taken	taking
know	knew	known	knowing
go	went	gone	going
be (am / are / is)	was / were	been	being

◆ A-A-B型

原形動詞	過去式	過去分詞	現在分詞
beat	beat	beaten	beating

◆ A-A-A型

原形動詞	過去式	過去分詞	現在分詞
bet	bet	bet	betting
shut	shut	shut	shutting

◆ A-B型：因助動詞沒有過去分詞和現在分詞的變化。

原形動詞	過去式
shall	should
will	would
can	could
may	might
must	had to
ought	------

◆ 常見的不規則動詞：英文中的不規則動詞數量並不多，因為

在後續單元的討論中，幾乎所有和動詞相關的文法規則都會涉及到動詞的變化，所以一定要將不規則動詞的變化記牢。下列是常見的不規則動詞：

原形	過去式	過去分詞	現在分詞
awake	awoke	awaken	awaking
be	was / were	been	being
bear	bore	born	bearing
beat	beat	beaten	beating
become	became	become	becoming
begin	began	begun	beginning
bend	bent	bent	bending
beset（圍攻）	beset	beset	besetting
bet	bet	bet	betting
bid（命令、致意）	bid	bid	bidding
bind（綁紮、約束）	bound	bound	binding
bite	bit	bitten	biting
bleed	bled	bled	bleeding
blow	blew	blown	blowing
break	broke	broken	breaking
breed	bred	bred	breeding
bring	brought	brought	bringing
broadcast	broadcast(ed)	broadcast(ed)	broadcasting

原形	過去式	過去分詞	現在分詞
build	built	built	building
burn	burned / burnt	burned / burnt	burning
burst	burst	burst	bursting
buy	bought	bought	buying
cast	cast	cast	casting
catch	caught	caught	catching
choose	chose	chosen	choosing
cling（附著、依附）	clung	clung	clinging
come	came	come	coming
cost	cost	cost	costing
creep（爬行）	crept	crept	creeping
cut	cut	cut	cutting
deal	dealt	dealt	dealing
dig	dug	dug	digging
dive	dived / dove	dived	diving
do	did	done	doing
draw	drew	drawn	drawing
dream	dreamed / dreamt	dreamed / dreamt	dreaming
drive	drove	driven	driving
drink	drank	drunk	drinking
eat	ate	eaten	eating

原形	過去式	過去分詞	現在分詞
fall	fell	fallen	falling
feed	fed	fed	feeding
feel	felt	felt	feeling
fight	fought	fought	fighting
find	found	found	finding
fit	fit	fit	fitting
flee	fled	fled	fleeing
fling（猛衝、拋摔）	flung	flung	flinging
fly	flew	flew	flown
forbid	forbad	forbidden	forbidding
forget	forgot	forgotten	forgetting
forego (forgo)（先行）	forewent	foregone	foregoing
forgive	forgave	forgiven	forgiving
forsake（背棄）	forsook	forsaken	forsaking
freeze	froze	frozen	freezing
get	got	gotten	getting
give	gave	given	giving
go	went	gone	going
grind（銼刮）	ground	ground	grinding
grow	grew	grown	growing
hang（掛死、絞死）	hung / hanged	hung / hanged	hanging

原形	過去式	過去分詞	現在分詞
hear	heard	heard	hearing
hide	hid	hidden	hiding
hit	hit	hit	hitting
hold	held	held	holding
hurt	hurt	hurt	hurting
keep	kept	kept	keeping
kneel（跪）	knelt / kneeled	knelt / kneeled	kneeling
knit（編織）	knit / knitted	knit / knitted	knitting
know	knew	known	knowing
lay	laid	laid	laying
lead	led	led	leading
leap（跳躍）	leaped / leapt	leaped / leapt	leaping
learn	learned / learnt	learned / learnt	learning
leave	left	left	leaving
lend	lent	lent	lending
let	let	let	letting
lie	lay	lain	lying
light	lighted / lit	lighted / lit	lighting
lose	lost	lost	losing
make	made	made	making
mean	meant	meant	meaning
meet	met	met	meeting

原形	過去式	過去分詞	現在分詞
misspell	misspelled / misspelt	misspelled / misspelt	misspelling
mistake	mistook	mistaken	mistaking
mow（割草收割）	mowed	mowed / mown	mowing
overcome	overcame	overcome	overcoming
overdo	overdid	overdone	overdoing
overtake	overtook	overtaken	overtaking
overthrow	overthrew	overthrown	overthrowing
pay	paid	paid	paying
plead（辯護、懇求）	pled	pled	pleading
prove	proved	proved / proven	proving
put	put	put	putting
quit	quit / quitted	quit / quitted	quitting
read	read	read	reading
rid（免除、擺脫）	rid	ridden	ridding
ride	rode	ridden	riding
ring	rang	rung	ringing
rise	rose	risen	rising
run	ran	run	running
saw（鋸）	sawed	sawed / sawn	sawing
say	said	said	saying

原形	過去式	過去分詞	現在分詞
see	saw	seen	seeing
seek	sought	sought	seeking
sell	sold	sold	selling
send	sent	sent	sending
set	set	set	setting
sew（縫）	sewed	sewed / sewn	sewing
shake	shook	shaken	shaking
shave	shaved	shaved / shaven	shaving
shear（修剪）	shore	shorn	shearing
shed （流下、蛻脫）	shed	shed	shedding
shine	shone	shone	shining
shoe（釘蹄鐵）	shoed	shoed / shod	shoeing
shoot	shot	shot	shooting
show	showed	showed / shown	showing
shrink（縮水）	shrank	shrunk	shrinking
shut	shut	shut	shutting
sing	sang	sung	singing
sink	sank	sunk	sinking
sit	sat	sat	sitting
sleep	slept	slept	sleeping
slay（殺害）	slew	slain	slaying
slide（滑）	slid	slid	sliding

原形	過去式	過去分詞	現在分詞
sling（拋射、投擲）	slung	slung	slinging
slit（割裂、劃破）	slit	slit	slitting
smite（擊敗、譴責）	smote	smitten	smiting
sow（播種）	sowed	sowed / sown	sowing
speak	spoke	spoken	speaking
speed	sped	sped	speeding
spend	spent	spent	spending
spill（溢濺）	spilled / spilt	spilled / spilt	spilling
spin（旋轉、紡織）	span / spun	spun	spinning
spit（吐出）	spit / spat	spit	spitting
split（分切）	split	split	splitting
spread	spread	spread	spreading
spring（彈跳）	sprang / sprung	sprung	springing
stand	stood	stood	standing
steal	stole	stolen	stealing
stick	stuck	stuck	sticking
stride（跨大步走）	strode	stride / stridden	striding
strike	struck	struck	striking
string（貫串）	strung	strung	stringing

原形	過去式	過去分詞	現在分詞
strive（努力）	strove	striven	striving
swear	swore	sworn	swearing
sweep	swept	swept	sweeping
swell（腫脹）	swelled	swelled / swol-len	swelling
swim	swam	swum	swimming
swing	swung	swung	swinging
take	took	taken	taking
teach	taught	taught	teaching
tear	tore	torn	tearing
tell	told	told	telling
think	thought	thought	thinking
thrive（致富、繁盛）	thrived / throve	thrived	thriving
throw	threw	thrown	throwing
thrust（推衝）	thrust	thrust	thrusting
tread（步行、踐踏）	trod	trodden	treading
understand	understood	understood	understanding
uphold	upheld	upheld	upholding
upset	upset	upset	upsetting
wake	woke	waken	waking
wear	wore	worn	wearing
weave（織）	weaved / wove	weaved / woven	weaving

原形	過去式	過去分詞	現在分詞
wed	wed	wed	wedding
weep	wept	wept	weeping
wind	wound	wound	winding
win	won	won	winning
withhold（抑制、保留）	withheld	withheld	withholding
withstand（抗拒）	withstood	withstood	withstanding
wring（絞擰）	wrung	wrung	wringing
write	wrote	written	writing

● **容易混淆的動詞：**語言的使用多因使用者的思維邏輯和所使用語言的限制，在用詞遣字上或有不同。中文說「吃藥」，英文就成take medicine；中文說「喝湯」，英文則說成eat one's soup！在參加國際性英語文測驗如托福多益或雅思時，一定要注意到上述的差異。下列是一些意思接近但在使用上常造成混淆的動詞。

1. accept / receive

▶When he was ill, he **received**（收到）lots of money，but he did not **accept**（接受）any.

2. affect / effect

▶The flood has seriously **affected**（影響）our life.
▶The change was **effected**（造成、開始）by the land reform（土地

改革）.

3. arise / arouse / rise / raise

▶New problems **arise**（發生、出現）everyday.
▶The music **aroused**（喚起、引起）an intense（強烈）feeling of homesickness（鄉愁）in him.
▶The sun **rises** in the east and sets in the west.
▶He **raised** his hand to ask the permission from the teacher.
他舉手徵求老師的允許。

4. assure / ensure / insure

▶The announcement（公告、宣稱）by the government further **assured**（保證、使人放心）us.
▶His hard work will **ensure**（確保）success to him.
▶He **insured** his house against fire（保火險）.

5. award / reward

▶The university **awarded**（授與）him an honorary degree（榮譽學位）.
▶How can I **reward**（獎勵）you for a job nicely done?

6. convince / persuade

▶She is **convinced**（深信不疑）of his innocence.
▶I finally **persuaded** him to stop smoking.
我終於說服他停止抽菸。

7. change / alter / vary

▶In autumn, the leaves **change** from green to yellow.
樹葉在秋天由綠變黃。
▶This article（物件）must be **altered**（修改）because the length doesn't fit.

▶ Temperature varies（變化）from region（地區）to region.

8. conserve / preserve / reserve

▶ We should try our best to conserve（保存）our natural resources.

▶ They are preserving（保護）world peace.

▶ We will reserve two tickets under your name for the show tomorrow. 我們明天將在你名下保留兩張戲票。

9. crash / crush / clash

▶ The lamp crashed（摔碎）to the floor and the bulb（燈泡）burst（破裂）.

▶ Don't crush（壓壞）this box because there is a cake inside.

▶ The two armies（軍隊）clashed（衝突）near the border（邊界）.

10. deny / refuse

▶ John denied（否定）that he had done it.

▶ The movie star refused（拒絕）to answer any personal questions（私人問題）.

11. doubt / suspect

▶ I doubt（懷疑某事不可能）it will rain this afternoon.

▶ I suspect（猜測；認為某事有可能）that he is responsible for the murder.（suspect若當名詞使用，重音在第一音節；若當動詞用，重音在第二音節。）

12. discover / invent

▶ Columbus discovered America in 1492.

▶ Edison invented the gramophone（留聲機）.

13. dress（穿上；以人為受詞）/ put on（穿上；以物為受詞）/ wear（穿上；表示一種狀態）

▶ This young lady **dressed** herself in black.
這年輕女子穿黑衣服。

▶ I **put on** my raincoat when it started to rain.
當天下雨時，我穿上雨衣。

▶ My father always **wears** black shoes.
我父親總是穿黑鞋。

14. earn / gain / win

▶ He **earns**（掙得）his living by working two jobs.

▶ He **gained** his reputation（贏得）by hard work.

▶ Our team **won**（獲勝）the first prize in the tournament（錦標賽）.

15. fall (fell、fallen) / fell (felled、felled砍伐)

▶ John **fell** down and broke his leg.
John跌倒且摔斷了腿。

▶ The wood-cutter（樵夫）**felled** a large tree.

16. found (founded、founded) / find (found、found)

▶ He tried to **find** his lost bag.
他試著找他遺失的袋子。

▶ He **founded** the company fifty years ago.
他50年前創立這公司。

17. hang (hanged、hanged) / hang (hung、hung)

▶ He was **hanged**（絞死）for the crime he had committed.

▶ He **hung**（懸掛）some pictures on the wall when he moved in the apartment.

18. hear（聽見；強調結果）/ listen（聽見；強調動作）

▶ He likes **listening** to music.

▶ He **listened** attentively（全神貫注）and **heard** nothing.

19. recall / remember / remind

▶ I do not **recall**（想起）your name but recognize your face.

▶ I **remember**（記得）reading that book when I was little.

▶ If I forget, please **remind**（提醒）me.

20. ignore / neglect

▶ He who **ignores**（視而不理）history is doomed（注定）to repeat it.

▶ He works extremely hard and **neglect** his health.
他非常努力工作且因此忘了他的健康。

21. replace / substitute

▶ He **replaced** paper money by gold.
他用金子來替代紙幣。

▶ He **substituted** paper money for gold.
他用紙幣來替代金子。

22. sit（坐；後加介系詞再加名詞）/ seat（坐；常用被動後加反身受詞）

▶ He **sat** at the desk working.

▶ He **seated** himself near the fire.

▶ Please be **seated**. (= Please sit down.)

■ 實用測驗

1. You must _____ me when I ask you a question.

   ① reply   ② answer   ③ replied   ④ answered

2. Lisa _____ two sons and two daughters.

   ① was born   ② bore   ③ has borne   ④ has born

3. She was never _____ with his talking.

   ① bore   ② bored   ③ born   ④ borne

4. Did John _____ from his illness?

   ① cure   ② recover   ③ recuperate   ④ regain

5. Please _____ the carpet in the living room.

   ① lied   ② lay   ③ laid   ④ lain

6. The auditorium _____ 3,000 viewers.

   ① sits   ② seats   ③ lis sitting   ④ is seating

7. Something that was strange occurred here last night. =

   ① Something strange was happened here last night.

   ② Strange something was happened here last night.

   ③ Something strange happened here last night.

   ④ Strange something happened here last night.

8. Many people think they can _____ what the weather is going to be like, but they hardly ever agree with each other.

   ① talk   ② cry   ③ tell   ④ speak

9. It _____ Mary a bundle to buy this antique dresser.

   ① cost   ② took   ③ spent   ④ made

10. The accident _____ on the morning of the sixth of this month.

    ① occurred   ② take place   ③ was held   ④ is happening

11. I'm sorry to be late for the meeting since my secretary _____ to tell me about your changing the schedule to the earlier time.

    ① decided   ② neglected   ③ refused   ④ ignored

12. When you drive through the main entrance, _____ a right as you enter the parking lot.

① make ② turn ③ do ④ change

13. It's the company's policy that every employee _____ to work in casual clothes on Friday.

① come ② be ③ dress ④ attend

14. If you're _____ Mr. Smith, he is away from the office this moment.

① looking for ② looking at ③ looking into ④ looking forward to

15. Most of us in this office _____ lunch at noon.

① make ② have ③ bring ④ go

16. I won't _____ to playing the radio at your desk if the volume is low.

① mind ② refuse ③ negate ④ object

17. If I say something bad about your work, you shouldn't _____ it personally.

① make ② think ③ believe ④ take

18. If you _____ long before leaving for the train station, the hotel will keep your luggage for you.

① exit ② depart ③ check out ④ move out

19. By law, we must _____ how much income tax to be deducted from your pay.

① calculable ② calculation ③ calculate ④ calculator

20. My friend in college is _____ marketing.

① studying ② researching ③ discussing ④ inquiring

■ 試題解析

1. ② must是助動詞，其後接原形動詞；但是「answer + 名詞」而「reply + to + 名詞」。

2. ③ 「生」bear的三式變化為bear、bore、born / borne；若用主動語態且其後沒有by時，要選borne。如 "She was _____ in a rich family." 時，則要選born。

3. ② 「厭煩」時選bored。

4. ② cure是「治癒」；recuperate是「復原」；regain是「重得」。

5. ② lie / lied / lied：說謊；lie / lay / lain：躺臥；lay / laid / laid：放置。

6. ② sit通常是不及物；若要當及物動詞用，需與介詞連用：sit on a chair、sit at table、sit for an exam等。在古英文中也有"sit yourself down"的用法。

7. ③ something、anything、nothing等字和形容詞連用時，形容詞需置於其後；happen沒有被動用法。

8. ① tell當「區別」用；speak則通常與語言連用。

9. ① 人 + spend + 時間 / 金錢；物 + cost + 人 + 金錢；事物 + take + 人 + 時間。

   John spent all his time on computer.

   John spent all his time in playing computer.

   The computer cost John a lot of money.

   The work took John whole day to finish.

10. ① 過去時間的被動語態。

11. ② neglect用於此處在句意上最合適。

12. ① make / take a right turn = turn right，前者的right是形容詞；後者的right是副詞。

13. ③ 因在句中有in casual 的修飾語，所以dress而非come才是正確的選擇。

14. ① look for：找；look at：看；look into：調查；look forward to：期盼。

15. ② have當「吃」用。

16. ④ mind後加Ving，但題目中有介詞to，所以要選④。

17. ④ take...personally：視為人身攻擊。

18.③ check out當「辦理退房」用。

19.③ 同樣的字根但有四種不同的詞性；在助動詞must後需選動詞。

20.① study「研讀」；若有major也可考慮但需與介詞in連用。

主詞與動詞間數的一致
(Agreement of Subject and Verb)

英文文法中有三個「一致」的規定：主詞動詞在單複數上需一致（I go., You go., He goes.），名詞和代名詞在互換時單複數的一致（My boss always wears suits to work; they look great on him. they代替suits，而him 則是my boss改成代名詞後的受格），以及複合句中動詞時態前後的一致（John went to see the movies last night, but he forgot to bring his wallet with him. "went"和 "forgot"都是過去式動詞）。

■ **本章重點**

● 主詞與動詞之間數的一致

主詞與動詞間數的一致

規定

● **主詞與動詞之間數的一致**

1. 兩個或兩個以上主詞用and連接，其後動詞通常用複數形

▶John and Mary work for the same company.
John與Mary在同一家公司工作。

▶Fire and water do not agree.
水火不相容。

2. 兩個或兩個以上的單數主詞用and連接，但視為單一的人、事物或觀念時，其後加單數形動詞

▶ **Curry and rice is** his favorite dish.

　咖哩飯是我最喜歡的一道菜。

▶ **A black and white cat is** lying by the door.

　一隻黑白相間的貓躺在門邊。

　比較 A black and a white cats are lying by the door.

　　　一隻黑貓和一隻白貓躺在門邊。

3. every、each、many a、more than one等字放在名詞前時，該名詞後需加單數動詞

▶ **Each** person in this office **has** his work to do.

　辦公室裡的每個人都有自己的事要做。

▶ **Many a** boy **likes** to play basketball.

　許多男孩喜歡打籃球。

　（many a = many；Many boys like to play basketball.）

▶ **More than one** worker **was** absent for work yesterday.

　昨天不只一個工人缺席了。（more than是複合副詞，用來修飾one。）

　比較 More workers than one were absent for work yesterday.

　　　（more是形容詞，用來修飾主詞workers。）

4. 兩個或兩個以上的單數主詞用and連接，而其前有如：each、every、many a、no等字時，後加單數動詞

▶ **Each** boy and (**each**) girl **has** his own chair and desk.

　每個男孩每個女孩都有自己的桌椅。

▶ **Every** man and (**every**) woman in the meeting **does** not necessarily

　agree with you.

　會議中的每個人不盡然同意你。

▶ **Many a** day and **many a** night has passed since she was last seen.

　自從最後一次見到她至今已經過了許多日子。

5. 兩個或兩個以上的主詞若用or、either...or...、neither... nor...、not only...but (also)... 連接時，動詞要跟最靠近的主詞一致

A or B	
Either A or B	+ V（與B一致）
Neither A nor B	
Not only A but (also) B	

▶ Either Jack or **I am** going to be there tomorrow.
　Jack或我明天會去那裡。

▶ Not only I but also **my family are** going to be there tomorrow.
　不只我還有我家人明天會去那裡。

▶ Neither Jack nor **his family are** saying anything.
　Jack和他的家人都沒說什麼。

▶ You, he or **I will** have to make the decision.
　不管你或我或他，一定有人要做決定。（因涉及意志未來，所以I之後要用will。）

▶ **Is Mary** or her friends to be blamed?
　是Mary還是她的朋友們該受責備？（疑問句中，動詞和前面主詞一致）

▶ Not Mary but **I am** to be blamed.
　不是Mary而是我該遭到責備。（若有肯定及否定主詞，動詞需與肯定主詞一致）

6. 兩個主詞若由as well as、no less than、together with、with、but、except、like等連接時，動詞要和第一個主詞一致

A as well as B	
A no less than B	
A together with B	+ V（需與A一致）
A with B	
A like B	

▶ The **boss** as well as his employees **was** invited to the convention.
老闆和他的員工都受邀參加大會。

▶ **Jack** no less than you **is** worried about the situation.
Jack和你一樣都擔心這種狀況。

▶ The **helmet** along with the motorbike **was** stolen last night.
安全帽和機車都被偷了。

▶ The **girls** like their mother **are** all dressed in black.
這些女孩和她們母親一樣都穿黑色。

▶ **Nobody** but you and your co-workers **has** ever made such a mistake.
除了你和你的同事外沒人犯這錯誤。

7. 表示「時間」、「重量」、「距離」或「價值」的複數名詞後需用單數動詞

▶ **Six months** is too short for anyone to learn English well.
六個月的時間對任何學英文的人而言都太短。

◆比較 Six months have passed since I last saw her.
從我最後見到她到現在已經六個月了。

▶ **Fifty pounds** is too much a burden for anyone to carry.
五十磅對任何人而言都太重了。

▶ **One hundred dollars** is not enough for a decent meal.
一百元是不夠吃頓像樣的飯。

◆比較 Millions of dollars were spent annually for nothing by the city government.
市政府每年都將數以百萬計的錢浪費在沒用的事上。

8. 複數形但單數義的名詞需與單數動詞連用

▶ The **news is** too good to be true.
消息好到難以相信。

▶ The **murderer's whereabouts remains** unknown.
謀殺犯的下落依然不明。

9. 有些複數形主詞其後需加複數形動詞

▶ These **clothes are** selling extremely well.
這些衣服的銷售好到不得了。

▶ **Riches are** nothing for the billionaire.
財富對億萬富翁而言不算什麼。

▶ The **wages** for interns **are** 95 dollars an hour.
見習生的時薪是一小時95元。

◆比較 The wage for a crime like this is death.
此種犯罪的代價是死刑。

10. 以Most of、Half of、Some of、Rest of、All of、Part of、A lot of / Lots of、Plenty of或分數，如Two thirds of當主詞時，若of之後的名詞是複數名詞用複數動詞，單數名詞則用單數動詞

▶ **Most of** my **co-workers are** from Taipei.
我大部分的同事都來自臺北。

▶ **Most of** my free **time is** spent on exercising.
我大部分的空閒時間都花在運動上。

▶ **Tow third** of my **savings has** been spent in buying electronic gadgets
我三分之二的儲蓄都花在新奇的電子小玩意上。

▶ **Two thirds** of the **students were** present even with the typhoon yesterday.
昨天雖然有颱風，但三分之二的學生都出席了。

▶ **A number of participants were** allowed to get in the show free of charge.
很多參與者都免費入場看表演。

▶ **The number of participants allowed** to get in the show free is limited to 15.
觀演民眾入場人數被限制在15人。

11. 集合名詞當主詞時，若取其「團體」意思用單數動詞；若取其「所有成員」意思則用複數動詞

▶ My **family is** a big one.
　我的家庭是個大家庭。

▶ My **family are** all well.
　我的家人都安好。

▶ The **committee consists** of 15 members, the **committee are** divided in their opinions.
　委員會由15人組成，成員們意見分歧。

12. 主詞若為用There / Here引導的句子，若其後是單數主詞用單數動詞，複數主詞則用複數動詞

▶ There **is a man** looking for you.
　有個人在找你。

▶ There **are two men** looking for you.
　有兩個人在找你。

▶ Here comes **an old lady.**
　來了位老太太。

▶ Here **come an old lady** and **her dog.**
　老太太和她的狗來了。

13. 不定詞、動名詞、名詞片語或名詞子句當主詞時，其後加單數動詞

▶ **To tell lies is** not my style.
　說謊不是我的風格。（不定詞當主詞）

▶ **Telling lies is** not my style.
　說謊不是我的風格。（動名詞當主詞）

▶ **Where to eat is** not important for me.
　在哪吃飯對我而言不重要。（名詞片語當主詞）

▶ **That the earth is round is** eternally true.
　地球是圓的是恆真的。（名詞子句當主詞）

■ 實用測驗

1. "How much meat do you need?" "Five pounds _____ quite enough."
   ① is ② are ③ has been ④ have been

2. The apartment with all its beautiful decorations and settings _____ mine.
   ① has been sold to ② have been sold to ③ has sold to ④ have sold to

3. Whether I go or I stay _____ none of your business.
   ① is ② are ③ shall be ④ will be

4. Learning a foreign language as well as the necessary skills on computer _____
   important nowadays.
   ① is ② are ③ has ④ have

5. The boss along with all his employees _____ looking forward to the coming of
   the year-end party.
   ① is ② are ③ has ④ have

6. She is interested in anything that _____ related to art.
   ① is ② are ③ has been ④ have been

7. I am sure neither you nor your family _____ happy about the result of your in-
   terview.
   ① is ② are ③ has ④ have

8. Much of what had been said _____ not true.
   ① was ② were ③ is ④ are

9. The majority of damage caused by the typhoon _____ easy to repair.
   ① is ② are ③ has ④ have

10. One of his dreams _____ to travel around the world one day.
    ① is ② are ③ has ④ have

11. Mary often _____ on a diet, but that doesn't last very long.
    ① go ② goes ③ went ④ has gone

12. Collecting rare coins _____ his lifelong hobby.
    ① is ② are ③ has been ④ have been

13. Every one of the boys _____ own idea about where to spend the coming week-end.

① have their   ② has one's   ③ has his   ④ have his

14. Among all the qualities, a must for any student _____ diligence.

① is   ② are   ③ has   ④ have

15. The parents as well as the children _____.

① has expressed their opinions   ② were look at the door   ③ prefers going out than staying at home   ④ have made the same choice

試題解析

1. ① 重量、時間、距離和價值取其總數，用單數動詞。
2. ① A with B時，動詞與A一致。
3. ① whether的名詞子句，其後用單數動詞。
4. ① 動名詞當主詞時，其後動詞取單數；A as well as B，動詞需與A一致。
5. ① A along with B時，其後動詞需與A一致。
6. ① that當anything的關係代名詞；anything為單數，故其後需加單數動詞。
7. ② neither A nor B時，動詞需與B一致。
8. ① much修飾不可數名詞，動詞取單數形，再加上動詞時態需與said一致，所以選①。
9. ① damage為不可數名詞，其後取單數形動詞；若是the majority of people時，其後需取複數形動詞。
10.① 雖然dreams是複數名詞，但其修飾語為one of，所以要選單數形動詞。
11.② often用來表示習慣，常與現在簡單式連用；主詞為第三人稱單數，所以選②。
12.③ 雖然動名詞當主詞時，其後取單數形動詞，但lifetime「一生」表示經驗，所以需與現在完成式連用。
13.③ every + 名詞時，不僅需與單數形動詞連用，更要將所有格的形式改成his。
14.① "a must"「一件必要的事」當主詞，其後取單數形動詞。
15.④ A as well as B後之動詞需與A一致。

筆記頁

 **時態** (Tense)

時態是動詞用來表示動作或狀態的時間關係。

■ **本章重點**

時態

未來簡單　現在簡單

現在完成
過去進行　　　12種時態形式

未來完成　　　　現在進行

過去完成

未來完成進行　　　未來進行　過去簡單

過去完成進行　現在完成進行

- ● 12種時態形式
- ● 現在簡單式
- ● 過去簡單式
- ● 未來簡單式
- ● 現在進行式
- ● 過去進行式
- ● 未來進行式

- ● 現在完成式
- ● 過去完成式
- ● 未來完成式
- ● 現在完成進行式
- ● 過去完成進行式
- ● 未來完成進行式

● 12種時態形式

1. 以 "eat" 為例，其時態如下

		簡單式	完成式	進行式	完成進行式
現在式		eats / eat	have / has+eaten	am + eating	have + been + eating
				are...	have...
				is...	has...
過去式		ate	had+eaten	was + eating	had + been + eating
				were...	
未來式		shall + eat	shall + have + eaten	shall + be + eating	shall + have + been + eating
		will...	will...	will...	will...

2. 以實際句子說明

I eat.（現在簡單式）

I ate.（過去簡單式）

I shall / will eat.（未來簡單式；shall表單純未來 / will表意志未來）

I am eating.（現在進行式）

I was eating.（過去進行式）

I shall be eating.（未來進行式；shall表單純未來 / will表意志未來）

I have eaten.（現在完成式）

I had eaten.（過去完成式）

I shall / will have eaten.（未來完成式；shall表單純未來 / will表意志未來）

I have been eating.（現在完成進行式）

I had been eating.（過去完成進行式）

I shall / will have been eating.（未來完成進行式；shall表單純未來 / will表意志未來）

● 現在簡單式（主詞 + V-s / V-es / V-ies）

1. 用來表示現在的動作、狀態或事實

▶ John **is** a conscientious worker.
John是位正直的工作者。

▶ China **is** larger than any other country in Asia.
中國比任何亞洲國家都大。

▶ Ms. Chen **teaches** English; she **is** an English teacher.
陳女士教英文，她是位英文教師。

2. 用來表示習慣性的動作

▶ I **get up** at six every morning.
我每天早上六點起床。

▶ The bus usually **runs** every five minutes.
公車每五分鐘一班。

▶ I **go** to the movies once a week.
我一個星期看一次電影。

> 🔊 小提醒
>
> 此種用法通常會與頻率副詞（always, usually, often...）
> 或表示時間的副詞（every..., once a + 時間…）等連
> 用。

3. 表示人格、職業

▶ He **is** a man of courage.
他是個勇敢的人。

▶ His father **runs** a bookstore.
他的父親經營一家書店。

▶ She **swims** very well.
她泳游得很好。

4. 表示不變的真理或格言

▶ Light **travels** faster than sound.
光速快過音速。

▶ The sun **rises** in the east and **sets** in the west.
太陽東邊升起西邊下降。

▶ Six times four **is** (**are**) twenty-four.
六乘四是二十四。

▶ Columbus **discovers** America.
哥倫布發現美洲。

5. 可用來代替未來式

▶ She **leaves** (will leave) for Japan tomorrow.
她明天啟程到日本。

▶ The ship **sails** on Sunday.
這艘船週日起航。

▶ My cousin **returns** next spring.
我表（堂）兄弟明年春天回來。

🎧 小提醒

此種用法的動詞多為表示「來往」或「預定」意思的動詞，如：go、come、leave、start、sail、arrive、reach、meet...，也會與表示未來時間的時間副詞：如tomorrow、next week、the day after tomorrow...連用。

表示「時間」或「條件」的連接詞，如：when、till、before、as soon as、if...所引導的副詞子句，通常動詞也會以現在式代替未來式。

▶ Let us tell him the fact when he comes back.
讓我們在他回來後告訴他實情。

▶ If it is fine tomorrow, I will visit you.
如果明天天氣好，我將會去探望你。

6. 若為下列動詞，如：hear、see、understand、forget、read、learn...時，也可以現在式代替未來式

▶ I **hear** that he has come back.
　我聽說他已回來了。

▶ I **forget** what you have told me before.
　我忘了你先前告訴我的事。

7. 若現在簡單式的主詞為第三人稱單數時，其後動詞尾應加-s 或-es

1 字尾是【ch, s, sh, x或z】時，加-es讀成【iz】。

pass - passes、catch - catches、wish - wishes、fix - fixes.

2 動詞字尾是子音+y時 ，去y加-ies讀成【z】。

cry - cries、worry - worries、try - tries.

3 動詞字尾若是母音+y時，直接加-s讀成【z】。

play - plays、say - says.

4 若動詞字尾是子音+o時，加-es讀成【z】。

do - does、go - goes.

5 其他動詞字尾加s讀成【z】。

know - knows、make - make.

● **過去簡單式（主詞 + V-d / V-ed / V-ied）**

1. 表示在過去的某一點或某一段時間內所發生的動作、狀態或習慣，通常與表示過去時間的副詞，如：ago、last week / month / year、yesterday、yesterday morning、this morning、just now、the other day等連用

▶ We **had** a company outing yesterday.
　我們昨天有公司郊遊。

▶I **saw** Mary two days ago.

我兩天前看過Mary。

▶My brother **studied** at this university from 1990 to 1994.

我兄弟1990到1994年之間在這所大學讀書。

▶Columbus **discovered** America in 1492.

哥倫布在1492年發現美洲。

◆比較▶ Columbus discovers America.　哥倫布發現美洲。（事實）

Columbus discovered America in 1492.　哥倫布在1492年發現美洲。（過去動作）

◆比較▶ 過去簡單式和過去進行式

I read a book last night.（動作發生在過去時間）

I was reading a book at nine last night.（動作在過去時間正在進行中）

2. "used to + v原形" 表過去的習慣；"be used to + v-ing" 表目前的習慣；"get used to + v-ing" 表將養成的習慣

▶I **used to get** up early (but I don't do that anymore).

我以前習慣早起。

▶I **am used to getting** up early now.

我現在已習慣早起。

▶I will have to **get used to getting** up early soon if I want to be on time for classes.

如果我要準時上課，我將來一定要早起。

3. 過去式和ever或never等副詞連用時，可等於現在完成式表示「經驗」

▶**Did** you **ever** see a tiger?

= Have you ever seen a tiger?

你曾看過老虎嗎？

▶I **never heard** of such a horrible story.

= I have never heard of such a terrible story.

我從沒聽過如此恐怖的故事。

● **未來簡單式：** 第一人稱單複數主詞 + shall + V原形；第二 / 三人
　　　　　　　　稱單複數主詞 + will + V原形。

1. 在未來某一點或某一段時間內將發生的動作、狀態或習慣。通常和表示未來時間的副詞，如：tomorrow、next week / month / year、_____ days from now等連用。

▶I **shall be** glad to meet you at the same time next year.

我將會高興在明年此時見到你。

▶He **will be** unable to pass the final exam tomorrow unless he studies hard.

如果他不努力讀書，他將無法通過明天的期末考試。

▶Jack **will graduate** from university 3 years from now.

Jack將在三年後從大學畢業。

2. 下列三種用法也可代表未來式

1 「be going to + v原形」：表示推測或預定的未來；可能會。

▶It **is going to rain** this afternoon.

明天將會下雨。

▶I **am going to study** harder next time.

我下次要更用功。

2 「be about to + v原形」：表示最近的未來；即將。

▶I **am about to** start on a journey.

我即將開始我的旅程。

▶The case **is** shortly **about to** be tried .

這件案子即將開始被審理。

3「be + to + v原形」：表示未來的預定，計畫或命令等；應
該。

▶My father **is to come** back next Sunday.
我父親應該在下週日回來。

▶You **are to knock** before you enter the room.
你在進入房間前應該先敲門。

3. 未來式又可分「單純未來」和「意志未來」；意志未來是指說話者（第一人稱）的意志

▶I **shall go** to the U.S. next year.
我將在明年去美國。

▶John **will study** abroad after he graduates.
John將在畢業後出國讀書。（單純未來：第一人稱單複數用
shall；第二人稱單複數及第三人稱單複數用will）

▶You **shall leave** when I tell you to.

▶I **will** not **go** until the last minute.（意志未來：第一人稱單複數
用will；第二及第三人稱單複數用shall）

● 現在進行式（主詞 + am / are / is + V-ing）

1. 表示目前正在發生、進行或繼續的一種動作或狀態。通常和 now或at present 連用

▶We **are studying** English grammar now.
我們現在正在讀英文文法。

▶A white and black dog **is lying** by the door.
一隻黑白相間的狗正躺在門口。

▶Jack **is typing** a letter at present.
Jack現在正在打信。

2. 用現在進行式表示動作的反覆、經常或習慣。通常與下列副詞，如：always、constantly、usually等連用

▶ The girl **is always smiling**.
這女孩總是微笑。

▶ He **is constantly complaining** his salary's being too low.
他一直埋怨薪水太低。

3. 表示「存在」、「所有」、「感情」、「感受」的動詞，如：be、consist、stand（在）、lie（位於）、have、possess、belong to、know、understand、agree、imagine、seem、forget、remember、suppose、desire、hope、wish、believe、love、hate、like、see、hear、smell、taste等不可使用進行式

▶ The hat belongs to me.（○）
這帽子是屬於我的。

The hat is belonging to me.（×）

＋ 例外
▶ He was having（吃）his dinner when we came in.
▶ He is seeing his girl friend off（送行）at the station.
▶ They are seeing the sights（觀光）of Tainan.
▶ The judge is hearing（審理）the case.

小提醒

現在簡單式用來表示具永久性、習慣性和固定性的動作；現在進行式則是用來表示具臨時性、偶發性和短暫性的動作。

▶ The earth moves around the sun.
地球繞著太陽轉。

▶ The falling leaves are moving in the wind.
落葉在風中飄動。

● 過去進行式（主詞 + was / were + V-ing）

1. 兩個過去的動作，某動作發生時另一動作正在持續中，持續者用進行式而發生者用過去簡單式

▶ He came across me while he **was taking** a walk in the park.
他在公園散步時碰到我。

▶ I **was watching** TV when he called last night.
當他昨晚打電話來時我正在看電視。

> 🔊 小提醒
>
> while通常與過去進行式的動詞連用，when則與過去簡單式的動作連用。
> 但We were reading while they were writing.
> （兩個同時在過去時間進行的動作；while當「而」使用）

2. 在過去某點時間或某段時間內正在進行或持續的動作

▶ We **were watching** the movies at eight o'clock last night.
我們昨晚八點正在看電視。

3. 表示過去的習慣或反覆的動作

▶ He **was always studying** late in the evening when he was a student.
當他是學生時總是讀書讀到很晚。

▶ She **was forever asking** her husband for money with which to buy new shoes.
她過去總是跟先生要錢去買新鞋。

● 未來進行式（主詞 + shall / will + be + V-ing）

1. 兩個未來動作，當某個動作正在進行時，另一動作發生，正在發生的用未來進行式，發生的用未來式

▶ I **shall be taking** a nap when you come back.
當你來時我將會正在睡午覺。

2. 在未來某個時間內將正在發生的動作

▶ I **shall** probably **be correcting** students' homework at this time tomorrow.
明天此時我將可能在改學生的作業。

● 現在完成式（主詞 + have / has + V-ed）

1. 表示現在剛完成的動作；也就是說，從過去某點時間發生到現在才完成的動作。通常與下列副詞，如：just、yet、already、up till now、recently、lately等連用

▶ I **have** just **come** back from school.
我剛從學校回來。

　　☆比較 I came back from school just now.

▶ I **haven't seen** him recently .
我最近沒看到他。

　　☆比較 I saw him recently.
　　　　　我剛剛看到他。

🔊 小提醒

> be動詞與go、come、rise、arrive、return、grow...等不及物動詞的過去分詞連用,也可表示動作的完成。
>
> ▶He is gone.
>
> 　= He has gone.
>
> 　他已離開。
>
> ▶He is fully grown.
>
> 　= He has fully grown.
>
> 　他已長大。

2. 表示到現在為止一生中所經驗到的事情。通常與下列副詞,如:never、ever、once、often、seldom、before、several times等連用

▶I **have never seen** a tiger.
我從沒見過老虎。

▶They **have talked** about you **before**.
他們曾提到你。

◆比較 They had talked about you before you came.
他們在你來之前曾談到你。(兩個動作前後發生)

▶The woman **has seen** that movie **many times**.
這女士已經看過好幾次那部電影了。

3. 表示從過去時間開始繼續到現在的動作或狀態。通常與下列副詞,如:since、for a long time、for years、How long...等連用

▶I **have known** him **since** childhood.
我從孩童時代就認識他。

▶**How long have** you **studied** English?
你學英文多久了?

▶I **have studied** English **for** six years.
我讀英文已有六年了。

🔷比較 It is four years since she left here.（總時間）

　　　　It has been four years since she left here.（持續時間）

4. 表示過去所發生的動作其結果影響到現在

▶Edison **has made** many important inventions.
愛迪生有許多重要的發明。

5. 表示時間或條件的副詞子句，用現在完成式代替未來完成式

▶I shall call on him when I **have finished** writing my letter.
當我完成工作後將去拜訪他。

▶If you **have done** your work, you will get your pay.
如果你做好工作就能拿到酬勞。

🔷比較 現在完成式和過去式

　　　　(A) He has eaten nothing since yesterday.（從昨天起）

　　　　　　He ate nothing yesterday.（昨天）

　　　　(B) He has been to Tokyo.（曾去過東京）

　　　　　　He has gone to Tokyo.（已去東京）

　　　　(C) He reached home just now（剛）

　　　　　　He is playing tennis just now（此刻）

　　　　　　We have just eaten dinner（剛吃完）

● 過去完成式（主詞 + had + V-ed）

1. 過去兩個動作做比較，先發生的用過去完成式而後發生的用過去簡單式

▶My brother lost his pen which I **had bought** for him.
我兄弟把我買給他的筆弄丟了。

▶ The train **had already** left when I arrived at the station.
當我到車站時火車已離開了。

2. 指過去某一段時間內,或過去某一點時間前所完成的動作或經驗

▶ He **had lived** here from 1990 to 1995.
他在1990到1995之間住在這裡。

▶ The rain **had stopped** before yesterday morning.
雨在昨天早上之前就停了。

◆比較 I bought a pen and lost it.（過去兩動作,依順序表達時,都用過去式）

I lost the pen which I had bought.（過去兩動作,晚發生的先說,早發生的後說,先說用過去簡單式,後說用過去完成式）

The teacher told us that Columbus discovered America in 1492.
（歷史事實雖先發生仍用過去簡單式。）

● 未來完成式（主詞 + shall / will + have + V-ed）

1. 兩個未來的動作,在某動作將發生時,另一動作已完成,完成之動作用未來完成式,而另一動作用未來式

▶ When you come back, I **shall have finished** my homework.
當你回來時,我將已完成我的作業。

▶ If you want to come to see me, I **shall have done** my homework immediately.
如果你要來看我,我將會立即把作業做好。

2. 表示到未來某一時間所完成或經驗的事情

▶ I **shall have lived** here for two years by next month.
到下個月我將在此居住滿兩年了。

▶ He **will have reached** Taipei by this time tomorrow.
明天此時他將到達臺北。

● **現在完成進行式（主詞 + have / has + been + V-ing）：**表示某一自過去某時開始，進行到說話的現在，而且會持續到未來的動作。

▶ I **have been waiting** for you since you left.
我從你離開就一直等。（如果有必要還會等下去）
▶ We **have been learning** English for six years.
我已經學了六年英文。（而且還會繼續學下去）

> 🔊 小提醒
>
> 現在完成是表示從過去開始到現在結束的動作；現在完成進行式則表示從過去開始進行到現在而且會持續到未來的動作。
> ▶ I have worked for ABC Company for 10 years. (but I am not working for it now.)
> ▶ I have been working for ABC Company for 10 yaers. (and am still working for it.)

● **過去完成進行式（主詞 + had + been + V-ing）：**從較早的過去持續到較晚的過去，比過去式更強調動作的持續。

▶ We **had been waiting** for about ten minutes when the bus came.
在公車來之前我們就已經等了十分鐘了。
▶ He **had been staying** at home when the murder happened.
當謀殺發生之前他就在家了。

● **未來完成進行式（主詞＋shall / will＋have＋been＋V-ing）：**
表示某動作已完成且持續到未來的某一時間。

▶ My family **will have been living** here for four years by next year.
我全家到明年就將在此居住滿四年了。

▶ It **will have been raining** for a week if it does not stop tomorrow.
如果雨明天還不停的話，雨就將下滿一個星期了。

> 🔊 小提醒
>
> 動詞章節中雖已對動詞的規則及不規則變化有詳盡說明，但因在上述時態討論中可看到時態的應用，除現在簡單式外，其他時態都會使用到動詞的過去式、過去及現在分詞，所以一定要反覆練習熟記。

實用測驗

1. The whole area was flooded because it _____ for weeks.

   ① rains ② has rained ③ had been raining ④ was taining

2. Education _____ him into a new person.

   ① transforms ② has transformed ③ has been transforming ④ will have transformed

3. These workers _____ for the company five years by the end of this year.

   ① will be working ② will have been working ③ will work ④ will have been worked

4. The kids won't go to bed until their father _____.

   ① returns ② will return ③ will return ④ return

5. There _____ some very bad news lately.

   ① is ② are ③ have ④ have been

6. When I went to his house last night, he _____ his dinner.

   ① has eaten ② was eaten ③ ate ④ was eating

7. Look! Someone _____ in the park.

   ① is dancing ② dance ③ to dance ④ dances

8. Keep an eye on the stove while I _____.

   ① go shopping ② go to shop ③ am do some shopping ④ will be doing some shopping

9. So far, we _____ a reply from the client.

   ① did not have ② are not having ③ haven't had ④ have had not

10. We have been informed about the outcome of the negotiation, but we shall never find out what _____ on behind the scenes.

    ① goes ② will go ③ went ④ will have been going

11. The students did something they _____ before; that is, they were absent at the same time.

    ① have had never done ② had had never done ③ has had never done ④ will have never done

12. My little brother is always good while my mother _____.

　　① looks　② will be looking　③ has been looking　④ is looking

13. I have seen the performance of "Cats" twice already. How many times _____ shown in this city?

　　① has it been　② has it　③ have it been　④ had it been

14. _____ you have bought some new books.

　　① I was seeing　② I see　③ I am seeing　④ I saw

15. Don't worry. If he said he _____ lend you the money, he will.

　　① shall　② will　③ would　④ should

試題解析

1. ③ 因在過去式was flooded之前的動作，所以要選過去完成式或過去完成進行式。

2. ② 因動作做到說話時已完成，所以選現在完成式。

3. ② 因為是到未來時間所完成的動作，所以選未來完成進行式。

4. ① 因為是until帶頭的時間副詞子句，而且是與「來去」等動詞相關的return，所以用現在簡單式代替未來簡單式。

5. ④ 因lately常與現在完成式連用。

6. ④ 兩個發生在過去時間的動作，耗時較長者用過去進行式；耗時較短者用過去簡單式。

7. ① look暗示某一動作正在發生中，所以選現在進行式，類似用法還有 listen；Listen! Someone is singing.

8. ① 因while常與進行式句子連用，若選項中am doing some shopping時也可以考慮。

9. ③ 因so far與現在完成式連用。

10. ③ 因協商結果現在已知，但其幕後運作為何則未知，過去的動作所以選過去簡單式。

11. ② 因為在were absent的動作之前有過的經驗，所以選過去完成式。

12. ④ 本為慣性的動作固當選現在簡單式，但又因while常與進行式連用，所以選現在進行式。

13. ① 表示經驗的被動語態，所以選現在完成式的被動用法。

14. ② 因see無進行式的用法，而選saw又和have bought之間在時態上不一致。

15. ③ 因與said需同時態，所以選would。

筆記頁

助動詞 (Auxiliary / Helping Verbs)

助動詞是用來幫助動詞的詞；若置於句首成疑問句，若與not連用成否定句，若與其他形式動詞連用成各種時態、語態和語氣。而有些助動詞如have或do也可以當主動詞用。

■ 本章重點

- be
- have
- do
- need / dare
- may / might
- can / could
- must
- shall / should / ought to
- will / would / used to

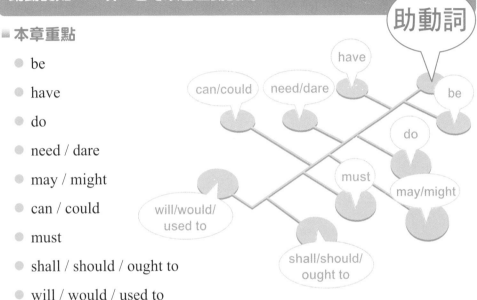

- **be**：「是」，「有」（與there連用當主動詞用）am / are / is / was / were與及物動詞連用形成被動語態；與現在分詞連用形成進行式；與不及物動詞的過去分詞連用有時也可表示動作的完成。

  ▶ The book **is written** by Mr. Smith.
  史密斯先生寫這本書。（被動語態）

  ▶ The boys **are playing** basketball now.
  男孩們現在在打籃球。（現在進行式）

▶He **is gone**.

　他走了。（表示現在的狀態）

　比較 He has gone.　他已走了。（表示動作的完成）

▶There **are** some apples on the table.

　桌上有些蘋果。

● **have**：have / has / had與過去分詞連用表示完成式。

▶My sister **has** just **come** home from school.

　我姊妹剛從學校回到家。

▶The work **had been finished** before he came back.

　工作在他回來前就完成了。

▶I **have been living** here since last year.

　我從去年起就住在這裡。

🔊 小提醒

「have」當主動詞用時的意思是「有」、「吃」、「要」等。

▶I **have** two brothers and one sister.

　我有兩個兄弟和一個姊妹。

▶I am **having** my lunch now.

　我正在吃午餐。

▶The teacher **has** her students be quiet in the classroom.

　老師要她的學生在教室內安靜。

● **do**：「do」當主動詞用時是「做」的意思，但在下列情形中則當助動詞用。

1. 形成疑問或否定句

▶ **Does** she come here every day?
她每天都來嗎？

▶ I **don't** want to stay here tonight.
我今晚不要待在這裡。

2. 用來加強語氣

▶ She **does like** you.
她的確喜歡你。

▶ I **did visit** you last night.
我昨晚的確去拜訪你。

3. 用來代替主要句子的動詞以免重複

▶ You run faster than I **do**.
你跑得比我快。

▶ He likes apples, and so **do** I.
他喜歡蘋果，我也喜歡。

▶ You don't like noise, and nor **do** I.
你不喜歡噪音，我也不喜歡。

4. 用來作倒裝句，通常與下列副詞，如：hardly、scarcely、rarely、never、little、only、seldom、well等連用

▶ **Never did** I see it again.
我再也沒看到它。

▶ **Well do** I remember her.
我很清楚地記得她。

▶ **Rarely has** John come to work on time.
約翰很少準時上班。

● **need / dare**：「need」與「dare」若當助動詞用時，主詞為第三人稱也不可加「s」。

▶ It **needs** to be done with care.
這需要謹慎處理。（主動詞）

▶ He **need / dare** not do it.
= He does not need / dare to do it.
他不需要 / 不敢做那事。（助動詞）

▶ He **dare not** travel alone.
他不敢獨自旅行。（助動詞）

▶ He did not **dare** (to) speak to her.
他不敢和她說話。（主動詞）

> 🔊 小提醒
>
> (A)「need not have + p.p.」表示過去不必做而做的事。
>
> ▶ You need not have said that. （你大可不必說）
>
> ✤比較 He need not have done it. （已經做了）
> He did not need to do it. （沒有做）
>
> (B)「need not」的過去或未來用「didn't have to」或「won't have to」表示。
>
> ▶ You did not have to say that.
>
> ▶ You won't have to say that.

● **may / might**

1. 表示許可

▶ **May** I leave now?　我能離開嗎？
Yes, you **may**.　是的，你可以。
No, you **mustn't**.　不，你不准。

2. 表示祈願

▶ **May** you be happy!
  祝你快樂！

3. 表示推測或可能

▶ The news **may** be true.
  這答案可能是真的。

▶ Work hard while you **may**.
  趁你還能時努力工作。

4. may 的慣用語

▶ You **may** well think so.
  你有理由這樣想。

▶ You **may** as well go at once.
  你最好立即就去。

🔊 小提醒

「may not」表示客氣的禁止；「must not」表示一般的
禁止；「shall not」表示強烈的禁止。

▶ You may not eat it if you don't like it.
  如果你不喜歡，你可以不吃。

▶ You must not smoke indoor.
  你不准在室內抽煙。

▶ You shall not talk back to your parents.
  你不准對父母親回嘴。

● can / could

1. 表示能力的意思，未來式可用shall / will be able to代替

▶ **Can** you swim?
  你能游泳嗎？

▶He **will be able to** finish this work by himself.
他能獨自完成工作。

2.「can be」在疑問句中表示強烈的懷疑；在否定句中表示否定的推測

▶**Can** the news **be** true?
這消息可能是真的嗎？

▶The bad news **cannot be** true.
這壞消息不可能是真的。

3.「can + have + p.p.」表示對過去或現在完成的事情之懷疑或否定的推測

▶**Can** he **have said** such rude words?
他可能說如此粗魯的話嗎？

▶He **cannot have done** such a terrible thing.
他絕不可能做如此可怕的事。

4.「Could you...」表示客氣的請求

▶**Could you** lend me your dictionary?
你能借我你的字典嗎？

> 🔊 小提醒
>
> can = may表示許可；can't = mustn't表示不可。
>
> ▶Can I leave now?
> 我能離開嗎？
>
> ▶Yes, you can (=may).
> 是的，你能。
>
> ▶No, you can't (=mustn't).
> 不，你不准。

5. can的慣用語

▶ I **cannot but** laugh.

我不得不笑。

▶ One **cannot be too** honest.

再誠實也不為過。

● must

1. 表示必須；「must not」表示禁止；「need not」表示不必

▶ **Must** I go now?

我一定要現在走嗎？

▶ Yes, you **must**.

是的，你一定要。

▶ No, you **need not**. You may go at any time you want.

不，你不需要。你任何時間想走都可以。

2.「must have + p.p.」表示對過去一種必然的推測

▶ It **must have rained** last night as the ground is wet.

昨晚一定下雨了因為地是溼的。

小提醒

must的過去式是had to

▶ I had to go there last week.

我上個星期必須去那裡。

● shall / should / ought to

1. 第一人稱用shall為單純未來；第二或第三人稱用shall則是受到他人牽制的意志未來

▶ I **shall** study abroad after I graduate from university.

▶ You **shall** do what you were told.

2. 時態需與主要句子中的動詞相同

▶ I say that I **shall** never forget your kindness.

▶ I said that I **should** never forget your kindness.

✛比較 He said, "I shall be leaving."

He said that he should be leaving.

3. 「should」當「應該」用時，可用「ought to」來代替，但意思較弱

▶ All of us **should** study hard.

▶ All of us **ought to** study hard.

4. lest＋S＋（should）＋V原形；「免得…」

▶ You have to work hard **lest** you (**should**) fail in the future.
你必須努力讀書免得未來失敗。

5. 「should」用以表示驚奇、悲傷、意外、後悔等感情的子句

It is / was strange / right / wrong… ＋ that ＋ S ＋ should ＋V原形 / have ＋ p.p.

▶ It is natural that she **should** be mad after she heard what you had said.
她在聽到你說的話後，生氣是自然的事。

▶ It is wrong that you **should** have kicked your kid brother in the game.
你在比賽中踢你弟弟是不對的。

6. 「should」用來表示意向或命令，通常用在如：desire、decide、intend、demand、order等動詞後的子句中

▶The doctor **demanded** that Mary (**should**) stop smoking.
醫生要求Mary戒菸。

7. 「should」用在疑問詞如：who、why、how等後面的從屬子句中

▶**Who** are you that **should** judge me!
你是誰啊敢來評斷我！

▶**Who should** write it by himself?
除了他外會有誰去寫它呢？

8. 「should have + p.p.」表示過去某事該做未做

▶I **should have study** harder when I was young.
我該在年輕時更努力讀書。

● **will / would / used to**

1. 第二人及第三人稱用will為單純未來；第一至第三人稱用will則為意志未來，用來表示說話者的意志

▶He **will study** abroad after he graduates from university.
他大學畢業後將出國讀書。（自己決定的未來動作）

▶I **will study** abroad after I graduate from university.
我在大學畢業後將出國讀書。（可能為他人的意志所造成的結果）

2. 表示強烈的決心或意向（=wish）

▶He **would** do it in spite of the difficulty.
他不計困難要做那事。

▶**Would** that I were in your place.
= I **wish** that I were in your place.

若我在你的位置就好了。

3. 表示客氣的請求

▶ **Would** you kindly do me a favor?

你能否幫我個忙？

▶ **Would** you mind opening the window?

你介不介意打開窗子？

4. 表示過去不規則的習慣；「used to」則表示過去規則的習慣

▶ I **would** sit up all night（有時熬夜） when I was in high school.

▶ I **used to** sit up all night（習慣熬夜） when I was in high school.

實用測驗

1. The machine ought to _____ a week ago.

   ① have fixed   ② be fixed   ③ get fixed   ④ have been fixed

2. "What has happened to Jack?" "I don't know. He _____ lost."

   ① may have gotten   ② might get   ③ can have gotten   ④ ought get

3. The girls don't want to go but the boys _____.

   ① do   ② are   ③ will   ④ be

4. You _____ your lesson from the last incident, but you didn't.

   ① would learn   ② dud not learn   ③ had not learned   ④ should have learned

5. It was necessary for John to go overseas last week.= He _____ to go overseas last week.

   ① used   ② has   ③ had   ④ ought

6. Judging from his accent, he _____ be an English man.

   ① mustn't   ② needn't   ③ can't   ④ won't

7. My watch keeps good time, but his _____.

   ① isn't   ② doesn't   ③ hasn't   ④ won't

8. It _____ for the ground is wet.

   ① must rain   ② must be going to rain   ③ must have rained   ④ must to rain

9. Which would you rather _____, go to the movies or stay at home watching TV?

   ① do   ② doing   ③ to do   ④ did

10. You had better _____ the client again just to make sure.

    ① call   ② to call   ③ calling   ④ called

11. You ought _____ careful when alone.

    ① be   ② to   ③ to be   ④ to have been

12. I have read more books in the past few days than I usually _____ in a whole year.

    ① am   ② will   ③ do   ④ have

13. When the girl heard the bad news, she could not _____.

    ① help crying   ② but to cry   ③ help cry   ④ but crying

14. Savings accounts pay the depositor interest but checking accounts _____.

    ① are not   ② do not   ③ have not   ④ will not

15. He said he didn't call, but I am sure he _____.

    ① does   ② did   ③ has   ④ had

試題解析

1. ④ 因有a week ago，所以選過去完成式的被動語態。

2. ① may / might + have + p.p.：可能，表過去可能的推測。

3. ① do代替先前所提的go。

4. ④ should + have + p.p.：該做未做的事。

5. ③ ought to / must的過去式為had to。

6. ③ 若題中有must be的選項時亦可。

7. ② doesn't代替keep；keep good time：準時。

8. ③ must + have + p.p.：對過去肯定的推測。

9. ① would rather + V原形：寧願。

10.① had better + V原形：最好。

11.③ ought to + V原形，be + 形容詞；若題目所強調時間為過去，則要選
     ④。

12.③ usually通常與現在簡單式連用，do則用來代替read。

13.① cannot help + Ving；cannot but + V原形。

14.② 助動詞do代替先行動詞pay。

15.② 前為否定，所以後面選肯定的助動詞。

筆記頁

語態 (Voice)

主詞是動作者稱為主動語態，主詞是動作的接受者稱為被動語態；只有及物動詞才有被動語態。被動語態的公式是：be動詞 + p.p.（動詞的過去分詞）；把它和其他時態或句型的公式結合即成。

■ **本章重點**

● 被動語態的形式

● 主動語態與被動語態互換

● 語態的用法

● 被動語態的形式

現在簡單式	am / are / is + p.p.	The box is opened by him. 他開這盒子。
過去簡單式	was / were + p.p.	The letter was written by him. 他寫信。
未來簡單式	shall / will + be + p.p.	You will be seen（接待）there by me. 我將會在那接待你。
現在完成式	have / has + been + p.p.	The work has been done by him. 他已做完工作。
過去完成式	had been + p.p.	My work had been done by me when she came. 當她來時，我已做完我的工作。

未來完成式	shall / will have been + p.p.	A letter will have been written by him before you return. 在你回來之前，他將會寫好信。
現在進行式	am / are / is being + p.p.	The letter is being written by him now. 他正在寫信。
過去進行式	was / were being + p.p.	A song was being sung by her when I came. 當我來時，她正在唱歌。

> 🦻 小提醒
>
> (A)未來進行式及所有的完成進行式都沒有被動語態。
> (B)被動語態並非中文語法中常有的形式，所以在英文
> 　　被動語態句子翻譯成中文時，還是用主動的說法；
> 　　千萬不要犯了「老師，他給我打」的笑話！

● 主動語態與被動語態互換

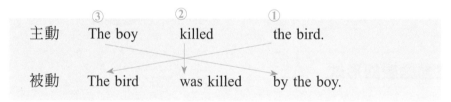

1 主動語態的受詞變為被動語態的主詞。

2 以主動語態的時態作為被動語態的動詞時態。

3 主動語態的主詞變為被動語態的受詞前加介詞如by等。

● 語態的用法

1. 不要把受詞補語當作被動語態的主詞，受詞補語要放在過去分詞的後面

▶I **made** him my assistant.

　= He **was made** my assistant by me.

　我讓他當我的助手。

▶We **elected** him our president.

　= He **was elected** president by us.

　我們選他當總統。

2. 有些授與動詞（give、teach、buy、send、tell ...）其後有兩個受詞（間接受詞通常指人，直接受詞通常指事物）；如果用間接受詞作被動語態的主詞，那直接受詞就成為保留的受詞；若以直接受詞作為被動語態的主詞，那間接受詞就成為保留的受詞

▶He **gave** me a new book.　他給我一本新書。

　= I **was given** a new book by him.（間接受詞me當被動語態的主詞）

　= A new book **was given** to me by him.（直接受詞a new book當被動語態的主詞）

▶I **made** her a cake.　我做個蛋糕給她。

　= She **was made** a cake by me.（間接受詞her當被動語態的主詞）

　= A cake **was made** to her by me.（直接受詞a cake當被動語態的主詞）

▶My boss **asked** me a question.　我老闆問我個問題。

　= I **was asked** a question by my boss.（間接受詞me當被動語態的主詞）

　= A question **was asked** of me by my boss.（直接受詞a question當被動語態的主詞）

🔊 小提醒

還記得英文五大基本句型嗎？

S＋V（完全不及物動詞）	The bird flies high in the sky.
S＋V（不完全不及物動詞）＋S／C（主詞補語）	She is very beautiful.
S＋V（完全及物動詞）＋O	I ate my dinner last night.
S＋V（不完全及物動詞）＋O＋O／C（受詞補語）	We elected him our class leader.
S＋V（授與動詞）+O（間接受詞）＋O（直接受詞）＝S＋V（授與動詞）＋O（直接受詞）＋ by／of／with…+O（間接受詞）	

3. 某些授與動詞，如：write、bring、do、make、pass等通常只能用直接受詞作被動語態的主詞

▶He **wrote** me a letter.　他寫信給我。

= A letter **was written** (to) me by him.（○）

I was written a letter by him.（×）

▶The new company **made** me an offer.　新公司提供我一個差事。

= An offer **was made to** me by the new company.（○）

I was made an offer by the new company.（×）

4. 「不及物動詞＋介詞」可作及物動詞。改變語態時，將介詞的受詞作被動語態的主詞，而介詞則放在過去分詞後

▶He **is looking** for his lost wallet now.

= His lost wallet **is being looked** for by him.

他正在找遺失的皮夾。

▶Mary **was reading** the book when Jack called.

= The book **was being read** by Mary when Jack called.

Jack打電話時，Mary正在看書。

5. 在主動語態裡，「使役動詞」（have、let、make...）或「感官動詞」（see、hear、feel、taste、smell...）後面的不定詞要將to省略；在被動語態中，to則不可省略

▶ I **saw** him enter the house.

= He **was seen to** enter the house by me.

我看他進入屋內。

▶ My father **made** me study hard.

= I **was made to** study hard by my father.

我父親叫我用功讀書。

6. 主動語態的動詞之受詞為名詞片語或子句時，其被動有兩種作法

1 用虛／形式主詞it代替名詞子句作為被動語態的主詞，而將主要句子的動詞改為被動的形式，但名詞子句不變，仍放在過去分詞的後面。

2 用名詞子句的主詞作被動語態的主詞，而將主要子句的動詞改為被動的形式，之後在將名詞子句的動詞改為不定詞並置於過去分詞之後。

▶ **They say** that he is a liar.

= **It is said** that he is a liar.

= **He is said** to be a liar.

據說他是個騙子。

▶ **People say** that failure is the mother of success.

= **It is said** that failure is the mother of success.

= **Failure is said** to be the mother of success.

據說失敗是成功之母。

7. 主動語態的主詞為表示「一般人」的意思的字,如:we、they、people、somebody、one...時,在改被動語態中,常將 by us、by them...等省略。同樣地,若將被動改為主動時,要視句意用we、they、you 等作為主動語態的主詞

▶We drink much water in summer.

= Much water is drunk in summer.

我們在夏天喝很多水。

▶English is spoken in the U.S.

= They speak English in the U.S.

人們在美國說英文。

8. 在被動語態中,表示行為的介詞,一般用「by」,但有些動詞會用其他的介詞代替by

▶Snow **covered** the mountain.

= The mountain **was covered with** snow.

雪覆蓋著山。

▶The Chinese opera **interests** the old lady.

= The old lady **is interested in** the Chinese opera.

這位老太太對京劇感興趣。

▶Everybody in Taiwan **knows** her.

= She **is known to** everybody in Taiwan.

她在臺灣眾所皆知。

▶The sight **frightened** us.

= We **were frightened at** the sight.

所見到的事嚇到我們。

🎧 小提醒

其他常出現在被動語態中的介系詞：

be +	acquainted（熟悉） equipped（裝備） pleased（高興） satisfied（滿意）	+ with
	disappointed（失望） excited（興奮） surprised（驚訝）	+ at
	dressed（穿著） interested（感興趣）	+ in
	devoted （獻身致力於） known （為…所知） married （與…結婚）	+ to

9. 有些動詞主動語態被動語態表示同樣意思

▶ He **married** Miss White.

= He **was married to** Miss White.

他娶了White小姐。

▶ My hat **blew** off.

= My hat **was blown off**.

我的帽子被吹掉了。

10. 否定句被動語態的作法

先以被動語態中新的主詞為準，選擇適當的be動詞，not保留，
再將主動語態中動詞的過去分詞放在not後即可。

▶ The hostess did **not invite** them.

= They **were not invited by** the hostess.

女主人並沒邀請他們。

11. 主動語態中有助動詞改被動將該助動詞保留,在其後加be 再把主動語態中的動詞的過去分詞放在be之後即可。被動 改主動時,去be並將p.p.改為原形動詞

▶ He **can finish** the work.

= The work **can be finished** by him.

他能完成這工作。

▶ It **ought not to be taken** by you.

= You **ought not to take** it.

你不該拿那個。

12. 主動語態為疑問句時,先依被動語態的主詞選用be動詞, 再把主動語態動詞的過去分詞放在主詞的後面

▶ Did John write the letter?

= Was the letter written by John?

John寫這封信嗎?

▶ Will John write the letter?

= Will the letter be written by John?

John將會寫這封信嗎?

1 完成式時選用適當形式的have助動詞,並在過去分詞前加 been。

▶ Haven't you done the work?

= Hasn't the work been done by you?

你做好這工作了嗎?

2 若是用疑問詞為主詞的疑問句,改被動時要將who改為by whom 並置於句首,其後接被動語態的主詞,再加適當形式的be動 詞,再加過去分詞。

▶ Who can make a kite?

= **By whom** can a kite be made?

誰做了這個風箏?

13. 附加問句時，只將敘述句改為被動語態，而後依被動語態另於句尾做附加問句，被動改主動亦同

▶They occupied that house, didn't they?

= That house was occupied by them, wasn't it?

他們佔住著這房子，不是嗎？

▶She doesn't like coffee, does she?

= Coffee isn't liked by her, is it?

她不喜歡咖啡，是吧？

14. 祈使命令句（主詞為第二人稱時），句前用let而其後接受詞，再接原形的be再加過去分詞

▶Open the door at once.

= **Let** the door **be** opened at once.

立即把門打開。

▶Don't take the book away.

= Don't let the book be taken away.

= Let the book not to be taken away.

別拿走這本書。

15. 祈使命令句（主詞為第一或第三人稱時）

▶Let him open the door at once.

= Let the door be opened by him at once.

讓他立即打開門。

▶Don't let him read such a book.

= Don't let such a book be read by him.

別讓他讀這樣的書。

> 🔊 小提醒
>
> ▶Let's go!　我們走吧！
> ▶Let us go!　讓我們走！

16. 雖然及物動詞才有被動語態，但下列及物動詞不適合用在被動語態中

例 become、beg、contain、cost、hold、have（有）、elude（躲避逃避）、escape、wqual、fail、fit、flee、get、lack、posses、resemble（類似）、suit（合適）、survive…

▶He lacks a sense of humor.
他缺少幽默感。

▶This dress fits you well.
這件衣服很適合你。

▶The plane holds about 250 people.
這飛機可載250人。

▶She resembles her sister in appearance but not in character.
她和她姊妹外表像，但性格不同。

■ 實用測驗

1. Lots of audiences were gathered outside the concert hall but only 50 _____.

   ① is admitted   ② are admitted   ③ was admitted   ④ were admitted

2. We had dinner at the new restaurant; the food was good but we we _____.

   ① were not well waited for   ② were not well taken care of   ③ were not well looked at   ④ were not well fed

3. After Mary _____ about the news, she ran home crying.

   ① would have been informed   ② would have informed   ③ had been informed ④ has been informed

4. All those condemned buildings _____ down within weeks.

   ① will be torn   ② will tear   ③ will have torn   ④ tear

5. More accidents _____ in summer than any other time in the year.

   ① happen   ② is happening   ③ are happened   ④ is happened

6. A fire _____ in our neighborhood a couple weeks ago.

   ① broke out   ② was broken out   ③ was breaking out   ④ had been breaking out

7. Computers are _____ by many students to replace notebooks.

   ① being used   ② benn used   ③ to be used   ④ been using

8. You shouldn't have referred to her as a big lady; she disliked _____ a big lady.

   ① calling   ② called   ③ being called   ④ to be called

9. To keep the view as pleasant as possible, most of the trees _____ when the roads are widened.

   ① preserves   ② must preserve   ③ should be preserved   ④ ought to have been preserved

10. He was made _____ it.

    ① do   ② to do   ③ did   ④ done

11. The lady was heard _____.

    ① to sing   ② sing   ③ had sung   ④ singing

12. The winner said that he was proud of _____ the first prize.

    ① award   ② being awarded   ③ be awarded   ④ awarded

13. Tens of thousands of apples _____ every year.

    ① are eaten　② are eating　③ has been eaten　④ had been eaten

14. I am the boss and I am not used to _____ what to do.

    ① be told　② be telling　③ tell　④ being told

15. I don't like _____ this way.

    ① to treat　② to be treated　③ treated　④ treating

試題解析

1. ④ 過去簡單式被動語態。

2. ② wait for 應改為wait on；looked at與well fed雖用法正確但與題意不符。

3. ③ 前後兩個動作：hear與inform，inform先發生，所以用過去完成式的被動語態。

4. ① 未來簡單式的被動語態；condemned buildings：危樓。

5. ① happen無被動語態的用法；take place亦同。

6. ① break out（發生）無被動語態的用法，所以選過去簡單式。

7. ① 現在進行式的被動語態。

8. ③ dislike後接動名詞；refer to ＋ 人 ＋ as...：把⋯稱為⋯。

9. ③ 因主詞為trees，所以用被動語態。

10.② 使役動詞主動時應與原形動詞連用，被動時則需與不定詞連用。

11.① hear其後本該接動名詞，但被動語態時要改成不定詞形式。

12.② 在介系詞of後，所以要選動名詞的被動語態。

13.① 因為有時間副詞every year，所以用現在簡單式的被動語態。

14.④ be used to後接動名詞。

15.② treat ＋ 人：對待；to be treated：被人對待。

筆記頁

語氣 (Mood)

英文動詞的語氣有三種：直述、祈使和假設。

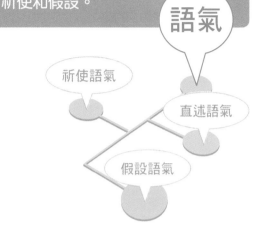

■ **本章重點**
  ● 直述語氣
  ● 祈使語氣
  ● 假設語氣

● **直述語氣**：用以敘述事實，一般可以敘述句、疑問句或否定句
　　　　　　　　的形式出現。

　　▶ The mother and her daughters are all dressed in red.
　　　母女都穿紅的。（敘述句）
　　▶ Don't you know the address?
　　　你不知道住址嗎？（疑問句）
　　▶ I don't know what his address is.
　　　我不知道他的住址為何。（否定句）

● **祈使語氣**：用來表達命令、請求和勸告等。

1. 表示祈願時皆用原形動詞；主詞為第三人稱時動詞不加s，沒有過去式

▶God save the Queen!

天佑女王！

▶Peace be with you!

和平與你同在！

▶Long live the Republic of China!

中華民國萬歲！

▶May you succeed!

希望你成功！

2. 對第二人稱的祈使句通常將主詞you省略，而用原形動詞引導即可

▶**Study** hard.

（你該）用功讀書。

▶**Get out of** here.

（你）出去。

▶**Be** kind to others.

（你該）對他人仁慈。

▶**Don't go** swimming alone.

（你）不可以單獨去游泳。

▶**Do keep** your promise.

（你）該守信用。

3. 對第一、第三人稱的祈使句，通常用let引導

▶**Let** me **help** you.

讓我幫你。

▶**Let** them **go** away.

讓他們走。

▶**Don't let** him **stay** here.

= **Let** him **not to stay** here.
別讓他待在這裡。

4. 祈使附加問句的作法

▶ Shut the window, will you?
關上窗戶，好嗎？

▶ Have a cup of coffee, won't you?
來杯咖啡，好嗎？

▶ Let's go fishing, shall we?
我們去釣魚，好嗎？

▶ Don't let them stay here, will you?
別讓他們待在這裡，好嗎？

5. 祈使句的特殊用法

▶ Stick to your principle （堅守原則）, and you will succeed.
  = If you stick to your principle, you will succeed.

▶ Study hard, or （否則）else you will fail.
  = If you don't study hard, you will fail.
  = Unless you study hard, you will fail.

▶ Another step forward, and （那麼） you shall be dead.
  = If you take another step forward, you shall be dead.

▶ Say what you will, I shan't trust you.
  = Whatever you may say, I shan't trust you.
說什麼我都不相信你。

● **假設語氣**：用來表示目的、願望、條件或假設等。

1. 用以表示與現在事實相反的假設

If + S +	were（所有be動詞）， 過去式動詞（所有動詞），	S +	should would could might	+ V原形

▶ If she **were** industrious, I should employ her.

(She is not industrious enough to be employed.)

如果她勤勉些，我就會僱用她。

▶ If I **had** a car, I would drive you to school.

(I don't have a car, so I can't drive you to school.)

如果我有車，我就會開車去上學。

2. 用以表示與過去事實相反的假設

If + S + had + p.p…,	S +	should would could might	+ have + p.p.

▶ If you **had** informed me of your departure, I would have seen you off.

(You didn't tell me of your departure, so I didn't see you off.)

如果你讓我知道你要離開，我就會去送行。

▶ If she could have smiled then, she would have smiled.

= If she had been able to smile then, she would have smiled.

(She didn't smile then.)

如果她那時能笑，她就會笑了。

3. 用以表示與未來事實相反的假設

If + S + were to + V原形…,	S +	should	+ V原形
		would	
		could	
		might	

▶ If I **were to** become a millionaire tomorrow, I would travel around the world.
　如果我明天成為百萬富翁，我就會去環遊世界。

▶ If the sun **were to** rise in the west, I would help you.
　如果太陽從西邊升起，我就會幫你。

若可能性極小（可疑或萬一）時，將were to改為should。

▶ If the sun should rise in the west, I would not talk to you.
　就算太陽從西邊升起，我也不會和你說話。

🔊 小提醒

如果能清楚分辨是與現在或過去事實相反的假設時，使用正確的句型不難；但若將兩個時間混雜在一起，那回答時就要小心：

If I knew the importance of study, I would be better off now.（與現在事實相反）

If I had known the importance of study, I would have been better off then.（與過去事實相反）

If I had known the importnce of study then, I would be better off now.（涉及過去和現在兩個時間；通常和today, now, at present等連用）

▶ Hadn't been urged by my high school teacher to pursue another career, I would never be what I am tody.
　若非當時我高中老師勸我找份工作，我今天絕無法如此。

第八章

語　氣

↓

假設語氣

-155-

4. 條件子句的連接詞if可以省略，此時用倒裝句（將動詞或助動詞放在主詞前）

▶If I were a bird, I could fly to you.

　= Were I a bird, I could fly to you.

　如果我是鳥的話，我就會飛去你那裡。

▶If he had known you address, he would have written to you.

　= Had he known your address, he would have written to you.

　如果他知道你的住址，他就會寫信給你。

下列片語多可使用上述用法：

In case that = Provided that = Supposed that = On condition that = Providing that = If

▶Provided that I had been here yesterday, I should have met her.

　= I should have met her on condition that I had been here yesterday.

　= Supposed that I had been here yesterday, I should have met her.

　如果我昨天在那裡，我就會遇到她。

5. 接在「wish (ed)」後面的名詞子句通常用假設語氣動詞

S + wish (would rather) that S +	were
	過去式動詞
	should / would / could / might + V原形

▶I wish that I were a king now.

　我希望我現在是個國王。

▶I wish that you had taken part in the meeting yesterday.

　我希望你昨天有參加會議。

小提醒

(A)I wish that…= Would that…= If only（若是…就好了）…

▶ I wish that I were a king.

= Would that I were a king.

= If only I were a king.

(B)I am sorry… = I regret … = It is a pity（很遺憾）…

▶ I wish you had taken part in the meeting yesterday.

= It is a pity that you did not take part in the meeting yesterday.

6. 在「as if」或「as though」後接假設語法的用法

	主詞 + were
	過去式動詞
主要句子 + as if / as though +	should / would / could / might + V原形
	had + p.p.
	should / would / could / might + have + p.p.

▶ She talks as if she knew you.
她說話的樣子好像她認識妳。

▶ It seems as though it might rain.
看來好像要下雨。

▶ He turned pale as if he had seen a ghost.
他臉變蒼白好像遇到鬼。

▶ It seems as though he had been here yesterday.
感覺上他昨天好像在這裡。

第八章

語　氣

↓

假設語氣

7. 「But for＋N」（若非…）

| But for＋N，
＝ Without＋N，
＝ If it were not for＋N，
＝ Were it not for＋N， | ＋ | 主詞 ＋ should / would / could / might ＋ V原形（與現在事實相反） |
| | | 主詞 +should / would / could / might ＋ have ＋ p.p.（與過去事實相反） |

▶ But for your help, I should fail.

　＝ If it were not for your help I should fail.

　若非你的幫助，我就失敗了。

▶ Without water, we could not live.

　＝ If there were no water, we could not live.

　若沒水，我們就活不下去。

▶ But for you, I should have been drowned.

　＝ If it had not been for you, I should have been drowned.

　若非你，我就淹死了。

▶ Without air, no creature could have lived.

　＝ If there had been no air, no creature could have lived.

　若沒空氣，沒有生物能存活。

> 🔊 小提醒
>
> 「But that ＋ 子句」通常也會有下列的用法：
>
> ▶ But that I am poor, I would marry her.
>
> 　＝ If I were not poor, I would marry her.
>
> 　＝ I would marry her except that I am poor.
>
> 　若非我窮，否則我就娶她。
>
> ▶ But that I am so busy, I would go with you.
>
> 　＝ If I were not so busy, I would go with you.
>
> 　＝ I would go with you except that I am so busy.
>
> 　若非我忙，否則我就跟你去。

▶ But that I caught her, she would have fallen.

= If I had not caught her, she would have fallen.

= She would have fallen except that I had caught her.

若非我抓住她，否則她就掉下去了。

8. 主要句子的動詞若表示吩咐、請求、建議等觀念時，動詞後的that子句的動詞要用should＋V；should通常可省略

例 advise、arange、ask、beg、command、direct、insist、intend、maintain（主張）、move（提議）、object（反對）、order、permit、pray、prefer、propose、recommend、request、require、suggest、want... 。

▶ He demanded that he (should) be given the right to express his opinion.
他要求該有表達意見的權利。

▶ The doctor advised that the patient (should) stop smoking.
醫生建議病人該停止吸菸。

▶ Jack moved that the meeting (should) be adjourned.
Jack提議會議應該延期。

9. It＋be動詞／感官動詞＋形容詞＋that＋S＋(should)＋V原形

▶ Is it necessary that the work (should) be done without delay?
= I don't know if it necessary to delay the work.
工作該不受任何耽擱嗎？

▶ It is important that she (should) go to see a doctor at once.
= I think it important that she (should) go to see a doctor at once.
她該立即去看醫生是非常重要的。

使用上述句型的形容詞有：

appropriate、advisable、better、desirable、essential、fitting
（貼切）、imperative、insistent、natural、normal、prefer-
able、strange、urgent、vital（極重要的）、desired、de-
manded、ordered、requested、suggested、recommended、
required。

10. 下列用法也有假設的意思在內

▶ With your advice, I should certainly succeed.

= If I had your advice, I should certainly succeed.

有了你的建議，我一定會成功。

▶ To see the man, you would like him.

= If you saw the man, you would like him.

看到那個人你一定會喜歡他。

▶ Brought up in a better family, he would not have done so.

= If he had been brought up in a better family, he would not have done so.

若在較好的人家長大，他絕不會如此做。

▶ The situation could be saved by immediate action.

= The situation could be saved if we took immediate action.

這狀況可經由立即的行動來拯救。

▶ I would have been bankrupted without your timely help.

= I would have been bankrupted if you had not helped me in time.

若非你即時的幫助，我就會破產了。

▶ Anybody who saw her there might take her for a maid.

= If anybody saw her there, he might take her for a maid.

任何看到她的人都會誤認她為女僕。

▶ What if she (should) fail to come?

= What would happen if she (should) fail to come?

萬一她不能來又如何？

11. 其他具有假設含義的用法還有

▶ She was ill that day; otherwise, she would have taken part in the meeting.

= If she hadn't been ill that day, she would have taken part in the meeting.

她那天生病，否則她就會出席會議。

▶ He felt tired yesterday, or he would have helped you.

= If he hadn't been tired yesterday, he would have helped you.

他昨天感到疲倦，要不然他就會幫你。

▶ He would have helped you, but he has been so busy.

= If he hadn't been so busy, he would have helped you.

若非他忙，否則他就會幫你。

▶ I would ask her out but I don't know her name.

= If I knew her name, I would ask her out.

如果我知道她的名字，我就會邀她出去。

▶ We would have done better under more favorable conditions.

= If the conditions had been better, we would have done better.

如果條件較好，我們會做的更好。

▶ All this would have been impossible ten years ago.

十年前這一切都不可能。

▶ That would have been considered miraculous in the past.

在過去，那會被視為奇蹟。

▶ A less brave man wouldn't have dared to jump into the river.

若膽子較小的人就不敢跳進河裡了。

▶ Who but a fool would believe that?

除了傻瓜還會有誰相信？

▶ It was so quiet; you could have heard a pin drop.

那時安靜到你能聽到針掉到地上。

■ 實用測驗

1. If only I _____ to speak English well then.

   ① learn ② learning ③ have learned ④ had learned

2. _____ it not for his idleness, he would be a successsful businessman.

   ① Is ② Was ③ Are ④ Were

3. If the trade were free, the more efficient producers _____ the less efficient producers out of business.

   ① push ② would have pushed ③ will push ④ would push

4. If it had not rained so hard yesterday, we _____ to Kenting.

   ① should have gone ② should go ③ go ④ went

5. It is necessary that this new invention _____ well controlled.

   ① is ② was ③ be ④ will be

6. If you _____ my advice, things will go more smoothly.

   ① follow ② received ③ accepted ④ hear

7. I would not change my mind if the sun _____ in the west.

   ① were to rise ② could rise ③ might rise ④ will rise

8. Had he heard this, he _____.

   ① had been very angry ② was angry ③ would have been very angry ④ will have been very angry

9. _____ my parents, I could not have become what I am today.

   ① Without ② But ③ Because ④ If

10. If the earth stopped moving, what _____?

    ① do you think would happen ② did you think will happen ③ do you think would be happened ④ did you think will be happened

11. Our teaching demanded that right _____ distinguished from wrong.

    ① be ② were ③ being ④ been

12. _____ you been here, you would find out that truth.

    ① Should ② Would ③ If ④ Had

13. What would he do if you _____ fail?

    ① should ② will ③ do ④ would

14. I wish that I _____ about this earlier.

　　① know　② knew　③ have known　④ had known

15. The doctor recommended that Jack _____ the new medicine.

　　① took　② taken　③ to take　④ take

■ 試題解析

1. ④ then表示過去的時間，所以用與過去事實相反的假設語氣。

2. ④ were it not for = if it were not for（若非）。

3. ④ 因有were；與現在事實相反的假設。

4. ① 與過去事實相反的假設。

5. ③ it is necessary that + S + (should) + V原形。

6. ① 因子句為未來式，所以用現在式來代替未來式。

7. ① 對未來而有的假設語氣。

8. ③ 與過去事實相反的假設。

9. ① 「若非」；如果選but，其後需加for。

10. ① 因有stopped，所以是與現在事實相反的假設。

11. ① 因動詞demanded後的should被省略。

12. ④ if省略，所以用倒裝句型。

13. ① 與未來相反的假設。

14. ④ earlier代表較早的時間；與過去事實相反的假設。

15. ④ 動詞recommend後的should省略，所以用原形動詞。

不定詞 (Infinitives)

不定詞的性質是to + V原形；不受主詞人稱和數的影響，to有時可省略。

■ 本章重點

● 不定詞的基本公式

● 不定詞的性質

不定詞

不定詞的性質

疑問詞+不定詞
=名詞片語

不定詞的
基本公式

省略「to」
的不定詞

不定詞的用法

不定詞的時態

獨立不定詞

不需表明不定詞
的主詞

● 不定詞的用法

● 疑問詞 + 不定詞 = 名詞片語

● 獨立不定詞

● 省略「to」的不定詞

● 不需表明不定詞的主詞

● 不定詞的時態

不定詞的基本公式

	主動	被動
簡單式	to write	to be written
完成式	to have written	to have been written
進行式	to be writing	X
完成進行式	to have been writing	X

● **不定詞的性質：** 不定詞具有動詞的性質，所以其後可加補語或受詞，也可以用副詞、副詞片語或副詞子句來修飾。

▶ For a student to get perfect scores is no easy matter.
學生拿滿分不容易。（no easy matter是不定詞to get perfect scores的補語）

▶ I expect you to be considerate when dealing with others.
我希望你和他人相處時能體貼些。（considerate當不定詞to be的補語）

▶ I should like to go there immediately.
我想立刻就去那裡。（there與immediately等副詞修飾不定詞to go）

● **不定詞的用法**

1. 不定詞可作名詞

1 當名詞用時，可當句中的主詞、動詞或介詞的受詞，以及補語。

▶ **To love** and **to be loved** is the greatest happiness on earth.
愛與被愛是世上最快樂的事。（主詞）

▶ She pretended **to be angry**.
她假裝生氣。（補詞）

▶ I intend **to study** harder this semester.
我這學期決心努力讀書。（受詞）

> 🦻小提醒
>
> 此用法時常與表示決心、努力、喜愛或討厭等意思的動詞，如：want、wish、like、intend等連用。

▶I make it a rule **to get up** early in the morning.

我規定自己早上早起。（it為形式／虛受詞，不定詞to get up是真受詞）

> 🔊 小提醒
>
> 適用上述用法的動詞還有：think、find、believe、con-sider、regard、deem（視為、認為）、take等。

▶She is about **to retire** this summer.

她將在今年夏天退休。

▶He desires nothing but **to see** you again.

（上述兩句不定詞當介詞如about、but、except、than之受詞，其他介詞皆不可以不定詞為受詞）

▶He does nothing but play all day. (=He only plays all day.)

他整日除了玩之外什麼都不做。

▶He desires nothing but to get close to Mary.

他除了想接近Mary外什麼都不想。

> 🔊 小提醒
>
> nothing but + V原形，「只是」；V + nothing but + to + V原形，「只是為了」。

2 下列動詞常以不定詞當受詞。

例 agree、afford（足以）、arrange、ask、attempt、bear（忍受）、beg、begin、bother、care、choose、consent（同意）、claim（聲稱、主張）、decide、demand、determine、endeavor（努力）、expect、fail、forget、guarantee、happen、hestitate、hope、love、long（可望）、manage、mean（意欲）、neglect、offer、plan、prepare、pretend、proceed（繼續）、promise、prove、refuse、remember、resolve（下定決心）、seek、seem、start、tend、threaten、trouble、try、undertake（承辦、承擔）、

volunteer。

3 下列動詞常以不定詞當受詞補語。

例 advise、allow、ask、beat、beg、compel（迫使）、command、encourage、entitle（給…的權利）、expect、forbid、force、get、hate、help、instruct（指令、訓令）、intend、invite、like、mean、need、oblige（迫使）、order、permit、persuade、prefer、press（施壓）、recommend、remind、request、teach、tell、temp（誘使）、trouble、urge、want、wish。

▶He likes his wife **to dress** well.
　他喜歡他太太穿的漂亮。（受詞補語）

▶He encouraged me **to study** abroad after I graduate.
　他鼓勵我畢業後出國讀書。

2. 不定詞當作形容詞，用於修飾名詞或代名詞，所以要放在所修飾的字之後

▶He is not a boy **to tell** a lie.
　他不是會說謊的男孩。（修飾受詞）

▶His ability **to learn** a foreign language is amazing.
　他學習外語的能力讓人感到驚訝。（修飾主詞）

▶He has no house **to live** in.
　他沒有能住的房子。（修飾受詞）

▶He is not the man **to blame** (=to be blamed).
　他不該受責。（用主動的不定詞代替被動的不定詞）

▶The news proved **to be true**.
　消息被證實是真的。（主詞the news的補語）

小提醒

　　be + 被動的不定詞表示「當然」（should）或「可能」
（can）。

▶You are to stay at home tonight.
　你要待在家裡。（主詞you的補語）

小提醒

　　be + 主動的不定詞表示未來的、溫和的命令或禁止。

不定詞常在下列名詞後當修飾語用。

例 ability、agreement、ambition、anxiety、attempt、campaign（戰
　　役、活動）、claim（聲明）、courage、decision、determina-
　　tion、effort、failure、intention、hope、motive、movement、
　　need、opportunity、plan、promise、readiness（願意）、reason、
　　refusal（拒絕）、reluctantce（不情願）、resolution（決心、果
　　斷）、right、struggle（鬥爭）、tendency、threat、time、way、
　　willingness、wish。

▶He feels a pressing need to become more independent.
　他迫切需要能更獨立。

▶She has an opportunity to earn more money.
　她有能賺更多錢的機會。

▶I have no wish to change.
　我沒有要改變的願望。

3. 不定詞當作副詞，用以修飾動詞、形容詞或其他副詞表示目的、結果、原因理由、條件或讓步

▶Men eat to live not live to eat.
　人吃的目的是活而非活的目的是吃。（to live 修飾 eat；to eat修飾live）

▶Don't be afraid **to ask** questions.

別怕問問題。（to ask question修飾 be afraid）

▶He is too old **to walk**.

他老到無法走路。（to walk修飾 too）

1 表示目的。

to + V原形

= in order to + V原形

= in order that + S + V。

= so as to +V 原形；that + S + V = so that + S + V

▶I studied hard **in order / so as to** make better grades.

= I studied hard in order that I might make better grades.

我為了能拿更好成績而努力讀書。

▶I get up early not **to be** late for work.

= I get up early **in order / so as not to** be late for work.

= I get up early lest I should be late for work.

我怕上班遲到而早起。

2 表示結果。

so + adj. + as to

= so + adj. + that + S + V

▶He is **so** rich **as to** buy a new house.

= He is so rich that he can buy a new house.

= He is rich **enough to buy** a new house.

他富有到可以買棟新房子。

▶She is **such** a pretty girl **as to** become a movie star.

= She is such a pretty girl that she becomes a movie star.

= She is so pretty a girl that she becomes a movie star.

她是如此美麗以至於她成為電影明星。

🔊小提醒

so as to表示目的；so + adj. / adv. as to則表示結果。

3 表示原因或理由的副詞不定詞，通常皆在感情形容詞或動詞之後。

▶ We thrill **to hear** of your success.
　我們很興奮聽到你的成功。

▶ He must be a fool **to turn** down a nice girl like her.
　他一定是個傻瓜才會拒絕像她一樣好的女孩。

4 表示條件或讓步的副詞不定詞。

▶ **To hear** you speak English, people might take you for an American.
　聽你說英文，大家可能會把你當美國人看。

▶ **To study** hard, you could not become a top student in one day.
　儘管你努力讀書，你無法在一天內就成為頂尖學生。

● 疑問詞（whom、which、what、where、when、how）＋ 不定詞 ＝ 名詞片語

▶ When to leave is not important to me.
　何時離開對我而言不重要。（when to leave 當主詞）

▶ I don't know what to do.
　我不知道做什麼。（what to do 當受詞）

● 獨立不定詞：某些不定詞片語因在句中與其他字間無任何關係，且處於一種獨立的地位。

▶ **To tell** the truth, I don't want to help you with your report.
　老實說，我不想幫你做報告。

▶ **To do** her justice, we must admit that she is kind and pretty.
　老實說，我們必須承認她是仁慈且漂亮。

類似用語：to be frank with you、so to speak（可謂）、strange to say、to be brief、sad to say（說來可悲）、to make matter worse、to begin with、to be sure（一定）、not to speak of（不用說）、needless to say（不待言）…。

● 省略「to」的不定詞

1. 知覺／感官動詞（see, hear, feel, watch, notice, observe, perceive, behold, look at, listen to, ...）及使役動詞（let, make, have, bid, help, ...）後面的不定詞在主動語態中需將to省略

▶ I **heard** the doorbell ring.
我聽到門鈴響。

▶ The little boy **watched** the bees fly from flower to flower.
小男孩看到這些蜜蜂從一朵花飛到另一朵花。

2. help後的to省略或不省略皆可

▶ He **helped** me (**to**) carry the suitcase upstairs.
他幫我把行李箱搬上樓。

3. 被動語態中的to不可省略

▶ The man **was seen to** enter the room.
我們看到這個人進入房內。

在and、rather than、or、than後慣用原形動詞；偶而也會用to的不定詞

▶ He would rather die than live in dishonor.
 = He would rather to die than to live in dishonor.
他情願死也不要活得不榮譽。

▶ He would prefer to saty home than to go out.
他情願在家也不要出去。

▶ I like to sit there and drink tea.
我喜歡坐在那喝茶。

4. 與下列片語連用時，不定詞中的to可省略：cannot but（不能不）、cannot help but（禁不住）、can't choose but（只好）、do nothing but（只會）、had better、would you please、may / might as well（倒不如）、would rather

▶ I cannot but admire him.
我不能不佩服他。

▶ I would sooner resign than work under that boss.
我情願辭職也不要替那種老闆做事。

在believe、consider、declare（宣告）、feel、find、imag-ine、know、prove、suppose、think、undersatnd等詞後，常跟「to be +形容詞 / 名詞 / 反身代名詞」連用，而且to be可省略。

▶ All her friends supposed her (to be) dead.
 所有她的朋友都以為她死了。

▶ I thought him (to be) an excellent choice for the job.
 我覺得他是做這工作的好人選。

▶ She imagined herself (to be) superior to others.
 她自以為高人一等。

● 不需表明不定詞的主詞

▶ I found that to talk with him was a waste of time.
我發現和他談話是浪費時間。

▶ It is wrong to tell a lie.
說謊是錯的。

▶ I want him to write his name correctly.
我要他正確地寫出他名字。

> 🔊 小提醒
>
> 不定詞的主詞通常用下列方式表示：
>
> ▶ It is difficult for me to study English.
>
> = I found studying English is difficult.
>
> = I had a hard time studying English.
>
> 我英文讀得很辛苦。
>
> ▶ It is very kind of you to say so.
>
> = It is very kind that you said so.
>
> 你如此說，真是很仁慈。

● 不定詞的時態

1. 在 seem、appear、be said、be thought（以為）、be supposed（認為）、be believed（相信）等表示推測的動詞後如用簡單式的不定詞，表示不定詞的時態與句子動詞的時態相同

▶ He **seems to** be rich.

= It seems that he is rich.

他似乎是有錢。

▶ He **was thought to** be rich.

= It was thought that he was rich.

大家覺得他是有錢。

2. 在seem、appear、be said、be thought、be supposed、be believed...等表推測的動詞後若接完成式不定詞，表示比句中動詞還早發生的動作

▶ They **seem to** have studied English for several years.

= It seems that they have studied English for several years.

他們像是讀了幾年的英文。

▶ He **was said to** have been rich.

= It was said that he had been rich.

據說他曾經有過錢。

3. 在表示希望、期待或答應等動詞，如：wish、hope、intend、expect、promise、want...後，如用簡單式的不定詞，表示比句中動詞較晚或在未來發生的動作

▶ He **promises to** help me.

= He says that he will help me.

他說他將會幫我。

▶ He **expected** me **to** come yesterday.

= He expected that I would come yesterday.

他期望我昨天會去。

4. 在表示希望、期待或意志的過去動詞，如：wished、hoped、desired、meant、intended後，若用完成式的不定詞，表示由於某種原因而沒有實現的動作

▶ They **intended to** have called on you, but they had been too busy.

他們本來昨天要打電話給你，但他們太忙了。

▶ I **wished to** have helped you, but I had no money.
我曾希望能幫你，但我沒錢。

◆比較 He hoped to have succeeded.
= He had hoped to succeed.
他希望成功但沒有成功
He hoped to succeed.
= He may or may not have succeeded.
他過去希望成功，現在則不知。

5. 不定詞後需接介系詞

▶ She is **easy to** talk to.
= It is easy to talk to her.
和她說話很自在。

▶ That swift river is dangerous to swim in.
= It is dangerous to swim in that river.
在流得很快的河流中游泳很危險。

6. 主詞 ＋ 祈使動詞（**tell**、**advise**、**ask**、**suggest**、**recommend**、**move**、**propose**、**insist**、**order**、**command**）＋ 受詞 ＋ 不定詞 ＝ 主詞 ＋ 動詞（同上）＋ **that** ＋ 主詞 ＋（**should**）＋ 動詞原形

▶ I told him to keep the room clean.
= I told him that he (should) keep the room clean.
我告訴他要保持房間乾淨。

▶ The doctor advised me to give up smoking.
= The doctor advised me that I (should) stop smoking.
醫生建議我戒菸。

7. It + be + 形容詞（easy、difficult、right、wrong、strange、odd、impossible、possible、natural、important、necessary、essential、imperative）+ for + one + 不定詞
= It + be V. + 形容詞（同上）+ 主詞 +（should）+ 動詞原形

▶It is natural for her to get angry.

= It is natural that she (should) get angry.

她生氣是件正常事。

▶It is right for me to stay at home tonight.

= It is right that I (should) stay at home tonight.

我今晚在家是件正確的事。

8. 主詞 + 不完全及物動詞 + it + 形容詞 + for + one + 不定詞 = 主詞 + 不完全及物動詞 + it + 形容詞 +that + 主詞 +（should）+ 動詞原形

▶I think it necessary for me to visit him.

= I think it necessary that I (should) visit him.

我想去拜訪他是應該的。

🔊 小提醒

常與不定詞連用的形容詞：able、amazed、angry、ashamed、astonished（驚訝）、clever、content（滿足的、滿意的）、cruel、destined（注定的）、disappointed、eager、fit、foolish、fortunate、frightened、glad、grieved（悲傷的）、happy、considerate、impatient、lucky、naughty、overjoyed（狂喜的）、pained、pointed（尖銳的、語言辛辣的）、prompt、proud、ready、relieved（如釋重擔的）、rude、sad、shocked、slow、unfortunate、unwise（不智的）、unwilling、willing、wrong。

▶That is not likely to happen.

那很不可能發生。

▶He was fortunate enough to have a good income.

他很幸運曾有好收入。

■ 實用測驗

1. I am sorry, but I forgot _____ the grocery you wanted.

   ① to buy ② buying ③ of buying ④ to have bought

2. When the situation calls you for help, you cannot but _____.

   ① to go ② going ③ go ④ to have gone

3. I do not know him well engouh _____ ask a favor of him.

   ① to ② so as to ③ as to ④ in order to

4. You seem _____ long hours under stress.

   ① to work ② to have worked ③ working ④ having worked-

5. I can hear the girl _____ in the next room.

   ① sang ② to sing ③ to singing ④ singing

6. The teacher told_____ home.

   ① us not to go ② we go not ③ us not go ④ us to not go

7. Hard as I tried, I still could not make myself _____ these English words.

   ① understanding ② understand ③ understood ④ to understand

8. He worked so hard in the office _____ to go home.

   ① that forgot ② he forgot ③ he forgets ④ that he forgot

9. Jack was made _____ his room.

   ① clean ② to clean ③ cleaned ④ to have cleaned

10. The words on the wall are _____ to be rcognized.

    ① to vague too ② to vague to ③ too vague to ④ too vague too

11. The earth was felt _____ when the earthquake occurred.

    ① shake ② shook ③ shakening ④ to shake

12. Do not let the baby _____ so long.

    ① crying ② cry ③ to cry ④ cried

13. The evil-looking man was seen _____ the girl's house.

    ① to enter ② entering into ③ entering ④ enter

14. I am sorry _____ with you all.

    ① not to be able to go ② to not be able to go ③ being not able to go ④ for going not

15. Would you like _____ for walk? I don't feel like _____ that.
    ① to go, to do ② going, going ③ to go, doing ④ doing, to go

■ 試題解析

1. ① forget + to + V原形：忘了去做…；forget + Ving：做了…但忘了，類似用法的字還有：remember, stop。

2. ③ cannot but + V原形，不得不。

3. ① enough to + V原形：足以…；so as to = in order to =為了…；as to = about：關於…。

4. ② 代表發生在說話之前的動作，所以用完成式。

5. ④ hear表示主動時，後加Ving。

6. ① 不定詞的否定用法是在to前加not。

7. ② make + oneslef + understand：讓自己了解…；make + oneself + under-stood：讓他人了解自己的話。

8. ④ so + adj. / adv. + that + S + V =如此…以至於…。

9. ② 使役動詞的被動語態需與不定詞連用；若主動則可將to省略。

10. ③ too + adj. / adv. + to + V原形：太…以至於…。

11. ④ 感官動詞（felt）的被動需用to + V原形。

12. ② 使役動詞主動後加V原形。

13. ① 感官動詞被動後加不定詞to + V原形。

14. ① 不定詞的否定需把not放在to之前。

15. ③ 都當「想」用但like + to + V原形，fell like + Ving。

動名詞 (Gerund)

> 動名詞的基本公式是V-ing；代表具有動詞性質的名詞。

■ 本章重點

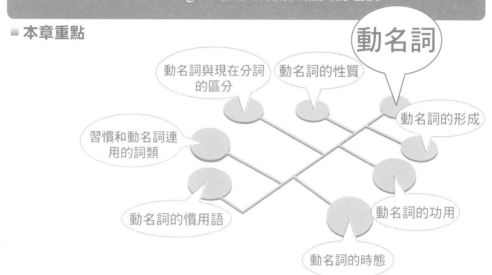

動名詞

動名詞與現在分詞的區分　　動名詞的性質

習慣和動名詞連用的詞類

動名詞的形成

動名詞的慣用語

動名詞的時態

動名詞的功用

- 動名詞的形成
- 動名詞的性質
- 動名詞的功用
- 動名詞與現在分詞的區分
- 動名詞的時態
- 習慣和動名詞連用的詞類
- 動名詞的慣用語

● **動名詞的形成**

	主動語態	被動語態
簡單式	doing	being done
完成式	having done	having been done

● **動名詞的性質**：動名詞可加補語，能有受詞，也可用副詞來修飾。

補語	The old man is proud of being rich. 老人以富有為傲。
受詞	Do you enjoy playing baseball? 你喜歡打棒球嗎？
主詞補語	One of his bad habits is eating too fast. 他壞習慣之一是吃得太快。 （too fast修飾動名詞eating）

● **動名詞的功用**：如名詞，可當句子的主詞、補語及動詞或介詞的受詞。

主詞	Reading English in the morning is a good habit. 早上讀英文是個好習慣。
動詞finish的受詞	Do you finish writing your letter? 你寫完信了嗎？
主詞補語	My hobby is collecting rare coins. 我的嗜好是蒐集稀有硬幣。
受詞補語	I saw flame rising and heard people shouting. 我看見火起也聽到人們大叫。

下列動詞後習以動名詞為受詞補語：catch（撞見、發覺）、have（使）、get（使）、keep（保持）、hear、find（發現）、feel（感覺）、leave（使）、start（開動）、notice（注意）、observe、watch（觀察）、set（處在某種特定狀態）。

▶I felt the house **shaking**.
　我感到房子在搖。

▶The jokes immediately set us **laughing**.
　這笑話立即讓我們開始笑。

▶I caught him **stealing** money from the old man.
　我抓到他從老人那偷錢。

▶Jack is fond of **walking** alone in the park.
　Jack喜歡一個人在公園散步。（介詞of的受詞）

▶His favorite exercise, **taking** a walk in the morning, is beneficial to his health.
　早上散步是他喜歡的運動，這對他的健康有益。（同位語）

●動名詞與現在分詞的區別

▶He is **reading**.
（reading 在is之後構成現在進行式，所以是現在分詞。）

▶He likes **reading**.
（reading 在動詞like之後，當動名詞做動詞的受詞。）

動名詞具名詞的性質，表示用途或目的；現在分詞具形容詞性質，表示動作或狀態。

a **sleeping** baby = a bay who is sleeping

（分詞：睡覺中的嬰兒）

a **sleeping** car = a car used for sleeping

（動名詞；臥車）

現在分詞的類例：a singing bird、a rising sun、a setting moon...。

動名詞的類例：a smoking room、a walking stick、a writing desk、drinking water...。

● 動名詞的時態

1. 簡單式的動名詞表示與動名詞和句子的動詞同時或較晚的動作或狀態

▶He is proud of his son's being rich.

= He is proud that his son is rich.

他對他兒子富有感到驕傲。

▶Are you sure of his being accepted?

= Are you sure that he will be accepted?

你確定他被接受了嗎？

2. 完成式的動名詞表示比句子的動詞早完成的動作或狀態

▶I regret having done so.

= I regret that I did / have done so.

我對做這事感到遺憾。

▶He denied having stolen my money.

= He denied that he had stolen my money.

他否認偷了我的錢。

● 習慣和動名詞連用的詞類

1. 後面僅可用動名詞做受詞的動詞

例 acknowledge、admit、advise、advocate（鼓吹、主張）、allow、anticipate、appreciate、avoid、complete、consider、contemplate（思量）、defer（延期）、delay、deny、detest（厭惡）、discuss、dislike、dread（害怕）、enjoy、ensure（保證）、escape、evade、excuse、facilitate（促成）、fancy（想像、喜歡）、favor（擁護）、finish、forbid、forgive、imagine、include、keep、loathe（厭惡）、mention、mind、miss（錯過）、pardon、permit、practice、postpone、practice、prevent、prohibit、propose、quit、recollect（回憶）、report、resent、renounce（放棄、拋棄）、resist、risk、suggest、tolerate（忍受）、understand等。

▶ She avoided seeing you.
她避免見到你。

▶ I have just finished typing a letter.
我剛打完信。

▶ He practices speaking English with an American.
他和美國人練習說英文。

▶ Please pardon my disturbing you.
請原諒我打擾你。

▶ She said that she had always detested watching bullfight.
她說她一向不喜歡看鬥牛。

2. 動詞片語（如：can't stand、can't help、feel like、give up、put off等）其後加動名詞或名詞

▶ I don't feel like doing anything.

我什麼事都不想做。

▶ I can't help laughing.
我無法不笑。

▶ He put off making any decision before he had more information.
他在有更多資訊前先延緩做決定。

3. 下列介詞或介詞片語後也常與動名詞連用

例 accuse...of（指控）、aim at、approve of（贊成）、be capable of、be afraid of、be interested in、be keen on（熱衷於）、be sick of（厭倦）、be sorry for、be tired of（厭倦）、be proud of、be responsible for、be engaged in（忙於）、charge...with（控告）、devote...to、dream of、excuse...of（原諒）、feel / be ashamed of、insist on、instead of、keep...from、persist in（堅持）、refrain from（忍住）、set about（開始著手）、stop...from、spend...in、suspect...of（懷疑）、think of。

▶ We are sorry for not having informed you of the decision.
我們很抱歉沒通知你這個決定。

▶ He should study instead of playing.
你該讀書而不是嬉戲。

4. 下列動詞片語中的to是介系詞，所以其後要加動名詞

例 add to、agree to、adhere to（堅持）、admit to、allude to（暗示）、amount to（等於）、attend to（照顧、處理）、bow to（順從）、cling to（堅守）、come to（涉及）、correspond to（等於）、confess to（承認）、consent to（同意、答應）、contribute to（有助於、促成）、object to（反對、不贊成）、resort to（訴諸）、revert to（恢復舊有關係）、refer to、relate to、submit to（屈服）、succeed to（繼承）、stick to、swear to（強調）、take to（開始從事）、trust to（依賴、依靠）、witness to（證實、出庭作證）、yield to（讓步、屈服）…。

▶ Keeping what belongs to others amounts to stealing.
將他人物品佔為己有視同偷竊。

▶ My father does not consent to my marrying a foreigner.
我父親不同意我娶（嫁）外國人。

▶ He admitted to having broken the window.
他承認打破窗子。

5. 可用「S＋V＋O＋動名詞」句形的動詞有：hear、listen to、look at、notice、see、smell等感官動詞，以及catch、find、imagine、keep、leave、set、start等動詞

▶ I found him writing at his desk.
我發現他在桌前寫字。

▶ I caught the boy stealing the oranges from my garden.
我抓到這男孩從我花園中偷橘子。

> 🔊 小提醒
>
> 可用「S＋V＋O＋不定詞」句形的動詞有：allow、ask、beg、command、compel、decide、determine、encourage、entreat、force、forbid、instruct、invite、lead、like、order、permit、persuade、press、remind、request、teach、urge、want、warn、wish...等。
>
> ▶ He urged me to stay here tonight.
> 他勸我今晚待在這裡。
>
> ▶ I persuaded him not to make this attempt.
> 我說服他不要去做此嘗試。

6. 下列形式片語（V＋N／pron.＋to）中的to也是介系詞，所以加動名詞

例 apply...to、attribute...to（歸因於）、acribe...to（歸因於）、abbreviate...to（縮寫為）、accustomed...to、confine...to（侷限

於）、commit...to（對…負責）、devote...to、dedicate...to、owe...to（歸功於）、prefer...to、reconcile...to（安於）、reduce...to（降低）、resign...to（聽任）。

▶ I have committed myself to helping people.
我致力於助人。

▶ You must accustomed yoursdelf to getting up early.
你一定要習慣早起。

▶ He has resigned himself to never being able to walk again.
他已接受永遠不能走路的事實。

> 小提醒

下列片語中的to也是介系詞，所以後加動名詞：

be accustomed to, be reduced to（淪落到）, be resigned to, to reconciled to, be devoted to, be used to…

▶ I am now quite reconciled to living in the country.
我現在非常安於住在鄉間。

▶ He was reduced to begging for food.
他淪落到乞討維生。

7. 在allow、permit、forbid...等動詞後，如有受詞接不定詞；如沒有受詞接動名詞

▶ My parents don't allow me to swim in the river.
我父母親不准我在河裡游泳。

▶ They don't allow our smoking here.
他們不准我們在此抽菸。

8. 主詞 + need / want / require / deserve / merit / ... + 動名詞（主動）/ 不定詞 / 名詞（被動）

▶ My clothes want washing.
= My clothes want to be washed.

我的衣服要洗了。

▶ His speech deserves applause.

= His speech deserves applauding.

= His speech deserves to be applauded.

他的演說值得喝采。

9. 主詞 + have + difficulty / trouble / fun / a hard time... + 動名詞

▶ I have difficulty writing English.

我在寫英文上有困難。

▶ He had a hard time finishing this work.

他辛苦地做完工作。

🎧 小提醒

有些動詞後接不定詞或動名詞意思不同：

(A) He stopped smoking. （停止抽菸）

He stopped to smoke. （停止去抽菸）

(B) I forget / remember mailing the letter. （忘記 / 記得已寄信）

I forget / remember to mail the letter. （忘記 / 記得要寄信）

(C) He tried to play the piano. （試著彈鋼琴）

He tried playing the piano. （試彈鋼琴）

(D) He ceased grumbling. （停止發牢騷）

He ceased to grumble. （不再發牢騷）

● 動名詞的慣用語

1. can't help + 動名詞
　 = can't help but + V
　 = can't but + V
　 = can't choose but + V
　 = have no choice but to + V （不得不）

　▶I can't help doing so.
　　= I can't help but do so.
　　= I can't but do so.
　　= I have no choice but to do so.
　　我不得不如此做。

2. be + worth + 動名詞
　 = be worthy of being + p.p.
　 = be + worthy + to be + p.p.
　 = It + be + worth one's while + 不定詞 / 動名詞
　 = It + be + worth while +不定詞 / 動名詞（值得）

　▶This book is worth reading.
　　= This book is worthy to be read.
　　= It is worth while to read this book. / It is worth while reading this book.
　　= It is worth our while to read this book. / It is worth our while reading this book.
　　這書值得一讀。

3. It is no use / good + 動名詞
　 = It is of no use / useless + 不定詞 （...是沒用的）

　▶It is no use crying over spilt milk.
　　= It is of no use to cry over spilt milk.

覆水難收。

4. There is no + 動名詞
= It is impossible / out of the question + 不定詞
= No one can + V原形 （無法…）

▶ There is no knowing what may happen.

= No one can know what may happen.

= We cannot know what may happen.
沒人知道接下來會發生什麼事。

5. It goes without saying that...
= It is needless to say that...
= It is quite obvious that...
= It need not be said that ... （…是不用說）

▶ It goes without saying that knowledge is power.

= It is needless to say that knowledge is power.

= It is quite obvious that knowledge is power.

= It need not be said that knowledge is power.
知識就是力量是無庸置疑的。

6. S + come / go / be near + 動名詞
= be almost + p.p. = nearly + V （幾乎）

▶ He came near being drowned.

= He was almost drowned.
他幾乎溺斃。

7. On / Upon + 動名詞
= When / As soon as / The moment that / The minute that / The instance that + 子句
= Once / Instantly / Immediately / Directly + 子句 （一…就…）

▶ On seeing a snake, she screamed.

= As soon as she saw a snake, she screamed.

= Directly she saw a snake, she screamed.

她一見到蛇就大叫。

8. be on / upon / at the point of + 動名詞
= be about +不定詞 （正要）

▶ It started raining when I was on the point of leaving home.

= It started raining when I was about to leave home.

我將要離家時就下大雨。

9. feel like + 動名詞
= should / would + like +不定詞 （想要）

▶ I don't feel like eating a big meal now.

= I should not like to eat a big meal now.

我不想吃大餐。

■ 實用測驗

1. I prefer reading books _____.

   ① than comics ② for joy ③ insteading of jogging ④ to jogging

2. None of us object to _____ John to the meeting.

   ① invite ② inviting ③ invited ④ have invited

3. Surfing on the net _____ very interesting.

   ① is ② are ③ to be ④ be

4. We spent nearly three full days _____ the 2010 Shanghai Expo.

   ① visit ② to visit ③ visiting ④ visited

5. When you find something in your writing that needs _____, do it at once lest you forget it.

   ① to be correcting ② correct ③ to correct ④ correcting

6. The curious kids kept on _____ questions while visiting the museum.

   ① ask ② asking ③ to ask ④ asked

7. When Mary heard the news of her passing the exam, she burst _____.

   ① into crying ② out to taers ③ crying ④ out crying

8. We should avoid _____ same mistakes again and again.

   ① to make ② make ③ made ④ making

9. The global economy is such a strange thing; there is no _____ what will happen next.

   ① know ② to know ③ known ④ knowing

10. It _____ that children should respect and obey their parents.

    ① appears to be ② goes without saying ③ should be avoided ④ seems

11. When people greet each other, _____ is customarily used.

    ① shaking hand ② to shale hand ③ handshake ④ handshaking

12. I can't imagine _____ all my life in my present job.

    ① work ② to work ③ working ④ to working

13. We will be looking forward to _____ you and your family soon.

    ① see ② seeing ③ to see ④ seen

14. The whole company are busy _____ for the coming promotion campaign.

　　① prepare　② preparing　③ prepared　④ to prepare

15. No one can prevent him _____ that girl even though we all know that they aren't

　　that compatible.

　　① from married　② from getting married　③ get marry　④ to marry

■ 試題解析

1. ④ prefer + Ving + to + Ving：喜歡…勝過…。

2. ② object to中的to為介系詞，所以後加動名詞。

3. ① 動名詞為主詞時，其後取單數形動詞。

4. ③ spend time / money (in) +Ving；spend time / money + on + 名詞。

5. ④ need + Ving表示被動。

6. ② kept on因為是介詞收尾，所以加動名詞。

7. ④ burst into tears = burst out crying：大哭。

8. ④ avoid 後加動名詞。

9. ④ There is no + Ving = It is impossible to...：無法…。

10. ② It goes with out saying that S + V...：…是不用說的。

11. ③ handshake是名詞，所以不需要用動名詞。

12. ③ imagine後加動名詞。

13. ② look forward to的to是介詞。

14. ② busy後加動名詞；the whole company代表「公司所有人」，所以動詞用are。

15. ② prevent + 人 + from + Ving；compatible：相容，相提並論。

筆記頁

分詞 (Participle)

分詞可分為現在分詞和過去分詞;主要功能在與助動詞結合而成不同的時態、語態和語氣的句型。現在分詞強調「主動進行」;過去分詞強調「過去完成」。

本章重點

- 分詞的形式
- 分詞的性質
- 分詞的用法
- 分詞構句
- 獨立分詞構句

分詞

分詞的性質

脫節的分詞　分詞構句　分詞的形式

分詞的用法

獨立分詞構句

分詞相關的慣用語

分詞構句的位置

- 脫節的分詞
- 分詞構句的位置
- 分詞相關的慣用語

分詞的形式

	不及物動詞	及物動詞(主動/被動)
現在分詞	going	writing / being written
過去分詞	gone	X / written
完成式分詞	having gone	having written / having been written

● **分詞的性質：** 分詞因具有動詞的性質，所以其後可加補語或受詞，也可以用副詞來形容；分詞和它的補語、受詞以及修飾語統稱為分詞片語。

▶ Being ill, he couldn't attend the class yesterday.
他昨天因生病無法上課。（修飾主詞）

▶ I saw a man wearing a straw hat.
我看到個戴草帽的人。（修飾受詞）

▶ I heard her singing merrily.
我聽到她快樂地唱歌。（修飾受詞）

● **分詞的用法**

1. 分詞形成各種進行式或完成式及被動語態

現在進行式	We are **studying** English grammar now. 我們現在正在讀英文文法。
過去簡單式被動語態	The letter was **written** by my sister. 我的姊妹寫了一封信。
現在完成式	I have **finished** my homework. 我已經做完功課。
現在完成式被動語態	The book has **been written** by my teacher. 我的老師寫了一本書。
現在完成進行式	I have **been living** here for five years. 我已在此住了五年。

2. 分詞當形容詞用時，放在所修飾的名詞或代名詞前或後。現在分詞表示「主動」、「進行」的意思，過去分詞則表示「被動」、「完成」的意思

▶ The boy sitting there is my cousin.

= The boy who is sitting there is my cousin.

坐在那裡的男孩是我的表（堂）兄弟。

▶ I saw a boy wearing a straw hat in the room.

= I saw a boy who wore a straw hat in the room.

我在房裡看到一個戴草帽的男孩。

▶ She is drinking boiled water.

她喝煮過的水。

▶ She served the boys fried eggs and ham.

她以火腿煎蛋款待男孩們。

▶ The teacher told us an exciting story.

老師告訴我們一個刺激的故事。

▶ There are a lot of fallen leaves in the park.

公園裡有許多落葉。

🔊 小提醒

有些現在分詞表示被動的意思

▶ Where is the wanting volume (the volume that is wanted)?

人家要的那冊書在哪？

▶ I can't find the missing papers (the papers which are being missed).

我找不到遺失的文件。

3. **分詞當主格補語用時，若由主詞作補語的主詞則用現在分詞；若不是由主詞當作補語的主詞，也就是被動的意思，則用過去分詞**

▶ The boy came running to see me.
　這男孩跑來見我。（the boy是補語running的主詞）

▶ The window was closed throughout the night.
　窗子整晚都關著。（the window則是接受close這個動作，所以用過去分詞表被動）

4. **分詞當作受格補語用時，如果由受詞當作補語的主詞則用現在分詞；如果不是由受詞擔任補語的主詞，也就是說被動的意思時，則加過去分詞**

▶ I found her working in the garden.
　我發現她在花園中工作。

▶ I like my egg half cooked.
　我喜歡我的蛋半熟。

5. **擬似分詞（Quasi-Participle）如同過去分詞，在名詞字尾加ed可當形容詞，表示「具有…」的意思。此類分詞可分四種類型**

(A)adj. + N.-ed
(B)數詞 + N.-ed
(C)數詞 + 表度量衡或價值的名詞
(D)N.-ed

▶ This boy is a gifted child.
　這男孩是資賦優異。

▶ I saw a long-armed monkey in the zoo.
　我在動物園見到一隻長臂猴子。

▶ He is a one-eyed man.
　他是個獨眼龍。

▶ This is a fifty-dollar hat.
這是頂值五十元的帽子。

> **類似**
>
> a kind-hearted mother（心地善良的母親）、a good-na-tured man（性情善良的人）、a hot-tempered girl（脾氣火爆的女孩）、a four-wheeled car（四輪傳動的車子）、a red-roofed house（紅屋頂的房子）。

6. 分詞當名詞用時，現在分詞或過去分詞前加定冠詞the可當名詞使用

例 the living (= the living men)、the dying、the wounded、the learned 等，但the accused、the unknown、the deceased（死者）、the condemned（沒收、禁止進入）等其後需用單數動詞。

▶ The hospital was crowded with the wounded from the accident.
醫院裡擠滿了意外事件的傷者。

▶ The learned are respected by all.
人人尊敬有學問的人。

▶ The accused was sentenced to death yesterday.
受審者昨天被判死刑。

▶ The deceased has already been buried.
死者早已入土。

▶ The condemned building was off limits
這危樓是閒人勿進。

7. 有些現在分詞放在形容詞前表示程度，來修飾形容詞。此時，現在分詞當副詞用

▶ It is boiling hot today.
天氣炎熱。

▶It was freezing cold this morning.
今早冷死了。

🔖類似

piercing (biting, searching) cold（刺骨的冷）、boiling (burning) hot（炎熱）、soaking (dripping) wet（溼透）、thumping (thundering) big / great（很大）。

● **分詞構句：**分詞構句兼有形容詞子句及副詞子句的功用。

1. 形容詞子句和分詞構句的互換

▶Do you know the girl sitting there?
= Do you know the girl who is sitting there?
你知道坐在那裡的女孩是誰嗎？

▶Jack bought a camera which was made in Germany.
= Jack bought a camera made in Germany.
Jack買了一部德國製的照相機。

2. 表示時間的分詞構句。此類用法可改成由when、before、after...所引導的副詞子句

▶Seeing the cat, the rat ran off.
= When the rat saw the cat, it ran off.
老鼠見到貓就跑走了。

▶Having prepared tomorrow's lessons, I went to bed.
= After I had prepared tomorrow's lessons, I went to bed.
準備好明天的課後，我就上床睡覺了。

3. 表示原因理由的分詞構句。此類用法可改成由as、since、because...所引導的副詞子句

▶ Being very tired, I could walk no more.

= As I was very tired, I could walk no more.

因為我累了我一步也走不下去。

4. 表示條件的分詞構句。此類用法可改為由if所引導的副詞子句

▶ Going straight for a while, you will find the bank on your right.

= If you go straight for a while, you will find the bank on your right.

再往前直走一會，你將會發現銀行在你右手邊。

5. 表示讓步的分詞構句。此類用法可改為由though、al-though、even if所引導的副詞子句

▶ Admitting what you say, I still think you are wrong.

= Though I admit what you say, I still think you are wrong.

雖然你說的有理，但我依然覺得你錯了

● **獨立分詞構句**：自己有一個意思上的主詞的分詞構句稱為獨立分詞構句。

▶ Night coming on , we started for home.

= When night came on, we started for home.

夜幕低垂，我們開始回家。

▶ The letter written, he went out for a walk.

= After the letter had been written, he went out for a walk.

信寫完，他外出散步。

1. 簡單式的分詞通常表示與句子動詞同時或略早的動作

▶ Taking a walk in the park, I met an old classmate.

= While I was taking a walk in the park, I met an old classmate.

當我在公園散步時，我遇到個老同學。

▶ Leaving here at five, he arrived home at ten.

= He left here at five and arrived home at ten.

他五點離開，十點到家。

2. 完成式的分詞通常表示比句子動詞早完成的動作

▶ Having finished the homework, he took a rest.

= As he had finished the homework, he took a rest.

因他已完成工作，他就休息了。

▶ The letter having been written, I mailed it.

= After the letter had been written, I mailed it.

我在信寫完後就寄出。

● **脫節的分詞**（**Dangling Participle**）：分詞構句中的主詞不是句子的主詞，而分詞構句也沒有意思上的主詞，此類分詞稱為脫節分詞。

▶ Looking up, an airplane was seen by me.（ ✕ ）

Looking up, I saw an airplane.（ ○ ）

我抬頭看見一架飛機。

▶ Being a fine day, we will go on a picnic.（ ✕ ）

It being a fine day, we go on a picnic.（ ○ ）

我們因天氣好而去野餐。

● **分詞構句的位置**

(A)放在句前，跟主詞間加上逗點。

(B)放在句尾，跟前面句子間加上逗點。

(C)如句子的主詞是名詞,放在主詞之後,前後加逗點。

▶Seeing me, Mary ran off.

= Mary ran off, seeing me.

= Mary, seeing me, ran off.

Mary看到我就跑了。

● 分詞相關的慣用語

例 generally speaking、judging from（依…判斷）、speaking / talking of（說到,談到）、take it for granted that...、granted that（假定）、roughly speaking、strictly speaking、frankly speaking、considering（以…而論）、concerning（關於…）、provided that（假如）、seeing that（既然）…。

▶Generally speaking, man is stronger than woman.

一般而言,男人較女人來的強壯。

▶Judging from the fact, he must be innocent.

依照事實判斷,他應該是無辜的。

▶I take it for granted that he can do it well.

我把他能把這事辦好視為理所當然。

▶Seeing that you have finished your work, you can take a rest.

既然你已做完工作,你可以休息。

■ 實用測驗

1. I am sorry to have kept you _____.

   ① to wait   ② wait   ③ waiting   ④ waited

2. Machines can almost do many amazing things when properly _____.

   ① program   ② programed   ③ to program   ④ programming

3. I found a cat _____ over by a car on the street.

   ① to run   ② run   ③ ran   ④ running

4. All the students, _____ those from oversea, will participate the meeting.

   ① included   ② including   ③ include   ④ to include

5. _____ their shoes in hands, the boys tried to cross the stream.

   ① Carry   ② To carry   ③ Carrying   ④ Carried

6. A _____ stone gathers no moss.

   ① roll   ② rolling   ③ rolled   ④ rolls

7. The summer vacation _____ over, the students came back to school and began the new semester.

   ① is   ② are   ③ being   ④ be

8. During the war, some people were injured, and some _____.

   ① miss   ② missed   ③ missing   ④ to miss

9. _____ as the movie is, I don't like it at all.

   ① Interested   ② Interesting   ③ Interest   ④ Interests

10. The building, _____ in Taipei, is officially named Y.C. Wang Building in memory of the late industrialist.

    ① locate   ② locating   ③ located   ④ to locate

11. You must concentrate when _____.

    ① you reading   ② are reading   ③ reading   ④ you were reading

12. He is still unable to make himself _____ in English; his English is too poor.

    ① understood   ② understand   ③ understanding   ④ to understand

13. Walking into the park, _____.

    ① a beautiful scenery was seen   ② we saw a beautiful scenery   ③ a beautiful scenery had been seen   ④ we had seen a beautiful senery

14. Weather _____, we will have an outing this weekend.

    ① permit   ② permits   ③ permitted   ④ permitting

15. People _____ in urban areas long for more living space.

    ① live   ② are living   ③ living   ④ will live

■ 試題解析

1. ③ keep + 受詞 + Ving：繼續使…做…。

2. ② 原句為 "when they are properly programmed"的副詞子句；被動語態。

3. ② 過去分詞表示被動。

4. ② 現在分詞片語修飾students。

5. ③ carrying表示主動。

6. ② rolling表示主動；滾石不生苔。

7. ③ 獨立分詞構句；分詞構句和主要句子的主詞不同。

8. ③ missing：失蹤；missed：錯過，想念。

9. ② interesting形容事物，interested形容人。

10.③ 建築物「位於」用被動；industrialist：工業家。

11.③ 原句為 "when you are reading"。

12.① make oneself undertsand：聽懂…；make oneself understood：讓人聽懂。

13.② 分詞構句和主要句子的主詞需一致。

14.④ weather permitting = if the weather permits。

15.③ 現在分詞修飾主詞；若再用動詞，本句就會有兩個動詞（live, long for）。

形容詞 (Adjectives)

用以修飾限定名詞或代名詞的字，通常可用來表示修飾對象的性質、狀態、數量等。其位置通常在修飾對象之前並由副詞、副詞片語和子句修飾之。形容詞和副詞在外觀上相似者極多如high；同字根所衍生出的形容詞可能會在字義上有所差異，如：loving、lovable、beloved和lovely。

■ **本章重點**

- 性狀形容詞
- 代名形容詞
- 數量形容詞
- 形容詞的位置
- 形容詞的比較
- 易混淆的形容詞

形容詞

形容詞的位置　代名形容詞

性狀形容詞

易混淆的形容詞

數量形容詞

形容詞的比較

● **性狀形容詞**

1. 敘述形容詞：凡表示性質、顏色、大小、狀態等形容詞

▶ I have never seen such a **large** apple.
我從沒見過如此大的蘋果。

▶ She is fond of wearing **white** dresses.
她喜歡穿白色衣服。

▶ He is more **kind** than **wise**.
與其說他聰明不如說他仁慈。

▶The book is very **interesting**.
這本書非常有趣。

2. 專有形容詞：由專有名詞轉用之形容詞，其第一個字母仍需大寫

▶Many foreigners enjoy **Chinese** food very much.
許多外國人很愛中國菜。

▶The boy knows the **English** language.
這男孩懂得英文。

▶It is a **Japanese** wooden bowl.
它是個日本木碗。

3. 物質形容詞：由物質名詞轉用之形容詞

▶It is an **iron** bar.
它是鐵棒。

▶I gave my sister a **gold** ring last Christmas.
我去年聖誕節給我姊妹一只金戒指。

4. 副詞形容詞：少數副詞也可當形容詞用

▶Last night, an **up** train collided with a **down** train.
昨晚一列北上列車和一列南下列車相撞。
（up和down當形容詞用）

▶We found the people **here** are very friendly.
我們發現這裡的人相當友善。
（地方副詞here當形容詞用）

5. 動詞形容詞：由現在分詞與過去分詞所形成的形容詞

▶It is a very **interesting** novel.
它是本非常有趣的小說。

▶That **broken** cup must be thrown away.
那破了的杯子必須要丟掉。

● **代名形容詞**：由各種代名詞轉用而成的形容詞。

1. 所有形容詞：由各種名詞或代名詞的所有格（如：my、your、his、her、its、our、their）轉用而成的形容詞

▶ This is **my** pen, that is yours.
　這是我的筆，那是你的筆。

▶ The company I am working for is famous for **its** long history.
　我所工作的公司是以悠久歷史著稱。

2. 指示形容詞：由指示代名詞（如：this、these、that、those）轉用而成

▶ **These** clothes are more beautiful than **those**.
　這些衣服比那些衣服漂亮。

▶ **This** grammar book is of great help for me to learn English.
　這本文法書對我學習英文幫助很大。

3. 不定形容詞：由不定代名詞（如：some、any、each、every、all、both another）轉用而成

▶ I remember seeing this movie at **some** theater
　我記得在某個戲院看過這部電影。

▶ Do you need **any** money?
　你需要任何錢嗎？

▶ There are trees on **either** side of the street.
　在道路兩邊都有樹。

4. 疑問形容詞：由疑問代名詞（如：who、whose、whom、which、what）轉用而成

▶ **Whose** hat is this?
　這帽子是誰的？

▶ **Which** book do you want to buy?
　你要買哪本書？

5. 關係形容詞：由關係代名詞（如：who、which、when、where）或複合關係代名詞（如：whoever、whatever、whichever...）所轉用而成

▶ I know an American boy **whose** name is Tom.
我認識一位叫Tom的美國男孩。

▶ Return the book to **whosever** name is on it.
把書還給名字在書上的人。

● **數量形容詞**：用以表示名詞或代名詞的數、量、程度。

修飾可數名詞：many、few、a few、several、enough、some、any、no、all、a lot of、lots of、plenty of、a number of...。
修飾不可數名詞：much、little、a little、enough、some、any、no、all、a lot of、lots of、plenty of、a（great） deal of...。

1. many只用來修飾複數可數名詞（普通名詞與集合名詞）；much只用來修飾單數不可數名詞（物質名詞與抽象名詞）

▶ Although he has **much** money, he has not **many** friends.
雖然他有許多錢，但他沒很多朋友。

▶ He bought **many** eggs and **much** butter.
他買了很多蛋和奶油。

> 🔊 小提醒
>
> Many students have passed the exam.
> = Many a student has passed the exam.
> 許多學生通過考試。

2. few / a few用來修飾複數可數名詞，few意思為「幾乎沒有」；a few則為「雖少尚有幾個」。little / a little用來修飾不可數名詞，little為「幾乎沒有」；a little為「雖少尚有少量」

▶ I have few friends in Taipei.
我在臺北沒幾個朋友。

▶ His writing is good, but it has a few spelling mistakes.
他寫的不錯，但仍有幾個拼字的錯誤。

▶ There is little hope for the sick boy.
這生病的男孩機會不大。

▶ I have a little money to help you.
我沒多少錢能幫你。

▶ Not a few (= A great number of) Chinese speak English as fluently as Americans do.
很多中國人英文說的像美國人一樣好。

▶ He has made not a little (= a great deal of) money by working hard.
他藉由努力工作賺了很多錢。

3. several用來修飾複數名詞；enough用來修飾複數名詞及不可數的單數名詞，放在修飾對象前後皆可

▶ The foreigner can speak several languages.
這位外國人能說多國語言。

▶ There are enough books (= books enough) in the library.
圖書館中有足夠的書。

▶ There is enough food (= food enough) for everyone.
有足夠的食物給每個人。

▶ I have time enough (= enough time) to finish the work.
我有足夠的時間來完成工作。

🔊 小提醒

enough若當副詞用時，只能放在修飾對象後面：

Is this box large enough for you?

4. some與any都可以用來修飾可數及不可數名詞，some修飾複數名詞時表示「有些」，修飾單數名詞時表示「某一個」，一般用於肯定；any的意思是「一些、有些」時用於否定句、條件句或疑問句，如用在肯定句則表示「任何一個」

▶ I drink **some** milk every morning.
我每天早晨都喝些牛奶。

▶ Go and get me **some** water.
去替我拿些水。

▶ Can you tell me if there is **any** difference between these two books?
你能告訴我這兩本書有差別嗎？

▶ Will you get me **some** water?
能給我拿些水嗎？

= Please get me **some** water.
請替我拿些水。

▶ **Any** kid is fond of eating candy.
任何小孩都愛吃糖。

= All kids are fond of eating candy.
所有小孩都愛吃糖。

5. all用來修飾可數與不可數名詞，放在定冠詞、指示形容詞及所有形容詞前

▶ **All** my friends are present at the party.
所有我的朋友都出席聚會。

▶ She has spent **all** the money.
她花了所有的錢。

▶ **All** those goods are supposed to be delivered yesterday.
所有商品理當昨天送達。

6. no用來修飾可數與不可數名詞。no + 單數普通名詞 = not a / an + 單數普通名詞；no + 複數名詞 / 抽象名詞 = not any + 複數名詞 / 物質名詞 / 抽象名詞

▶ There is **no** friend to help you.

= There is not a friend to help you.

你沒任何朋友幫你。

▶ There are **no** schools in this town

= There are not any schools in this town.

這城裡沒有任何學校。

▶ He has **no** courage to do it

= He has not any courage to do it.

他沒勇氣去做它。.

▶ He gave us **no** time to think it over.

= He did not give us any time to think it over.

他沒給我們時間去思考。

7. 基數詞（one, two, three ...）當形容詞時，接可數名詞

▶ There are **two** oranges in the basket.
籃子裡有兩顆橘子。

▶ He is a man of **three** scores of years.
他是個六十歲的人。

8. 序數詞（first, second, third ...）當形容詞時，通常與the連用

▶ Sunday is **the first** day of the week.
週日是一週裡的第一天。

▶ December is **the last** month of the year.
十二月是一年的最後一個月。

I will give the present to whoever comes first.
我會把禮物給第一個來的人。（first為副詞）

9. 倍數詞（half, double, treble / triple, four times ...）

▶He bought a second-hand car at **half** of the price.
他用一半的價格買了二手車。

▶I'll come back **half** an hour (= a half hour) later.
他半個小時後就會回來。

▶He is **double** her age.
他的年紀是她的兩倍。

After the war, many things cost almost double.
戰後許多東西的價格都加倍。（double是副詞）

● **形容詞的位置：**幾乎所有的形容詞都放在所修飾的名詞前面，修飾且限定修飾名詞；部分形容詞在動詞後面，說明主詞的性質或狀態。

▶John is an honest boy.
John是誠實的男孩。

▶He is reading an interesting book.
他讀的是本有趣的書。

▶Roses are red and violets are blue.
玫瑰是紅的，紫羅蘭是藍的。

▶The good news made them happy.
好消息讓他們高興。

🔊 小提醒

> 若形容詞為a...形式的形容詞（如：alive、afraid、alone、asleep、awake、aware、ashamed...）時，一定要做後位修飾：
>
> ▶ The boy is asleep.
>   這男孩睡著了。
>
> ▶ The fish is alive. (= This is a living fish.)
>   魚是活的。
>
> ▶ They are ashamed of what they have done.
>   他們對所做的事感到羞愧。

1. something、anything、everything、nothing、someone、anyone、everyone、somebody、anybody、everybody、nobody等不定代名詞及who、what等疑問代名詞，形容詞需置其後

▶ Do you have **anything new**?
  你有新的東西嗎？

▶ I saw **nobody else** in the room. Who else came?
  我在房內沒見到別人。還有誰來？

2. 數詞（one, two ...）與deep、high、long、old、thick、wide等形容詞連用時為後位修飾

▶ The boy is fifteen years **old**.
  這男孩是十五歲大。

▶ The box is 15 inches **long**, 10 inches **wide**, and 20 inches **high**.
  = The box is 15-inch in length, 10-inch in width, and 20-inch in height.
  這盒子是15吋長、10吋寬和20吋高。

3. 兩個以上形容詞修飾同一個名詞時，放在名詞前後均可

This pretty and diligent girl is my cousin.

= This girl, pretty and diligent, is my cousin.

這個漂亮勤勉的女孩是我表（堂）妹。

4. 形容詞後帶有修飾語時，該形容詞放在被修飾名詞之後

▶ Pay more attention to cross the street full of traffic.

過街時要多小心來往車輛。

▶ This is lake famous for its scenery.

= This lake is famous for its scenery.

這湖以美景著稱。

5. 片語或子句做形容詞時均放在名詞之後

▶ The old man with grey hair is my grandfather.

有灰髮的老人是我的祖父。

▶ The man (who) just returned from New York is my teacher.

剛從紐約回來的人是我的老師。

▶ It was the wallet (that) he dropped.

他掉的是皮夾。

6. 修飾指示代名詞those的形容詞需置於其後

▶ Those who present were all surprised by the bad news.

出席的人都對這壞消息感到驚訝。

▶ Among those invited were some ladies.

在所有受邀請的人當中有些是女士。

7. last、next或following修飾表示時間的名詞時，置於修飾對象前後皆可

▶ John called on me last Sunday.

= John called on me on Sunday last.

John上週日打電話給我。

▶We are going to have a picnic next Sunday.

= We are going to have a picnic on Sunday next.

我們下週日將有個野餐。

8. 形容詞需放在不完全不及物動詞（be動詞，感官動詞）及完全不及物動詞後當主詞補語或受詞補語

▶The mountain is high and the sea is deep.

山高海深。

▶The rose smells sweet.

玫瑰聞起來很香。

▶A good boy will make his parents proud.

這好男孩將會使他父母親驕傲。

▶The thunder struck him dead.

雷劈死了他。

🔊 小提醒

下列形容詞多用此種用法：be afraid of、be ashamed of、be aware of、be sure of、be content with、be unable to、awake、asleep、alive、alike、drunk、sunk…。

▶Man is afraid of death.

人怕死。

▶He is ashamed of himself.

他對自己感到慚愧。

▶I am unable to solve the problem.

我不能解決問題。

▶He is drunk.

他喝醉了。

◆◆比較◆ A drunken man was lying in the street.
一個喝醉的人躺在街上。

9. 形容詞放置的位置

1 a / an / the + n.

a / an / the + adj. + n.

a / an / the + adv. (very, too, much) + adj. + n.

what / many / such / quite / rather + a(n) + adj. + n.

how / so / as / too + adj. + a(n) + n.

all / both + the + n.

▶ What a diligent student John is!

= How diligent a student John is!

John真是個勤勉的學生啊！

▶ He is as kind a boy as you are.
他像你一樣仁慈。

▶ I have never seen such an honest boy as he.

= I have never seen so honest a boy as he.

我從沒見過像他一樣誠實的人。

2 代名詞形容詞 + 數量形容詞 + 敘述形容詞。同種類的形容詞修飾同一名詞時，字短在前，字長在後，關係越密切越靠近名詞。

▶ I bought these two old books from that shop.
我從那家店買了這兩本舊書。

▶ Those three lazy boys were punished.
那三個懶惰的男孩接受懲罰。

▶ The old man told the boy an easy and interesting story.
那老人對那男孩說了個簡單且有趣的故事。

▶ He is walking along a long, straight street.
他正沿著一條長又直的路走。

3 一般形容詞可依下列原則放置：

冠詞 — 所有格 — 指示形容詞 — 不定形容詞 — 數量 — 性狀 — 大小 — 長短 — 新舊 — 顏色 — 專有形容詞 — 材料

▶It is a small Japanese wooden bowl.
這是一個小的日本木碗。

▶That tall old English gentleman is a professor.
那個高大的老英國紳士是位教授。

● 形容詞的比較：

形容詞會因所修飾對象的數量而分為原級、比較級和最高級。

▶She is very beautiful.　她很漂亮。

▶She is more beautiful than her sister.　她比她姊妹更漂亮。

▶She is the most beautiful of all her sisters.　她是所有姊妹裡最漂亮的。

比較級與最高級的形成可分：

1. 規則變化

◆ 在原級形容詞的字尾加-（e）r成比較級，加-（e）st成最高級。

1 單音節或少數兩音節的形容詞（尤其是字尾為 -er, -ow, -le），在原級形容詞的字尾加er成比較級，加est成最高級。

原級	比較級	最高級
young	younger	youngest
great	greater	greatest
clever	cleverer	cleverest
narrow	narrower	narrowest

2 單音節或少數兩音節的形容詞，字尾已有e者，只在原形形容詞的字尾加r成比較級，加st成最高級。

原級	比較級	最高級
wise	wiser	wisest
large	larger	largest
simple	simpler	simplest
gentle	gentler	gentlest

3 單音節或少數兩音節的形容詞，其字尾為【子音 + y】時，將y改為i，其後加er成比較級，加est成最高級；字尾為【母音＋y】時，只在字尾加er成比較級，加est成最高級。

原級	比較級	最高級
happy	happier	happiest
heavy	heavier	heaviest
gay	gayer	gayest
gray / greyer	grayer / greyer	grayest / greyest

4 單音節的形容詞，其字尾為【短母音 + 單子音】時，重寫字尾的子音再加er成比較級，加est成最高級。

原級	比較級	最高級
hot	hotter	hottest
big	bigger	biggest
sad	sadder	saddest
wet	wetter	wettest

◆ 在原級形容詞的前面加more成比較級，加most成最高級。

1 大多數的兩音節形容詞（尤其是字尾為-ful、-less、-ive、-ous、-ing、-did、-ed、-able、-ible），以及三音節以上的形容詞，在原級形容詞前加more成比較級，加most成最高級。

原級	比較級	最高級
useful	more useful	most useful
careless	more careless	most careless
active	more active	most active
famous	more famous	most famous
loving	more loving	most loving
splendid	more splendid	most splendid
learned	more learned	most learned
eatable / edible	more eatable / edible	most eatable / edible

2 以-y、-ow、-er、-le為結尾的兩音節形容詞，通常用-er、-est成比較或最高級。

原級	比較級	最高級
dirty	dirtier	dirtiest
hollow	hollower	hollowest
tender	tenderer	tenderest
simple	simpler	simplest

3 三個音節以上的形容詞，全部在原級前加more成比較級，加most成最高級。

原級	比較級	最高級
beautiful	more beautiful	most beautiful
difficult	more difficult	most difficult
horrible	more horrible	most horrible
interesting	more interesting	most interesting

4 複合字通常用more, most成比較與最高級。

原級	比較級	最高級
up-to-date	more up-to-date	most up-to-date
good-natured	more good-natured	most good-natured
well-to-do	more well-to-do	most well-to-do

◆ 原來用-er或-est形成比較級或最高級的形容詞，當用作be動詞的補語時且具有下列意思時，要用more及most表示。

1 比較同一人或物的不同性質。

▶ She is more shy than unsocial.

= She is rather shy than unsocial.

與其說不善社交不如說害羞。

▶ She is more proud than vain.

= She is rather proud than vain.

與其說虛榮不如說驕傲。

2 加重語氣時。

There was never a kinder and juster man.

= There was never a man more kind and just.

3 「No more 或 Not any more + 形容詞」。

▶ I am no more / not any more mad than you are.

我不比你瘋。

2. 不規則變化

(1)

原級	比較級	最高級
good	better	best
well		
bad	worse	worst
ill		
many	more	most
much		
little	less	least

▶ The war was going from bad to worse.
戰事每況愈下。

▶ She has little, he has less, and I have the least.
她有一點，他有的更少，我則是最少。

(2)

原級	比較級	最高級	
old	older	oldest	（年紀）
	elder	eldest	（輩分）
late	later	latest	（早晚）
	latter	last	（先後）
far	further	furthest	（程度）
	farther	farthest	（距離）

eldest daughter / son　　（長女 / 子）

oldest sister / brother　　（大姊 / 大哥）

▶ It's not farther than a mile from here.

離這裡不到一哩。

▶ I have no further question to ask you.

我沒更進一步的問題要問。

▶ I will talk to you later.

我等下和你說。

▶ He spent his latter part of the day reading.

他把一天剩下的時間花在讀書。

▶ This is the latest news from the U.S.

這是從美國來的最新消息。

▶ This is the last news from the U.S.

這是從美國來的最後消息。

3. 含有原級與比較級形容詞的慣用語

not so much as (= not even)（甚至於不……）

not so much...as (= not...but rather)（與其說…不如說…）

比較級 + and + 比較級（漸漸）

the + 比較級…, the + 比較級（愈…愈…）

no more than (= only)（只）

not more than (= at most)（至多）

no less than (= as much / many as)（和一樣多）

not less than (=at least)（至少）

sooner or later（遲早）

more or less (= somewhat)（多少，有些）

still / much the less（更不用，何況）

none the less = not the less = no less（仍舊，依然）

▶He cannot so much as write his own name.
　他連自己的名字都不會寫。

▶He is not so much a scholar as a teacher.
　與其說他是學者不如說是老師。

▶It's getting colder and colder.
　天氣越來越冷。

▶The older we grow, the wiser we become.
　人越老越有智慧。

▶He has no more than fifty dollars.
　他只有五十元。

▶He has not more than fifty dollars.
　他至多有五十元。

▶She is no less beautiful than her sister.
　(= She is as beautiful as her sister.)
　她和她姊妹一樣漂亮。

▶He will succeed sooner or later.
　他早晚會成功。

▶Most people are more or less selfish.
　人多少有些自私。

▶I don't love him the less for his faults.
　= I don't love him the less because he has faults.
　= He has faults, but I love him none the less.
　雖然他有錯，但我愛他卻依然不減。

4. 含有最高級形容詞的慣用語

do one's best（盡全力）

at best（充其量）

at least（至少）

not…in the least （一點也不）

at (the) latest（最遲）

at (the) earliest（最早）

at (the) most（至多）

at one's best（全盛時期）

make the most / best of（盡量利用）

at (the) worst（最壞）

最高級 + but one（第二）

for the most part（一般地，大部分）

▶ He did the best to finish the work on time.
　他盡最大努力準時完成工作。

▶ I can earn fifty dollars a week at best.
　我一星期最多賺50元。

▶ He can earn fifty dollars at least.
　他至少能賺50元。

▶ This book is not the least difficult.
　這書一點也不難。

▶ We must be there by 10 at (the) latest.
　我們最遲十點要到這裡。

▶ We shall lose only sixty dollars at worst.
　我們最多損失60元。

▶ I can pay only fifty dollars at (the) most.
　我最多只能付50元。

5. 形容詞各級間的互換

1 原級與最高級。

> as + adj. + as any + N. = the + 最高級

▶ She is as famous as any painter.
　= She is the most famous of all the painters.
　她是所有畫家中最出名的。

> as + adj. + a(n) + N. + as ever + V.
> = the + 最高級adj. + N. + that ever + V.

▶ This is as big an animal as I have ever seen.
= This is the biggest animal that I have ever seen.
這是我見過最大的動物。

> never + such / so + adj. + N.（複）/ a（n）N.（單）+ as + N.
> = S + V. + the 最高級形容詞 + that + ever +...

▶ I have never seen such a big animal as this.
= This is the biggest animal that I have ever seen.
這是我見過最大的動物。

> no... so + adj.....as + one = one...+ the最高級形容詞

▶ Nothing is so precious as health.
= Health is the most precious thing.
健康是最珍貴的東西。

2 比較級與最高級間的互換。

> S + V. + 比較級adj. + than + any + other + N（單）
> = S + V. + 最高級adj. + of + all + N（複）

▶ He is greater than any other English poet.
= He is the greatest of all English poets.
他是所有英國詩人裡最偉大的。

> S + never + V....+ 比較級adj. + than + N.
> = S + V. + the + 最高級adj. + that + ever + V.

▶I have never seen a picture more amusing than this.

= This is the most amusing picture that I have ever seen.

這是我所看過最有趣的電影。

> Nothing is + 比較級adj. + than + N.
> = N. + is + 最高級adj.

▶Nothing is more precious than time.

= Time is the most precious thing.

時間是最珍貴的東西。

3 原級與比較級間的互換

> S + be + less + adj. + than + …
> = S + be + not + so +原級adj. + as +…

▶It is not so cold as it was yesterday.

= It is less cold than it was yesterday.

今天沒昨天冷。

> S(1) + be + not + so + 原級adj. + as + S(2)
> = S (2) + be + 比較級adj. + than + S(1)

▶She is not so wise as her sister.

= Her sister is wiser than she.

她姊妹比她聰明。

4 原級間互換

as... as possible = as... as one can

▶The robber ran away as fast as possible.

= The robber ran away as fast as he could.

強盜盡可能地快速逃跑。

倍數 + the + N. + of +...= 倍數 as + adj. + as...

▶This is twice the size of that.

= This is twice as large as that.

這是那的兩倍大。

the same + N. + as = as + adj. + as

▶He is the same height as his brother.

= He is as tall as his brother.

他和他兄弟一樣高。

5 比較級間互換。

no more A than B = not A any more than B

▶He is no more a poet than I am.

= He is not a poet any more than I am.

= I am not a poet, nor is he.

我倆都不是詩人。

no / not more than

▶ He is no / not more diligent than you are.
他沒比你更勤勉。

the + 比較級adj. + S + V. the + 比較級adj. + S + V.
= as + S + V. + 比較級adj. S + V. + 比較級adj.

▶ The higher up you go, the colder it becomes.
= As you go up higher, the weather becomes colder.
你爬得越高，天氣就變得越冷。

prefer N. to + N. = like... better than...

▶ She prefers tea to coffee.
= She likes tea better than coffee.
她喜歡茶勝過咖啡。

superior / inferior to = better / worse than

▶ This book is superior to that.
= This book is better than that.
這本書比那本書好。

senior / junior to = older / younger than

▶ My brother is two years junior to me.
= My brother is two years younger than I.
= My brother is younger than I by two.
我兄弟比我小兩歲。

6 最高級間互換。

> the very + 最高級adj.
> = much the + 最高級adj.
> = by far the + 最高級adj.

▶ Gold is the very most valuable of all metals.

　= Gold is much the most valuable of all metals.

　= Gold is by far the most valuable of all metals.

　金子是最有價值的金屬。

6. 注意

1 在比較級用法中，若出現 "of the two"時，比較級前需加the。

▶ He is the taller of the two.

2 在最高級形容詞前需加the；最高級副詞前則不需。

▶ He is the fastest runner of all.

　他是所有跑者裡最快的一個。

▶ He runs fastest of all.

　他在所有人裡跑得最快。

3 相同事物之間才可比較。

▶ The ears of the cats are usually shorter than dogs. （✕）

▶ The ears of the cats are usually shorter than those of dogs. （○）

　貓的耳朵通常比狗的耳朵短。

▶ The weather in Taiwan is milder than Japan. （✕）

　The weather in Taiwan is milder than that in Japan. （○）

　臺灣的天氣較日本的天氣溫和。

4 用very修飾原級；用much / far修飾比較級；用the very / much the 修飾最高級。

▶ Mary is very kind.

Mary很仁慈。

▶ Mary is much kinder than her sister.

= Mary is far kinder than her sister.

Mary比她姊妹仁慈多了。

▶ Mary is the very kindest of all her sisters.

= Mary is much the kindest of all her sisters.

Mary是她所有姊妹裡最仁慈的。

● 易混淆的形容詞

1. 就如同易混淆的動詞一樣，有些形容詞也會因外型相似而造成混淆

alone（獨自的），lonely（孤獨的），lonesome（冷清的）

alive（活的），living（有生命的），live（活的、現場的）

beastly（禽獸的），bestial（獸慾的）

childlike（天真的），childish（幼稚的）

clean（清潔的），clear（清澈的）

continual（時斷時續的），continuous（連續的）

considerate（體貼的、體諒的），considerable（應考慮的、相當大的）

contemptuous（輕視他人的），contemptible（受輕視的）

comical（好笑的、滑稽的），comic（喜劇的）

corporeal（實體的），corporal（身體的）

desirable（值得的、合意的），desirous（渴望的）

dead（死的），deadly（致命的），deathly（死一般的）

distinct（清晰的），distinctive（有特色的）

economical（節儉的），economic（經濟的）

electrical（電的、與電有關的），electric（電的、帶電的），electronic（電子的）

efficient（效率高的），effective（有結果的），effectual（有效的）

frightful（可怕的、討厭的），frightened（害怕的）

gentle（溫柔的、高貴的），genteel（假斯文的）

hard（艱苦的），hardy（能吃苦耐勞的）

healthful（有益健康的），healthy（健康的、衛生的）

historic（有歷史意義的），historical（歷史的）

honorary（名譽上的），honorable（值得尊敬的）

imaginary（虛構的），imaginable（可以想像的），imaginative（富有想像力的）

immortal（不朽的），immoral（不道德的）

industrial（工業的），industrious（勤勞的）

intelligent（聰明的），intelligible（可理解的、清楚的）

intense（強烈的），intensive（密集的）

like（相像的），likely（可能的），alike（相像的）

▶ Jack is like his father in many ways.

▶ Jack and his father are alike in many ways.

lineal（直系的），linear（直線的）

lovely（可愛的、美好的），loveable（討人喜歡的）

manlike（有男子氣概的、強壯的），mannish（像男人的）

massy（堅實的），massive（巨大的）

notable（著名的、顯著的），notorious（惡名昭彰的）

pictorial（圖畫的），picturesque（有戲劇效果的）

popular（流行的），populous（人口稠密的）

practical（實際的），practicable（可行的）

respectful（恭敬的），respectable（可敬的），respective（各自的）

sensitive（敏感的），sensible（明智的、可感覺到的）

sensual（感官的），sensuous（好色的）

successful（成功的），successive（連續的）

tolerant（寬容的），tolerable（可忍受的）

uninterested（不感興趣的），disinterested（無私的）

valueless（無價值的），valuable（有價值的），invaluable（無法估價的）

2. 除了外型相似所造成的混淆之外，意義相似也會造成形容詞的混淆

1 previous、original、former、prior

▶ I am unable to attend because of a previous engagement.
我因事前有約所以無法出席。

▶ I prefer your original plan to this one.
我喜歡你前個計畫勝過這個。

▶ She's back to former self again.
她又恢復老樣子。

▶ They have a prior claim to the property.
他們對這房地產有優先權利。

2 heavy、large、huge、vast

▶ The result of the final exam was a heavy blow（重大打擊） to John.

▶ Jack has a large appetite（胃口好）.

▶ Instead of money and estate（地產），Jack inhertited（繼承） huge debts.

▶ His business empire was truly vast.
他的事業帝國的確很大。

3 late、the latter、the latest、the last

▶ One of my favorite speeches is the inaugural address（就職演說） made by JFK（約翰甘迺迪）.

▶ One can travel there by ship or plane; most people choose the latter.（後者）

▶ Mary is always dressed in the latest（最新） fashion.

▶The last（最後） bus leaves in 5 minutes.

4 used、useless、useful、usefulness

▶This is a used car.（二手車）

▶His foolish idea is useless at all.

▶What you said just now is quite useful.

▶The old car had outlived（壽命長過）its usefulness（用處）.

5 likely、possible、probable

▶Jack is not likely（不可能）to come.

▶Success is possible, but hardly probable.（有可能但機率性不大）

6 dead、dying、deathly、deadly

▶He has been dead for almost ten years.

▶The terminal patient（末期病人） is dying soon.

▶She is dying to（渴望） know the truth.

▶The whole theater was in a deathly silence（死寂） after the performance.

7 worth、worthy

▶He felt his life was no longer worth（不值得） living.

▶Her achievement is worthy（價值） of the higest praise.

8 lone、lonely、alone

▶He lives like a lone（孤獨）wolf.

▶He lives alone（獨自） but he never feels lonely（孤單）.

■ 實用測驗

1. The defeated boxer looks _____.

   ① hurt more than frightened ② more hurt than frightened ③ more hurting than frightening ④ more hurting than frightened

2. Usually, students in Taiwan have _____ vacation in the summer.

   ① a two-month ② a two months ③ a two month's ④ a two months'

3. _____ participants came to this seminar than last year.

   ① Few ② A few ③ Fewer ④ Quite a few

4. You can always learn _____ from anyone anytime anywhere.

   ① some useful thing ② something useful ③ somethings useful ④ something usefully

5. I have always _____ glad that grandfather lived with us while he was still alive.

   ① be ② being ③ been ④ to be

6. Tom _____ his brother in many ways.

   ① alike to ② look like ③ is like ④ is likely

7. She is _____ taller than her sister.

   ① very ② much ③ more ④ many

8. He is _____ the two boys.

   ① taller than ② the taller in ③ the taller of ④ the taller between

9. Jack looked _____.

   ① angrily the people around him ② tired and restless ③ exciting and embarrassing ④ the girl he loved

10. About _____ of the students were absent yesterday.

    ① two third ② two thirds ③ twos third ④ twos thirds

11. Mr. Smith's luggage is not so heavy as _____.

    ① Mr. Nelson ② Mr. Nelson's ③ that of Mr. Nelson's ④ those of Mr. Nelson's

12. He is smarter than _____ in the class.

    ① all the boys ② the all boys ③ all the other boys ④ all boys

13. The table is _____ that one.

    ① as two times as long   ② as lont two times as   ③ two times as long as

    ④ long as two times than

14. This is the most interesting movie _____.

    ① that I saw   ② that I have ever seen   ③ that I had seen   ④ that I have seen

15. Did he do _____ he could?

    ① the much best   ② very the ebst   ③ best the very   ④ the very best

■ 試題解析

1. ② more A than B = not so much A as B：與其說A不如說B。

2. ① 數字+單數名詞=形容詞。

3. ③ participants為可數名詞，than須與比較級連用，所以選③。

4. ② something／anything／nothing...等字後接形容詞。

5. ③ glad是形容詞，須置於be動詞後；現在完成式的用法。

6. ③ 「相似」：look like = be like = be similar to。

7. ② much修飾比較級形容詞。

8. ③ the +形容詞比較級 + of the two。

9. ② 感官動詞look後加形容詞；若選①或③則因look為不及物動詞而需要介系詞，選④則需改成過去分詞。

10. ② 分數的分子用基數，分母用序數；若分子大於1時，分母需加s。

11. ③ 同質事物之間才可比較。

12. ③ 因為用比較級，所以只能有兩個比較對象；he和all the other boys是兩個比較的對象。

13. ③ 倍數的基本用法。

14. ② 最高級形容詞需用關係代名詞that；且表示經驗，所以現在完成式中須加ever。

15. ④ the very／much the + 形容詞最高級。

副詞 (Adverbs)

用來修飾動詞、形容詞或句中其他的副詞。若要以外型來判斷，符合「形容詞 + ly」的規定的才是副詞。同樣字根所衍生出的不同副詞在意義上會有不同。

■ 本章重點

● 副詞的功能
● 副詞的位置
● 副詞的形成
● 常用副詞的用法
● 副詞的比較

● 副詞相關的慣用語
● 容易混淆的副詞

副詞

副詞的位置

常用副詞
的用法

副詞的比較

副詞的功能

副詞的形成

容易混淆的副詞

副詞相關
的慣用語

● **副詞的功用：**修飾動詞、形容詞及副詞。

▶She speaks English very fluently.　她英文說得流利。

（副詞 fluently 修飾動詞 speak，副詞 very 修飾副詞 fluently）

▶My father came yesterday.　我父親昨天來。

（時間副詞 yesterady 修飾動詞 came）

▶It is a very lovely day.　今天天氣很美好。

（形容詞 lovely 修飾名詞 day，副詞 very 修飾形容詞 lovely）

● 副詞的位置

1. 表示態度或方法的副詞，如：well、hard、fast、quietly、slowly、happily、merrily、fluently、beautifully、diligently、bravely...等其位置為

1 不及物動詞 + adv.

▶ The old man lives alone but happily.
老人快樂地獨居。

2 及物動詞 + 受詞 + adv.

▶ The lifeguard saved the child from drowning.
救生員拯救了溺水的小孩。

> 🎧 小提醒
>
> 若以名詞子句為受詞，或受詞後有子句或片語來修飾時，副詞放在動詞與受詞之間。
> I can't understand clearly what you have written in that letter.
> 我無法清楚地了解你在那信中所寫的是什麼。
> I heard clearly a sound like that of my sister.
> 我清楚地聽到像是我姊妹發出的聲響。

2. 表時間的頻率副詞，如：always、often、usually、seldom、never、ever、hardly、scarcely、generally、sometimes、suddenly...等其位置為

1 adv. + V.

▶ My family always goes out for dinner on Sundays.
我家人總是在週日外出晚餐。

2 be + adv.

▶ I am always on time for class.
我上課總是準時。

3 助動詞 + adv. + 主要子句

▶ She has never forgotten your favor to her.
　她從未忘記你對她的恩惠。

3. 表示時間的副詞，如：tomorrow、yesterday、...ago、be-fore、last ...、every ...等其位置一般置於句尾，但若為了強調時也可置於句首。

▶ I usually go to the movies once a week.
　我通常每週看一次電影。

▶ For six years, we have been studying English.
　我們已讀了六年的英文。

4. 表程度的副詞，如：very、terribly、much、little、too、just、rather、almost、pretty...等其位置為adv. + V. / adj. / adv.

▶ He did the work very well.
　他事做得很好。

▶ I would rather stay at home than go out on the rainy day.
　下雨天我寧願待在家裡，也不要出門。

▶ The girl is quite pretty, isn't she?
　這女孩很漂亮，不是嗎？

5. 當兩個以上的副詞修飾同一對象

1 同種類的副詞，小單位 + 大單位。

▶ I was born on July 14 in 1990.
　我生在1990年7月14日。

2 不同種類的副詞則依：
　A. 地方 + 時間
　B. 地方 + 方法 + 時間
　C. 狀態 + 地方 + 時間

▶ I was there at the party last night.
　　我昨晚在聚會中。

▶ My father returned home by air yesterday.
　　我父親昨晚搭飛機回家的。

▶ He has been very seriously ill in the hospital for some time.
　　他已經因嚴重地不適住院一段時間了。

6. 如on、off、up、in等介詞副詞,若動詞的受詞為名詞時,放在該受詞前後皆可;若受詞為代名詞時,要放在該受詞後

▶ She took off her coat.
　　= She took her coat off.
　　她脫掉帽子。

▶ She wore a hat, and she took it off after entering the room.
　　她戴了一頂帽子,進屋後,她把帽子脫掉。

▶ She put the hat on.
　　= She put on the hat.
　　她戴上帽子。

▶ A car came and picked me up.
　　一部車來接我。

7. 為了加強語氣,有時可把否定副詞放在句首,但要把助動詞放在主詞的前面(倒裝句)

▶ Hardly had I left the house before it began to rain.
　　我一離開房子就下雨了。

▶ Never in my life have I been so ashamed of myself.
　　我一生從沒如此慚愧過。

> 🔔 小提醒
>
> 若句中沒有助動詞或be動詞時,在主詞前加助動詞do。
> I remember the story well. = Well do I remember the story.
> 這故事我記得很清楚。

● 副詞的形成

1. 大部分副詞是在形容詞後加「-ly」而成

例 quick - quickly、wise - wisely、loving - lovingly、undoubted - undoubtedly。

2. 當形容詞字尾是「y」時，把y改成i再加上ly即可

例 happy - happily、easy - easily、pretty - prettily。

> 🔊 小提醒
>
> 單音節的形容詞字尾是「-y」時，把y改為i再加ly或不把y改成i而直接加ly皆可。
>
> gay - gaily / gayly
>
> dry - drily / dryly

3. 當形容詞字尾是「-le」時，把e改為y即可

例 possible - possibly、simple - simply、humble - humbly。

➕ 例外 sole - solely, whole - wholly

4. 當形容詞字尾是「-ll」時，只加上y即可

例 full - fully、dull - dully。

5. 當形容詞字尾是「-ue」時，去e加上ly即可

例 true - truly、due - duly。

6. 當形容詞字尾是「-ic」時，加ally即可

例 automatic - automatically、democratic - democratically。

7. 有些ly結尾的字可同時當形容詞與副詞用

▶ This is a monthly (adj.) magazine.

這是一份月刊。

This is published monthly (adv.).

這是每月發行一次。

▶ Ill (adj.) news travels fast.

壞事流傳地快。

Don't speak ill (adv.) behind one's back.

別在背後說人壞話。

▶ A well (adj.) man should not lie in bed.

健康的人不該懶在床上。

He speaks English well (adv.).

他英文說得好。

▶ She leads a fast (adj.) life.

她生活步調快。

She lives fast.

她生活放蕩。

▶ I have enough (adj.) money to buy the house.

我有足夠的錢買房子。

This room is large enough (adv.) for all participants.

這房間大到可容納所有出席者。

▶ I am sorry to give you so much (adj.) trouble.

我很抱歉給你惹這麼多麻煩。

I was much (adv.) troubled by the news.

我深受這消息的困擾。

▶ My family are all early (adj.) risers.

我全家人都是早起者。

I get up early (adv.) in the morning.

我早上很早起。

▶ It is too late (adj.) to go there.
現在去那已太晚。

He sat late last (adv.) night.
我昨晚熬夜。

▶ This is the only (adj.) way to do it.
這是做那事的唯一方法。

He can only (adv.) do his best.
他只有盡力了。

▶ The chair is three feet high (adj.).
這椅子有三呎高。

Birds fly high (adv.) in the sky.
鳥高高地飛在天上。

🔊 小提醒

(A)有些以 -ly結尾的字並不是副詞而是形容詞：
　　lively（活潑的）、fatherly（慈愛的）、costly、
　　lovely、cowardly、earthly（塵世的）、lonely、ugly、
　　silly、friendly...。

(B)有些以 -ly結尾的詞既是形容詞又是副詞：
　　likely、deathly、monthly、kindly、early、weekly、
　　cleanly、yearly、daily、deadly...。

(C)有些形容詞也做副詞用，根據它在句中的作用來決定
　　詞性：
　　fast、firm、near、clean、hard、quick、clear、high、
　　slow、close、late、straight、direct、low、wrong、
　　enough、much、wide、far...。

● 常用副詞的用法

1. 「very」、「much」，原形形容詞與副詞用very；比較級形容詞或副詞用much或far；最高級形容詞或副詞用much the 或the very

▶The book is very useful in studying English.
這本書在讀英文上很有用。

▶The earth is much larger than the moon.
地球比月球大得多。

▶This pen is the very / much the best of all.
這筆是所有裡最好的。

> 🔊 小提醒
>
> (A)現在分詞或當純粹形容詞的過去分詞用very；被動語態中的過去分詞用much。
> > ▶He told me a very interesting story.
> > 他告訴我個很有趣的故事。
> > ▶He was wearing a very surprised expression.
> > 他臉上帶著一種非常訝異的表情。
> > ▶He was much remembered by everyone.
> > 他被所有人牢記在心中。
> (B)修飾動詞或介詞片語時只能用much或very much。
> > ▶She was much at a loss about what she should do.
> > 對她該做什麼感到迷惑。

2. 「ever」

1 ever當「曾經」時，通常用在疑問句。

▶Have you ever been to Japan?
你去過日本嗎？

2 ever當「始終，常是」時，通常用在肯定句。

▶Parents are ever ready to help their children.
父母親始終待命幫助子女。

3 ever當「無論如何」時，可用於否定句、疑問句或條件句。

▶Be it so humble, there is no place like home.
就算不耀眼，也沒有其他地方像家。

▶If you ever come to Taiwan, be sure to call me.
如果你來臺灣，一定要打電話給我。

4 ever表示「讓步」時通常與慣用語連用。

▶He is as great a scientist as ever lived.
他是有史以來最偉大的科學家。

5 ever用在最高級形容詞後的關係子句。

▶This is the best book that I have ever read.
這是我所讀過最好的書。

3. 「once」

1 once表示「曾經，昔時」時，通常用在肯定句，且放在動詞前。

▶Have you ever been there? Yes, I have once been there.
你去過那嗎？有啊！我曾去過一次。

2 once表示「一次，一遍」時，通常放在句尾。

▶I have been there once.
我曾去過那裡一次。

3 once也可表示「一旦，無論如何」。

▶If the fact once becomes known, he will be hold responsibly for it.
如果事情一旦曝光，他一定會被要求負起責任的。

4. 「enough」、「too」

1 enough修飾動詞、形容詞或副詞時,要放在修飾對象之後;too
要放在修飾對象之前。

▶The little boy can speak English well enough.
這小男孩能說好英文。

▶My father works too hard.
我父親工作太辛苦。

2 「enough to + 動詞」表示肯定的結果;「too...to...+ 動詞」則
表示否定的結果。

▶The boy is honest enough to be trusted.
這男孩誠實到足以讓人相信。

▶The old man is too old to work.
這老人老到無法工作。

5. 「needs」、「necessarily」:needs must表示「必定,不得不」;must needs表示「偏要」

▶A soldier needs must go where duty calls.
士兵因責任不得不去任何地方。

▶He must need go away when I want him.
當我需要他時他偏要走。

6. 「already」、「yet」:already用在肯定句或疑問句,若特別強調時也可放在句尾。yet用在否定句或疑問句,通常都放在句尾

▶I have already known the news.
我已經知道這消息了。

▶You are half an hour late already.
你已遲到半小時了。

▶Has the class begun yet? No, not yet.
課開始了嗎?還沒。

因yet本身就有否定意思，所以不可以和not連用。

I haven't eaten my lunch yet.　我還沒吃午餐。

Yet, I haven't eaten my lunch.　但是，我還沒吃午餐。

I have yet eaten my lunch.　我還沒吃午餐。

7.「ago」、「before」、「since」

1 ago表示從現在起到某時間以前，前面需有表示時間的字，與過去簡單式連用。

▶My sister left home two days ago.
我姊妹兩天前離家。

2 before表示從過去某時間算起，其前也可和時間連用，此時通常與過去完成式或其他時式連用。

▶He said that he had paid me the money five days before.
他說他五天前就把錢還給我了。

▶I didn't know the news before.
我之前不知道這消息。

▶I have seen the movie before.
我以前看過這電影。

3 since當副詞用時，可代替ago或before；當介詞或連接詞用時跟現在完成式連用。

▶I heard the story long since (=ago).
我很久以前聽過這故事。

▶He did it many years since (=ago).
他很多年前做了那事。

▶I haven't seen her since I left school.
我從離開學校就沒見到她。

8. 「there」、「here」

1 there後跟動詞，如：be、seem、appear等連用時，此時there當虛主詞。

▶ There are three new buildings in the city.
城裡有三棟新建築。

2 there當「那裡」時當副詞。

▶ I haven't seen anyone there.
我在那沒見到任何人。

3 here若和名詞連用時需用倒裝句形；與代名詞連用時則用一般句形。

▶ Here comes the bus.
= Here it comes.
公車來了。

9. 「only a few」表示「只有些許」；「quite a few」表示「很多」

▶ Only a few students were absent today.
今天只有幾個學生缺席。

▶ Quite a few people are coming today.
今天不少人來。

10. 「short」表示「不足地、突然地」；「shortly」表示「很快地」

▶ The bus stopped short.
公車突然停住。

▶ He will be back shortly.
他很快就回來。

11. 「high」表示「高」；「highly」表示「非常地」

▶ The eagle flew high.
老鷹飛得很高。

▶He is highly pleased.
　他非常高興。

12.「late」:「晚」;「lately」:「最近」

▶I got up late this morning.
　我今早起晚了。

▶I haven't seen him lately.
　我最近沒見到他。

● **副詞的比較:**表示程度、份量、態度及方法的副詞,如同形容
　　　　　　　詞一般,也有原級、比較級和最高級的變化。

▶He studies diligently.　他努力地讀書。

▶He studies more diligently than you.　他比你更努力地讀書。

▶He studies most diligently of us all.　他是我們裡面讀書最努力地。

1. 單音節與少數兩音節的副詞在字尾加er成比較級,加est成最高級

例 soon - sooner - soonest、hard - harder - hardest、early - earlier - earliest

➕例外 well - better - best、much - more - most、little - less - least

2. 多數兩音節及字尾為ly的副詞,在其前加more成比較級,加most成最高級

例 bravely - more bravely - most bravely、carefully - more carefully - most carefully。

➕例外 ill / badly / poorly - worse - worst; far - farther / further - farthest / furthest

▶We are so tired that we could go no farther
　我們如此累,以至於無法再繼續行走。

▶ We will discuss the matter further
我們需更進一步地討論這事。

> 🔊 小提醒
>
> ▶ It is not safe to go any further / farther.
> 繼續走下去，是不安全的。
> ▶ Further (=besides, moreover), there is another thing still more important.
> 再者，另一件事更重要。

3. 修飾like或love時用原級副詞very much，比較級或最高級時，like與better / best連用；love與more / most連用

▶ My mother likes (loves) me very much.
我母親很愛我。

▶ He likes me better than you.
他喜歡我勝過喜歡你。

▶ I like summer best.
我最喜歡夏天。

▶ Does your mother love you more than your sister?
你母親喜歡你勝過喜歡你姊妹嗎？

▶ Does your mother love you most among all your sisters?
你母親在妳的所有姊妹中最喜歡妳嗎？

4. 最高級副詞前的the通常被省略，可是若其後接of...時，the可省略也可不省略

▶ He came latest.
他最後到。

▶ He studies (the) hardest of all students.
他是所有學生裡最用功的。

5. 原級副詞的比較

▶ Tom works as hard as Mary (does).
Tom和Mary一樣努力。

▶ Tom doesn't work so hard as Mary (does).
= Mary works harder than Tom.
Tom的努力不比Mary。

6. 比較級副詞的比較

▶ Henry drives less carefully than Tom.
Henry開車不如Tom小心。

▶ John studies more diligently than all other students.
= John studies more diligently than any other student.
John比其他任何學生都努力。

◆比較 He drives the most carefully of the three.
= He drives more carefully than all the others.
= No one drives so carefully as he.
沒人開車比他還小心。

▶ Tom speaks English most fluently in the class.
Tom在班上英文說得最流利。

▶ No other student studies so diligently than John.
= No other student studies more diligently than John.
= John studies more diligently than all the other students.
= John studies more diligently than any other student.
= John studies the most diligently of all the students.
沒有任何學生比John還勤勉。

● 副詞相關的慣用語

▶ He is quite well off (=rich) now.
他現在有錢了。

▶He is worse off (=poorer) than ever.

他從沒如此窮過。

▶He gave me advice and money as well (=too).

= He gave me money as well as advice.

= He gave me not only advice but also money.

他不僅給我錢也給我建議。

▶You may well give up the plan.

= You have good reason to give up the plan.

你有足夠的理由放棄這計畫。

▶You may as well go at once.

= You had better go at once.

你最好趕緊走。

▶I am more or less tired of your long talk.

= I am somewhat tired of your long talk.

我對你的長篇大論多少有些厭煩。

▶The trip will take ten days, more or less .

= The trip will take about ten days.

這旅程大約是十天。

● 容易混淆的副詞

1. very、much、quite、too

▶My argument is very convincing.

我的論點相當有說服力。

▶We are much excited by the news of his success.

他成功的消息讓我們非常興奮。

▶She is quite selfish.

她相當地自私。

▶It is too hard for me to play soccer.

踢足球對我而言相當困難。

2. fairly、quite、rather、pretty四個字的程度一個比一個強

▶ He is fairly rich, but his brother is rather poor.
他相當富有，但他弟弟卻很貧窮。（通常fairly有褒意而rather則帶貶意）

▶ The show opened last night on Broadway was pretty good one, but I think the leading female actress was rather thin.
昨晚上演的百老匯戲劇相當好，但我覺得女主角太瘦了。

3. also、too、as well、either：also、too、as well多用在肯定，其中also用於句中而too用於句尾；either用於否定句

▶ She noy only sings, she plays the piano as well.
她不僅歌唱得好，琴也彈得好。

▶ I was in Japan last year, too.
我去年也在日本。

▶ I, too, know where we can find John.
我也知道哪裡可以找到John。

▶ I also play the flute.
我也吹笛子。

▶ I don't like the result, either.
我也不喜歡這結果。

4. most、mostly、almost：most構成形容詞和副詞的最高級；mostly則為「在多數狀況下」；almost當「幾乎」用

▶ This is the most (adj.) exciting game I have ever seen.
這是我見過最刺激的比賽。

▶ This is the most (adv.) exciting game.
這是最刺激的比賽。

▶ He mostly gets up late on Sundays.
他週日都晚起。

▶She slipped, almost fell.
她腳滑差點跌倒。

5. already、still、yet

▶He had already left when I called.
當我打電話時他已離開。

▶He was two days late already.
他已經晚了兩天。

▶Has he gone to work already?
他已經去工作了嗎？

▶I still don't understand what you meant.
我仍不了解你的意思為何。

▶He is still energetic at the age of eighty.
八十歲了他依然活力十足。

▶I've been thinking for hours, but I still can't make up my mind.
我已經想了好幾個小時，但我依然無法做出決定。

▶Has the mailman come yet?
郵差還沒來？

▶Those oranges are not ripe yet.
橘子還沒熟。

6. all together、altogether：all together（總共）；altogether（整體來說）

▶All together forty participants had been admitted to the conference.
總共有四十人被准許參加會議。

▶It is altogether out of the question.
就整體而言是不可能。

7. anyhow、somehow、somewhat：anyhow（無論如何）； somehow（以某種方式）；somewhat（有幾分）

▶ The house was locked and I couldn't get in anyhow.
這房子被鎖上了，我怎麼弄都進不去。

▶ We shall get to our destination somehow.
我們總會到達目的地。

▶ I was somewhat surprised when Mary told me she was going to get married.
當Mary告訴我她要結婚時，我多少有些訝異。

■ 實用測驗

1. Mary was _____ sad to say anything.

   ① too much   ② so muc   ③ too   ④ so

2. Atomic energy plays an _____ important role when the world is in danger of possible power shortage.

   ① increasing   ② increasingly   ③ increasedly   ④ increased

3. You have been _____ with your brother.

   ① angrily unreasonable   ② unreasonably angry   ③ angrily unreasonably

   ④ unreasonably angrily

4. With the introduction of computers in teaching and learning, we can pick up information and knowledge _____ than ever.

   ① much easily   ② much more easily   ③ more easilier   ④ much more easlier

5. If the proposal is worked out _____, everybody will benefit from it.

   ① thoroughly   ② excellently   ③ willingly   ④ wonderfully

6. Are you _____ for these giant sandwiches?

   ① enough hungry eat   ② enough hungry to eat   ③ hungry enough to eat

   ④ hunger enough to eat

7. His parents wrote him _____ while he was studying abroad.

   ① in regular   ② of regularly   ③ with regularity   ④ be regular

8. Jack is used to _____ for his girlfriend whenever they have a date.

   ① wait patiently   ② waiting patiently   ③ waiting patient   ④ wait patient

9. The more you learn, the more _____ you can land on a good job.

   ① easily   ② easy   ③ ease   ④ easiness

10. John came _____ than all the others.

    ① later   ② latest   ③ latter   ④ last

11. Jean _____ ever drinks coffee; she likes tea instead.

    ① hard   ② hardly   ③ greatly   ④ nearly

12. The children ran _____ when they heard their father's opening the door.

    ① downstair   ② downstairs   ③ to downstair   ④ to downstairs

13. The passer-by found that the driver _____ so he telephoned for an ambulance immediately.

① who was injured　② who had been injured　③ seriously injured　④ was seriously injured

14. Great minds _____.

① think to like　② thinks alike　③ think alike　④ think likely

15. Which of these five books do you like _____?

① more　② better　③ most　④ best

■ 試題解析

1. ③ too + adj. / adv / + to +V原形：太…以至於…。

2. ② increasingly「與日俱增地」為副詞，用來形容動詞play。

3. ② 副詞 + 形容詞。

4. ② much修飾more；more修飾easily；easily修飾pick up（習得）。

5. ① 四個選項都是副詞，但就題意而言，①「徹底地」最合適。

6. ③ enough to需置於形容詞後；「…到足以…」。

7. ③ 介系詞 + 抽象名詞 = 形容詞 / 副詞；with regularity = regularly。

8. ② be used to + Ving。

9. ① 副詞修飾動詞land on「得到」。

10. ① 比較級的副詞需用①；latter：「後者」。

11. ② hard：「辛苦地」；hardly：「幾乎不」。

12. ② 副詞不可與介系詞連用。

13. ④ the passer-by是子句的主詞，was injured是動詞；副詞seriously需置於was 和injured之間。

14. ③ 「英雄所見略同」。

15. ④ 副詞最高級不可與the連用。

介系詞 (Prepositions)

介系詞以名詞、代名詞或名詞片語為其受詞，表示該受詞與句中其他字的關係。

■ **本章重點**

- 介系詞學習重點歸類
- 介系詞片語
- 介系詞的位置
- 介系詞的用法

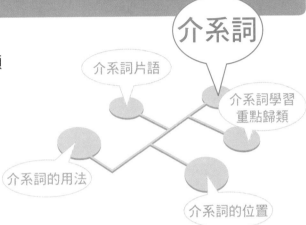

● **介系詞學習重點歸類：** 對所有學習語文的人而言，介系詞所帶來的問題可能比任何詞類都多！

1. 許多介系詞的意思不止一個。以after為例

▶ We rested after lunch.（之後）

▶ The cat is after the mouse.（追逐）

▶ He was angry after the way she acted.（因為）

▶ This is a painting after Picasso.（有…之風）

▶ She worked night after night.（連續）

2. 不同的介系詞可能會有同樣的意思

▶ She is disappointed in her new job.

▶ She is disappointed with her new job.

有時介系詞之間可以互換，但有時它們的用法規定卻又是相當嚴謹。

He is fascinated with his new job.

He is interested in his new job.

He is bored by / with his new job.

3. 介系詞與其他字連用時可能意思大有不同

make up your bed（整理）

make up your face（化妝）

make up your mind（決定）

make up a story（編撰）

make up a list（列出）

make up the difference（補齊）

make up last week's homework（補足）

make up for the lost time（彌補）

make up with your girlfriend（重修舊好）

4. 介系詞有時更可以當其他詞類使用

I want to learn the ins and outs of prepositions.（in / out當名詞用；詳情）

The hospital has only a few in patients.（in當形容詞用；住院病人）

There is a down side to his idea.（down當形容詞用；缺點）

I heard they were upping the price.（up當動詞用；抬高）

5. 常見的介系詞

例 about、above、across、after、against、along、among、around、at、before、behind、below、beneath、beside、between、beyond、but、by、despite、down、during、except、for、from、in、inside、into、like、near、of、off、on、onto、out、outside、over、past、since、through、throughout、till、to、toward、under、underneath、until、up、upon、with、within、without。

● **介系詞片語**：介系詞片語是由介系詞加受詞所組成的字群，其功用為當形容詞或副詞用，有時也可當名詞用。

▶The man at the door is my friend.

在門口的人是我的朋友。（介系詞片語當形容詞）

▶I always take a walk in the park.

我總是在公園散步。（介詞片語當副詞用）

▶From 9 to 5 is the usual working hours for most people.

對多數人而言，上班時間是朝九晚五。（介詞片語當名詞用）

🔈 小提醒

(A)片語介詞則為幾個字組合成一個片語當介詞用，通常以介詞結尾。

　　▶In spite of her illness, she kept on working.

　　儘管她生病，她繼續工作。

　　（in spite of及kept on是片語介詞）

　　▶You can succeed by means of working hard.

　　你可藉由努力工作而成功。

　　（by means of是片語介詞）

　　▶My house is not far from my school.

　　我家離學校不遠。（far from是片語介詞）

(B)常見的片語介詞有：according to（= in accordance with）、ahead of、along with、apart from（除了…之外）、as for / to（就…而言）、at home in（精通）、at the end of、because of、but for (= except for)（若非）、by means of、due to、for fear of（唯恐）、for lack of、for the good of、for the purpose of、for the sake of、in care of（= c / o；轉交）、in case of、in common with（相同）、in comparison with、in exchange for（交換）、in honor of（紀念）、in regard to、in search of、in spite of、instead of、in terms of、 in the course of...（在…過程中）、in the event of（倘若）、in the light of（按照、根據）、on account of、on good terms with（與…友善）、on behalf of（代表）、on the part of（在…方面）、on the point of（即將）、owing to、thanks to（因為、由於）、together with、with a view to、with the exception of（除…外）…。

● 介系詞的位置

1. 可分開動詞（動詞 + 介副詞）的受詞如果是代名詞時，受詞一定要插在兩個字中間；如果受詞是名詞，分開或不分開皆可

▶ Mark turned on the radio.

= Mark turned the radio on.

Mark打開收音機。

Mark turned on it.（×）

Mark turned it on.（○）

(A)常見的介副詞有：on、up、off、away...。

(B)常用的片語，如：look up、give up、pick up、put on、turn on、turn off、take off、find out、take away...。

2. 不可分開動詞 （動詞 + 介詞 + 受詞）的受詞不管是名詞或代名詞，一律放在介詞之後

▶ Look at the dog.

Look at it.　看那隻狗。

(A)常見的介詞有：in、of、at、about...。

(B)常用的片語，如：run out of、look at、listen to、think about、talk about、care about...。

3. 若受詞為疑問詞時，介詞置於句尾

▶ What are you laughing at?
你在笑什麼？

▶ Where did that old man come from?
那老人從哪裡來？

4. 若受詞為關係代名詞時，介詞也要置於句尾

▶ That is the book (which) we are looking for.
那是我們在找的書。

▶ This is the town (that) my family and I live in.
這是我和我家人居住的城市。

● 介系詞的用法

1. 表示「時間」的介詞

1 at：表示一點或短時間，用於時刻、正午、午夜、何時及年紀。

▶ He works at night.
他晚上工作。

▶ He came home at ten last night.
他昨晚十點回家。

▶ We are studying at present.
我們現在在讀書。

▶ I am not working at the moment.
我現在沒有在工作。

2 on：特定時間；日期或一週日。

▶ He is punctual, he always arrives on time.
他準時，他總是準時到達。

▶ She is coming on Monday.
她將在週一來。

▶ I heard that song on my birthday.
我在生日時聽到那首歌。

▶ Be here at ten o'clock on the dot.
十點整到這裡。

3 in：較長時間；年、月、季節、世紀、上下午或傍晚。

▶ He lived in the sixteenth century.
他活在十六世紀。

▶ That singer was popular in the eighties.
那歌手在80年代受歡迎。

▶ We came here in fall.
我們在秋天時來的。

4 till / until…為止。

▶ You must wait till your father returns.
你必須等到你父親回來。

▶ The party will last until ten.
聚會將持續到十點。

5 by：在某個期限前；在…以前。

▶ You must hand in your report by Friday.
你必須在週五前交報告。

▶ By the time you get there, we will have left.
你到那裡時，我們將已經離開。

6 from：從…起。

▶ She works from 6 to 8 everyday.

她每天從六點工作到八點。

7 since：從過去某時到現在；從…以來。

▶ I have been studying since yesterday.
我從昨天起就在讀書。

▶ They have been here since last Thursday.
他們從週四起就在這裡。

8 for：一段時間（後多與數詞連用）。

▶ I have not eaten anything for 24 hours.
我已有24小時未進食。

▶ They have been here for a week.
他們在此已經一個星期了。

9 during：在…期間。

▶ I had visited many places during my summer vacation.
我在暑假期間到訪許多地方。

▶ She slept during the football game.
她在美式足球賽中間睡著了。

10 through / throughout：在…期間（從頭到尾）。

▶ I had worked hard through the summer vacation.
我整個暑假期間都在工作。

▶ He slept throughout the day.
他整日都在睡覺。

11 before：在…之前；after：在…之後。

▶ I started before sunrise and arrived after sunset.
我在日出之前出發，在日落之後到達。

12 within：在…之內。

▶ They will be here within ten minutes.
他們將在10分鐘內到這裡。

13 beyond / past：在某時之後。

▶ Our guests stayed beyond midnight.
我們的客人在午夜後到達。

14 towards：接近某時。

▶ It was towards evening when she called.
她在近傍晚時打電話。

2. 表示「地方」的介詞

1 in：在…之內。

▶ We are playing in the park.
我們在公園內嬉戲。

▶ He sat in the chair and watched television.
他坐在椅上看電視。

2 on：在…上面。

▶ The folder is on the desk.
這檔案夾在桌上。

▶ Our house is on the left side of the street.
我們家在街的左邊。

▶ He came over on his bike.
他騎腳踏車來。

3 over：在…正上方（直接）。

▶ The clouds are right over my head.
雲正在我頭上。

4 under：在…正下方（直接）。

▶ I had my book under my armpit .
我把書夾在腋下。

5 above：在…之上（廣義）。

▶The airplane flew above my house.
　飛機從我房子上方飛過。

6 below；在…之下（廣義）。

　▶The sun had set below the horizon.
　　太陽落在地平線下。

7 by / beside：在…之旁。

　▶I love to have a house by the sea.
　　我喜歡一棟在海邊的房子。

　▶Mary sat beside me.
　　Mary坐在我旁邊。

8 before：在…之前。

　▶My father likes to walk before us.
　　我父親喜歡走在我們前面。

9 after：在…之後。

　▶My mother does not like it but she still walks after my father.
　　我母親雖不喜歡，但她仍走在我父親的後面。

10 behind：在…之後。

　▶There is a small garden behind the house.
　　屋後有個小花園。

11 around：環繞、圍繞。

　▶All sat around the campfire after supper.
　　所有人晚餐後圍繞營火坐著。

12 betweem：在…之間（兩者）。

　▶John sat between Mary and me.
　　John坐在Mary和我之間。

13 among：在…之間（兩者以上）。

▶He tried to hide among the crowd.
他試著躲在人群中。

14 to：到…去。

▶Mary went to Japan last week.
Mary上週去日本。

15 from：從…。

▶How far is it from here to next city?
從這裡到下個城市有多遠？

16 up：向上；向北。

▶Mary ran up the hill.
Mary跑上山。

17 down：向下；向南。

▶Jack lived down the road.
Jack住在路的下頭。

18 into：進入…之內。

▶Jack was walking into the room when I saw him.
當我看到Jack時，他正走進房間內。

19 out of：從…出來。

▶Mary was running out of the room when I saw her.
當我看見Mary時，她正跑出房間。

20 through：穿過。

▶The new highway runs through the mountains.
新的公路穿過群山中。

21 across：橫過、越過。

▶The children went across the street in twos and threes.
孩子們三三兩兩的過街。

▶The toys were scattered（散布）across the floor.
玩具散得整個地板都是。

22 at：小地方；in：大地方。

▶I live at No. 65 on Zhungxiao E. Road in Taipei.
我住在忠孝東路65號。

▶The whole family is at the beach.
全家人都在海灘。

3. 表示「行為或手段」的介詞

1 by：置於被動語態後；經由、藉由。

▶The speech delivered by Mr. Chen was excellent.
陳先生所發表的演說棒極了。

▶I go to work by bus.
我搭公車去工作。

2 with：用…工具。

▶Painters pain with brushes.
畫家用畫筆作畫。

3 about：與…有關；常與careless、charming、crazy、cruel、good、honest、kind、mean、nasty、nice、rude、selfish、sweet、thought-ful、understanding等連用。

▶She was really crazy about her boyfriend.
她真的很迷她的男友。

4 on：在…的主題；常與easy、hard、rough、soft、strict、tough連用。

▶The new teacher is tough on his students.
新老師對他的學生很嚴厲。

4. 表示「材料」的介詞

1 of：做成成品時材料性質不變者。

▶The table is made of wood.
這桌子是木頭做的。

2 from：做成成品時材料性質改變者。

▶The liquor is made from rice.
這酒是米做的。

3 in：用…。常與write、speak、answer等字連用。

▶The transcript is written in ink.
這文稿是用墨水寫的。

▶Can you answer in Chinese?
你能用中文回答嗎？

5. 表示「原因、理由」的介詞

1 from：因為外在原因。

▶He died from the wound.
他因傷而死。

2 of：因為內在原因。

▶He died of cancer.
他死於癌症。

3 at：用在表示驚訝喜悅的動詞後表示「因聽到、看到…而」。

▶I was surprised at the news.
我對這消息感到訝異。

▶He became angry at her words.
他因她的話而生氣。

4 for：一般理由；接受獎勵或懲罰的原因。常與famous、noted、blame、punish、reward等字連用。

▶The city is famous for its snacks.
這城市以小吃零食著稱。

▶He was punished for his dishonesty.
他因不誠實而受處罰。

6. 表「目的」的介詞

1 for：為了⋯。

▶What is the tool used for?
這工具是幹什麼的？

2 after：所追求的目的。常與seek、run、search等字連用。

▶Jack has been working hard all his life only to seek after rich and fame.
Jack勞碌一輩子，只不過是為了追求名利。

3 on：為了⋯。常與business、tour、journey、trip、picnic等名詞連用。

▶My boss went to New York on business.
我老闆因公事去紐約。

7. 表「結果」的介詞

1 to：由某動作所造成的結果。

▶Mary's heart was broken to pieces after being dumped by her boyfriend.
從被男友拋棄後，Mary的心就碎了。

2 into：變化的結果。

▶Please translate this English passage into Chinese.
請把這段英文翻譯成中文。

8. 表示「比較」的介詞

1 to：比較。

▶ I prefer tea to coffee.
我喜歡茶勝過咖啡。

▶ Air is to man what water is to fish.
水之於魚如空氣之於人。

2 with：比較、對照。

▶ He tried to compare his computer with mine.
他試著拿他的電腦和我的比。

3 by：比較兩者之間的差距。

▶ My brother is older than I by five.
我哥哥比我大五歲。

9. 表示「單位」的介詞

1 at：程度或價值；at +單價，for +總價。

▶ He drove at a speed of 45 miles an hour.
他以45英哩的時速開車。

▶ The cakes are sold at 10 dollars a piece.
這些蛋糕一個賣10塊錢。

▶ The cakes are sold for 100 dollars.
這些蛋糕總共100元。

2 by：度量衡單位；以…計。

▶ Cloth is sold by the yard.
布以碼來賣。

▶ This apartment is rent by the week.
這公寓按週收租。

3 for：價格。

▶How much did you pay for the car?
你為這車付了多少錢？

10. 表示「來源、起源」的介詞

1 from：來自…。

通常與come、result、derive（衍生）等字連用。

▶Where did you come from?
你從哪來？

▶Do you know where this word derived from?
你知道這字起源為何？

2 out of：由…而出。

▶Plants grow out of the earth.
植物從土裡長出來。

3 in：在…（文字）…。

▶I read it in the book.
我在書裡讀到這個。

▶She found an article in the magazine.
她在雜誌中找到一篇文章。

4 on：在…（電子媒體）…。

▶I heard it on the radio.
我從收音機中聽到這個。

▶They saw him on television.
他們在電視上看到他。

11. 表示「分離」的介詞

1 from：禁止、防止…做…。常與stop、keep和prevent等字連用。

▶Nothing can keep me from talking to her.
沒有任何事物能阻止我和她說話。

2 of：⋯的。常與rob、relieve、deprive（剝奪）、cure等字連用。

▶ No one can deprive our pride of us.
　沒人能剝奪我們的尊嚴。

3 off：分離、分開。常與break、chop、cut、pick、pull、saw、send、shave、take、tear、throw等連用。

▶ John broke off with his girlfriend.
　John和他女友分手了。

4 out of：⋯出來。常與come、drive、get、go、grab、move、pour、pull、push、rip、sip、squeeze、take、tear等連用。

▶ Get those clothes out of the suitcase.
　把那些衣服從行李箱中拿出來。

12. 表示「關於」的介詞

1 of：關於某人事物的存在。

▶ He spoke of the book the other day.
　他那天提到這本書。

2 about：關於某人事物的詳情。常與advise、agree、ask、bother、brag（吹噓）、care、complain、contact、do、dream、fight、forget、harass（騷擾）、hear、inform、joke、know、laugh、lie、pray、remind、say、wonder、write、yell等連用。

▶ The kids were yelling about how they wanted to celebrate the New Year.
　孩子們大聲嘶吼著他們想慶祝新年的方法。
▶ He talked about the book the other day.
　他那天談到這本書。

3 on：與某主題有關；後多與名詞連用。

▶He has spent all his money on video games.
他把所有錢花在電玩上。

4 in：與某主題的作法有關；後多與動名詞連用。

▶He has spent all his time in playing video games.
他把所有時間花在打電玩上。

5 over：與…有關。常與argue、battle、cry、fight、grieve、puzzle、sigh、worry等連用。

▶They argued over whether they should go or not.
他們對於是否該去，有所爭執。

13. 表示「具某些特色；描述」的介詞

1 about：有部分特質。

▶There is something cute about him.
他有些可愛之處。

▶I'd not see anything funny about that remark.
我不覺得那說詞有任何好玩的地方。

2 above：較…好。

▶He is above cheating.
他不會說謊。

3 like：和…一樣。

▶He is just like his father.
他和他父親一樣。

4 of：有些潛在的特質。

▶They are people of low morals.
他們是沒道德的人。

5 with：有實體特質。

▶He is a man with a broken arm.
他是獨臂俠。

■ 實用測驗

1. The new building was finished _____ the morning of January 1st.
   ① in　② at　③ on　④ during

2. How did he go to America? He went _____ boat.
   ① by　② in　③ on　④ thorugh

3. Which candidate are you voting _____?
   ① at　② to　③ for　④ against

4. You must keep this secret; it's _____ you and me.
   ① between　② among　③ of　④ with

5. _____ the basketball team, Jack is the best.
   ① Between　② Among　③ Of　④ With

6. The main feature begins _____ 10 o'clock.
   ① in　② on　③ at　④ within

7. The flood deprived him _____ his family.
   ① of　② with　③ out of　④ within

8. That store sells everything _____ the lowest price.
   ① at　② in　③ with　④ of

9. The young lady dressed _____ blue _____ gold buttons.
   ① in, with　② in, in　③ with, with　④ with, in

10. You may gain tremendously _____ your hard working.
    ① of　② under　③ from　④ on

11. Jack returns the day _____ tomorrow.
    ① after　② before　③ in　④ on

12. The driver was blamed _____ the accient.
    ① on　② for　③ from　④ of

13. My sisters has been gossiping _____ the phone for the past three hours.
    ① in　② on　③ at　④ by

14. _____, that boy knew nothing about soccer.
    ① To my surprise　② With his surprise　③ For my surprise　④ In his surprise

15. We are traveling _____ a speed of 90 miles an hour.
    ① at　② of　③ in　④ on

試題解析

1. ③ 特定日子用on。

2. ① 交通工具用by。

3. ③ vote for：投贊成票；vote against：投反對票，本題選③較合邏輯。

4. ① 兩者之間。

5. ② 全體球員應是比兩人還多。

6. ③ 短時間；main feature：正片。

7. ① 剝奪。

8. ① 所有商品的個別價位。

9. ① dress in：穿著。

10.③ 由…處得到。

11.① two days after tomorrow：大後天；day before yesterady：前天；two days before yesterady：大前天。

12.② 因…受責。

13.② We discussed the matter over the phone.（用電話討論事情。）

We discussed the matter on the phone.（在電話上討論事情。）

14.① 讓我吃驚的是。

15.①。

筆記頁

連接詞 (Conjunctions)

用來連接單字、片語或子句的詞稱之。一般可分為對等連接詞及從屬連接詞,若將副詞轉用成連接詞又稱準連接詞。
對等連接詞用來連接對等的字、片語、或子句;從屬連接詞用以引導從屬子句,並將主要句子和從屬子句連接起來成為一個複句。

■ **本章重點**

● 對等連接詞

● 從屬連接詞

● 準連接詞

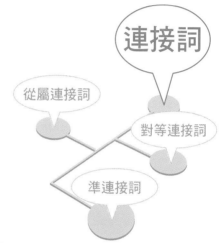

● **對等連接詞**

1. 「and」、「both...and...」、「or」

▶ His room is always at sixes and sevens.
他的房間總是亂七八糟的。

▶ The satellite could be seen before dawn and shortly after midnight.
可以在凌晨前或午夜後看到人造衛星。

▶ He has (both) the time and the money to take it easy.
他有錢有閒去放輕鬆。

▶ This movie is at once (=both) interesting and instructive.
這是部有趣且富有教育性的電影。

▶ What would you like, coffee or tea?
你要什麼,咖啡還是茶?

1 在否定意思的句子中，要連接兩個對等的部分時，需用or不能用and；但若要連接兩個否定子句時，就要使用and。

▶He didn't speak loudly or clearly.
他說得既不大聲也不清楚。

▶No one saw you or your sister.
No one saw you, and no one saw your sister, either.
沒人見到你，也沒人見到你姊妹。

2 注意下列的用法：

▶Study hard, and （那麼） (=then) you will succeed.
= If you study hard, you will succeed.
如果你努力讀書，那麼你就會成功。

▶Put on you overcoat, or （否則） (=otherwise) you will catch cold.
= If you don't put on your overcoat, you will catch cold.
= Unless you put on your overcoat, you will catch cold.
穿上外套，否則你會著涼。

▶He can't read, and he can't write, either.
= he can't read, nor can he write.
他既不能讀也不能寫。

3 both A and B中的A或B必須是對等的字、片語或子句。

▶Exercise is good both for body and mind. （×）
▶Exercise is good for both body and mind. （○）
▶Exercise is good both for body and for mind. （○）
運動對身心都好。

2. 「as well as」、「no less than」：用此連接的字、片語或子句時較強調前者，若連接兩個主詞時，動詞需與前者一致

▶Baseball is played by girls as well as by boys.
女孩能像男孩一樣打棒球。

▶The teacher no less than the students longs for a holiday.

老師和學生一樣都渴望假日。

▶ He as well as you is guilty.
　他和你一樣有罪。

3. 「not only (merely)...but also...」：用此連接詞所連接的字、片語或子句較強調後者，如連接兩個主詞時，動詞需與後者一致

▶ Not only you but also he is in the wrong.
　不僅是你，他和你一樣是錯的。

▶ I not only heard it but also saw it. （O）
　我不僅聽到也看到。

▶ Not only I heard it but saw it. （X）

> 小提醒
>
> 若把not only至於句首，主詞與動詞需要用倒裝句型。
> Not only did we dine together, but we also danced together.
> = We not only dined together, but also danced together.
> 我們不僅一起用餐，也一起跳舞。

4. 「but」、「yet」、「still」三者皆表示相反或對照的意思；含意yet強過but，而still則最強。

▶ He is sick, but he will soon be well.
　他生病了，但他很快就會康復。

▶ He worked hard, yet he failed.
　他努力工作，但他失敗了。

▶ I see your point; still, I don't agree with you.
　我了解你的論點，但我仍無法認同。

5. 「for」、「because」

for用來表示理由，因為對等連接詞所以連接兩個對等子句；because為從屬連接詞用來引導副詞子句。for不可放在句首而必須置於兩個對等子句之間；because引導的子句若表示強調時則不受此限。for不可以用來回答問句。

▶He was absent yesterday, for he was ill.

　= He was absent because he was ill yesterday.

　= Because he was ill, he was absent yesterday.

他昨天缺席因為他生病了。

6. 句子的連接

₁肯定

▶He can swim, and I can, too.

　= He can swim, and so can I.

他能游泳，我也能。

▶He is a Chinese, and I am, too.

　= He is a Chinese, and so am I.

他是中國人，我也是。

▶They went early, and we did, too.

　= They went early, and so did we.

他們去早了，我們也是。

₂否定

▶He will not go, and I will not, either.

　= He will not go, and neither will I.

　= He will not go, and nor will I.

他不會去，我也不會。

▶He doesn't have a pen, and I don't / haven't, either.

　= He doesn't have a pen, and neither do / have I.

　= He doesn't have a pen, and nor do / have I.

他沒有筆，我也沒有。

● 從屬連接詞

1.「that」：用that所引導的名詞子句一般不能作介詞的受詞，當主詞用時that不可省略；當受詞時則可省略

▶ That the earth is round is known to us.

= It is known to us that the earth is round.

地球是圓的是眾所皆知的。

▶ I hope (that) all will go well.

我希望一切順利。

比較 His worry is that he might go blind.　他擔心的是他可能失明。（主詞補語）

The news that he was killed proved false.　他被殺的消息證實是假的。（主詞同位語）

🔊 小提醒

except / save that（除了）、but that（若非）、in that（=because）所引導的是副詞子句。

▶ She knew nothing except that she was there.

她除了在那之外其他什麼都不知道。

▶ He would have helped us but that he was short of money.

= He would have helped us if he hadn't been short of money.

要不是他沒錢，否則他會幫我們。

2.「whether」、「if」：由此兩連接詞所引導的名詞子句意思相同；whether後可加or或or not而if則通常不接。只有whether子句可當介詞的受詞，if子句則不可

▶ He asked whether / if I was going.

= He asked whether I was going or not.

他問我是否要去。

▶ He was worried about whether he passed the exam.

= He was worried if he passed the exam.

他擔心他是否通過考試。

3. 引導形容詞子句的連接詞常以that、which、who為主；若當受詞用時可省略

▶ The student who answered the question was John.

回答問題的學生是John。

▶ The book (which) you lent me was interesting.

你借我的書很有趣。

4. 引導副詞子句的連接詞

1 表條件。

▶ If / In case it is fine tomorrow, I will go.

如果明天天氣好,我將會去。

▶ He will come unless it rains.

除非下雨,否則他將會來。

2 表時間。

▶ After he goes, we shall eat.

他離開後,我們將吃飯。

▶ Think well before you decide.

你決定前想清楚。

▶ It has been three months since we parted.

自從我們分手到現在已三個月了。

▶ When I go there, I shall see him.

當我到那時,我將看到他。

▶ Please be quiet while I am talking to you.

當我和你說話時請保持安靜。

補充 常見句型

(A) ...not...until...（直到…才…）

  = It is not until... that + 子句

  = Not until... + S + V...

▶We do not know the value of health until we lose it.

  = It is not until we lose health that we know the value of it.

  = Not until we lose health do we know the value of it.

直到我們失去健康，我們才知道它的價值。

(B)As soon as / The moment + 子句..., S + V（一…就…）

  = S + had no sooner / hardly / scarcely + p.p... than / when...

  = No sooner / Hardly / Scarcely + had + S + p.p... than / when...

▶As soon as he saw me, he ran off.

  = He had no sooner seen me than he ran off.

  = No sooner had he seen me than he ran off.

他一看到我就跑走。

3 表地點。

▶Where there is a will, there is a way.
有志者事竟成。

4 表原因。

▶I did not go because it rained.
我沒去是因為下雨。

▶Since / Now that you ask, I will tell you.
既然你問了，我就告訴你。

5 表結果。

▶He is so kind that everybody likes him.
= He is such a kind man that everybody likes him.
他是如此仁慈，所以所有人都喜歡他。

6 表目的。

> so that / in order that + 子句（為了…）

▶ He studies hard so that / in order that he may pass the exam.
他為了通過考試努力讀書。

> lest + S +（should）+ V原形（唯恐）

▶ He works hard lest he （should） fail the exam.
他努力讀書唯恐在考試中失利。

7 表比較。

▶ She is as beautiful as her sister.
她和她姊妹一樣漂亮。

▶ She is younger than her sister.
她比她姊妹年輕。

8 表讓步。

> Though / Although + S + V, S + V...

▶ Although he is a teacher, he can't know everything.
= Teacher as he is, he can't know everything.
儘管他是位老師，他不可能什麼事都知道。

▶ Though he worked hard, he failed.
= Hard as he worked, he failed.
儘管他努力，但他失敗了。

🔊 小提醒

注意名詞放句首時，不可加冠詞。

(A)In spite of / Despite + N...., S + V...

▶ He went fishing in spite of the rain.
　　儘管下雨，他仍去釣魚。

(B)疑問詞 + ever..., S + V...

　　= No matter + 疑問詞..., S + V...

▶ No matter what you (may) do, you must do it well.

　　= Whatever you do, you must do it well.

　　不管你做什麼，你一定要把它做好。

▶ No matter how hard it may be, I must try.

　　= However hard it may be, I must try.

　　不管它有多難，我必須試一試。

9 表狀態。

▶ As men sow, so will they reap.
　　一分耕耘一分收穫。

▶ He speaks as if he were a teacher.
　　他說話的方式就好像他是個老師。

10 表對比。

▶ He went out, while I stayed at home.
　　他外出而我待在家裡。

● **準連接詞**：是副詞而不是連接詞，通常用來表示兩種觀念之間的邏輯關係。因為是副詞，所以不能接兩個句子，所以其前用分號「；」後用逗號「，」。

▶ She was very tired; nevertheless (yet, still, however), she kept on working.
儘管她很累，她繼續工作。

▶ He is brave; moreover (besides, furthermore, in addition), he is kind.
他是勇敢的，除此之外，他也仁慈。

▶ I've never been to Hong Kong; therefore (thus, hence, consequently),
I don't know much about it.
我從沒去過香港，因此，我對它知道不多。

▶ You must hurry; otherwise, you will be late for your train.
你要快點，否則，你會趕不上火車。

1. 準連接詞的功用

1 表示「理所當然」。

例 of course、naturally、not to mention、needless to say、surely、certainly。

2 表示「明白，的確」。

例 clearly、obviously、apparently、without doubt、categorically（=absolutely）。

3 表示「換個說法」。

例 that is、that is to say、in other words、namely、as it were、so to speak、to put it plainly、to put it briefly、to put it precisely、more accurately、to put the matter simply、to put it more concretely、broadly speaking、generally speaking、strictly speaking、to be precise、to put it in another way、to put it other way around、rather than。

4 表示「陳述原因」。

例 for this reason、on account of、for this purpose、due to、owning to、thanks to、because of。

5 表示「舉例」。

例 for example、for instance、for a fine example、as an example、as an illustration、to take the case of...、to take a hypothetical（假設的）

example、as of in...。

6 表示「比較」。

例 compared with、in comparison with、by comparison、in contrast、by contrast、in contradiction to、without comparison、take in this light。

7 表示「陳述觀點」。

例 regarding、with regard to、with respect to、in respect to、as for、in the matter of、concerning、in this respect、at this point、viewed in this light、in terms of、related to the...、from the standpoint of...。

8 表示「某種狀況」。

例 in that case、in the case of、in these circumstances、in this connection、under the present conditions、at present、accidentally、unfortunately、regardless of...。

9 表示「條件」。

例 after due consideration、in principle、otherwise、or else、essentially、not any longer、if not all、if not、instead、in general、basically、except that、except for。

10 表示「改變話題」。

例 incidentally、by the way、now。

11 表示「陳述相反事實」。

例 however、yet、although、while、on the other hand、on the contrary、to the contrary、in spite of、for all that、nevertheless、still。

12 表示「追加內容」。

例 moreover、furthermore、basides、over and above、what is more、further、in addition、in addition to、over and beyond、additionally、added to this、also、beyond that、again、incidentally。

13 表示「陳述相反或類似事物」。

例 in the same way、also、as well、likewise、similarly、by the same token。

14 表示「提出反對」。

例 but then、to be sure、indeed、admittedly、after all、all the same、and yet、even then。

15 表示「依據某個觀點」。

例 according to、on the basis of...。

16 表示「陳述事實」。

例 in fact、actually、indeed、as a matter of fact。

17 表示「簡要說明」。

例 to sum up、summing up、in short、to put it briefly、in brief、briefly、thus far、anyway。

18 表示「陳述結果」。

例 thus、therefore、accordingly、as a consequence、as a result、as it turned out。

19 表示「陳述結論」。

例 finally、lastly、eventually、in conclusion、all in all、as a whole、by and large、on the whole、overall、inevitably、necessarily、at last、as has been noted、as I have said、in any event。

20 表示「順序」。

例 first / firstly、second / secondly、third / thirdly、finally、in the first place、in the second place、only in the final place、for one thing...for another...、the first and foremost、as a beginning、at the outset、to begin with、then、next、at the same time、in turn。

21 表示「前者；後者」。

例 above、the following、give above、as shown below、as I said earlier、as I said at the beginning、as has been pointed out、as I mentioned in the previous...、as discussed in...、as we have seen、the former、the latter、as follows、as mentioned above、the following。

22 表示「限制」。

例 at least、to say the least、by definition、in my understanding、within the limits of...。

23 表示「引用」。

例 in _____'s phrase、to use _____'s term、to quote from _____。

24 表示「位置」。

例 here、above、below、next、on the other side。

25 表示「經過時間」。

例 at the moment、in the past、over the past _____、in the future、afterward、later、immediately、at once、promptly、in a short time、soon、suddenly、briefly、temporarily、tentatively、by degrees、gradually、frequently、during。

🔊 小提醒

了解上述準連接詞的用法和涵意，不僅會在寫作文時讓文句之間連接得體，甚至在閱讀冗長的文章時，也可藉由對上述字詞的了解，來預期甚至於分辨上下句子或段落之間是否朝同樣方向或不同方向發展。這種能力在參加托福測驗時尤顯重要。

■ 實用測驗

1. The man is poor, _____ he is generous.

   ① either　② but　③ except　④ neither

2. You won't be on time _____ you hurry up.

   ① besides　② unless　③ without　④ except

3. Rich _____ he is, the old man is not happy.

   ① as　② like　③ though　④ even if

4. We finished early _____ we started late.

   ① as well　② even though　③ such as　④ so that

5. Some people are born with talents _____ others don't.

   ① when　② while　③ where　④ why

6. He must have been out; _____, he would have heard the door bell ring.

   ① except that　② or else　③ but that　④ otherwise

7. It makes no difference to me _____ he will help me or not.

   ① whether　② when　③ how　④ why

8. We are late, _____ we have to hurry.

   ① so　② therefore　③ because　④ as

9. I don't like coffee. I don't like tea. So I like _____.

   ① anything except coffee and tea　② coffee only　③ either coffee or tea

   ④ neither coffee nor tea

10. It is getting dark; _____, I am sleepy.

    ① besides　② beside　③ except　④ in addition to

11. It was _____ weather that we all went out for a walk.

    ① so fine　② so a fine　③ such fine　④ such a fine

12. _____ I arrived at school, it began to rain.

    ① As soon as　② When　③ Hardly had　④ As long as

13. _____ the bad weather, we decided to go out.

    ① If　② Despite　③ Unless　④ Though

14. This is not imagination, _____ reality.

    ① but　② except　③ besides　④ nor

15. Although he is poor, _____.

① but he is honest ② and yet he never lies ③ he works hardly to succeed

④ he won't steal

■ 試題解析

1. ②。

2. ②。

3. ①。

4. ②。

5. ② while「然而」。

6. ④ 因前有分號,所以選連接副詞。

7. ① whether...or not...:「是否」。

8. ① 不可以選②是因為前有逗號。

9. ④ 因like是肯定用法,所以要用否定的neither...nor...。

10.① 因有分號;in addition to = additional =「額外的」。

11.④ so + adj. + a / an + 名詞 = such + a / an + adj. + 名詞。

12.① as soon as:一…就…。

13.②。

14.① not...but...:不是…而是…。

15.④ although不可與but連用;其他選項意思不合題意。

冠詞 (Article)

冠詞可分不定冠詞與定冠詞，前者用於非特定單數可數名詞前，a用於發音是子音開頭的字前；an用於發音是母音開頭的字前。定冠詞the用於特定的單複數名詞前，在子音前讀作【ðə】，在母音前讀作【ðɪ】。

冠詞在英文中出現的次數最頻繁；但因對其後字義的影響極大，所以千萬不可大意！

■ **本章重點**

- 不定冠詞
- 定冠詞
- 冠詞的省略

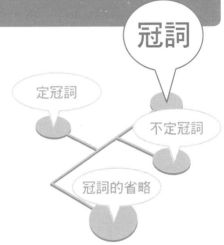

●不定冠詞（a / an）

▶ I picked up **a** book on my way home.
我在回家路上買了一本書。

▶ I eat **an** egg every day.
我每天吃一顆蛋。

1. 用在不特定的單數可數名詞之前

▶ **A** dog is standing in front of my house now.
一隻狗現在站在我家前面。

▶There are **an** orange and a banana on the table.

桌上有一顆橘子和一根香蕉。

小提醒

> 單數可數名詞前，除了在特定狀況下，一定要加不定
> 冠詞！

2. 不定冠詞放在介詞of之後，表示the same「同樣的」的意思

▶Those children are **of an** age.

= Those children are of the same age.

那些孩子是同年齡。

▶Birds **of a** feather flock together.

= Birds of the same feather flock together.

物以類聚。

3. 不定冠詞表示整體時，有any「任何」的意思

▶Being **an** honest man is better than being a wealthy man.

做個誠實的人勝過做個有錢的人。

▶**A** soldier must obey orders.

任何士兵都必須服從命令。

4. 表示「一個」的意思

▶I have **a** brother and two sisters.

我有一個兄弟和兩個姊妹。

▶They have **a** class in the morning, and three in the afternoon.

他們上午有一節課，下午有三節。

5. 表示per、each「每一…」或certain「某個」的意思

▶I write to my parents once **a** (each) week.

我一週寫信給我父母親一次。

▶ He can type fifty words a (every) minute.
他一分鐘可以打50個字。

▶ A Mr. Brown called on me last night.
昨晚有位Brown先生來拜訪我。

▶ The cost for the room is fifty dollars a head.
這房間的價錢是每個人頭五十元。

● 定冠詞

▶ The apple I had last night was very sweet, but the orange wasn't.
昨晚我吃的蘋果很甜，但橘子則不是。

1. 在句中第一次提到的單數普通名詞前用不定冠詞，再次提及時用定冠詞；雖第一次提到，但若為彼此所共知的事物仍要用定冠詞

▶ I have a dog and the dog is called Lucky.
我有隻狗，這狗的名字是Lucky。

▶ I will meet you at the park.
我將會在公園和你見面。

2. 宇宙間獨一無二的東西前用定冠詞

例 the sun、the moon、the earth、the sky、the air...；表示方向或方位的名詞前也要用定冠詞，如：the east、the right、the front、the back...。

▶ The sun rises in the east and sets in the west.
太陽東邊升起西邊落下。

▶ Turning to the right, you will find the post office.
向右轉，你會找到郵局。

> 🔊 小提醒
>
> earth、moon、sun不是專有名詞，所以不需大寫。

3. 「only」、「very」、「same」等形容詞及最高級形容詞或序數前用定冠詞；名詞後如有形容詞或形容詞子句來修飾時，其前也需用定冠詞

▶ He is the strongest man that I have ever seen.

他是我見過最強健的人。（最高級形容詞）

▶ This is the house where I was born.

這是我出生的房子。（形容詞子句）

▶ Tokyo is the capital of Japan.

東京是日本的首都。（主詞補語）

▶ Henry Ford is the first man that starts mass production.

亨利福特是第一個開始量產的人。

4. 「the + 單數普通名詞」可代表全體，但 "man" 及 "woman" 不屬此範圍。「the + 單數普通名詞」可等於抽象名詞

▶ The horse is more useful than the cat.

= Horses are more useful than cats.

馬比貓更有用。

▶ Man is usually stronger than woman.

男人通常比女人來得強壯。

▶ The pen is mightier than the sword.

文字比武力更有力量。

> 🎧 小提醒
>
> the pen（文）、the sword（武）、the mother（母愛）、
> the head（理性）、the heart（情）、the patriot（愛國
> 心）。

◆比較 They are the teachers of our school.（全體老師）

They are teachers of our school.（部份老師）

5. 「the + 形容詞」用做複數普通名詞或集合名詞時，主詞後加複數動詞。「the +形容詞」當抽象名詞時，主詞後用單數動詞

▶ The wounded were carefully being taken care of after the doctor came.

醫生來後，受傷的人都被仔細照顧。

▶ The rich are nor necessarily better than the poor.

富人不一定比窮人更好。

▶ The true is higher than the beautiful.

= Truth is higher than beauty.

事實勝過美麗。

> 🔊 小提醒
>
> the accused（被告）、the deceased（死者）、the un-known（陌生人）、the condemned（被定罪者）所形成的普通名詞後需加單數動詞。
>
> ▶ The accused is a well-known politician.
> 被告是一位知名的政治人物。

6. 計量單位前用定冠詞

▶ Sugar is sold by the pound.

糖論磅賣。

▶ We pay our rent by the month.

我們每月付房租。

▶ You can rent the bicycle by the hour.

你可以以小時為單位租腳踏車。

7. 於全體國民的名詞前用定冠詞

▶ The Chinese are industrious people.

中國人是勤勉的人。

語言的名稱前不加定冠詞，但其後若接有"language"時要加。

▶He can speak French well.

= He can speak the French language well.

他法文說得很好。

8. 專有名詞若有修飾語如 "...of..." 時加定冠詞

例 The City of Taipei（臺北市）、the University of Iowa（愛荷華大學）、the Edison of today（今日的愛迪生）…。

9. 河流、港灣、海峽、海洋、船名、群島、半島、山脈、公共建築物、書刊、雜誌、聯邦國家名稱、沙漠、條約等前加定冠詞

例 the Yellow River（黃河）、the Taiwan Strait（臺灣海峽）、the English Channel（英吉利海峽）、the Pacific（太平洋）、the Philippines（菲律賓群島）、the Alps（阿爾卑斯山脈）、the White House（白宮）、the Time（時代雜誌）、the United Daily（聯合報）、the United States（美國）…。但以人名為書名時不加，Robinson Crusoe（魯賓遜漂流記）。

10. play the + 樂器

▶Mary plays the piano very well.

Mary鋼琴彈得很好。

11. the + 身體部位

▶Jack took me by the arm.

Jack抓住我的手臂。

▶He hit me on the head.

他打我的頭。

● 冠詞的省略

1. 名詞在句中當呼喚語時，通常不加冠詞

▶ Boys, don't make so much noise.
孩子們，不要製造如此多的噪音。

▶ Waiter, bring me a cup of coffee, please.
服務生，請拿杯咖啡給我。

2. 說到家庭某一成員時，其名詞前不加冠詞但需大寫

▶ I don't know whether Mother will return next week.
我不知我母親是否下週會回來。

▶ Father has gone to Japan for business.
我父親因公去日本。

3. 表示官位、稱號、身份的普通名詞放在人名前不加冠詞

▶ People elected Mr. Ma president.
人們選馬先生當總統。

4. 餐名、運動名稱及顏色名稱前均不加冠詞

▶ I was having lunch when she called.
她打電話來時我正在吃午餐。

比較 The lunch I am taking is delicious. 我在吃很可口的午餐。

▶ He is good at playing tennis.
他網球打得好。

▶ She is dressed in red.
她穿著紅衣裳。

5. 單獨的島嶼和山峰的名字前不加定冠詞

Formosa（臺灣）、Mount Everest（聖母峰）、Mount Ali（阿里山）…。

6. 樂器本身加冠詞，但若代表學科時則不加

▶ He plays the piano very well.
他鋼琴彈得非常好。

▶ He teaches piano and violin.
他教鋼琴和小提琴。

實用測驗

1. "Is he an American?" "No, He is _____ European."

   ① a　② an　③ the　④ one

2. The workers are paid _____.

   ① by the week　② for the week　③ to a week　④ in a week

3. Mr. Lee is _____ teacher I mentioned to you.

   ① a　② an　③ the　④ this

4. What kind of _____ do you like?

   ① movie　② the movies　③ the movie　④ a movie

5. A cow is _____ as a horse.

   ① strong as an animal　② as a strong animal　③ as strong an animal

   ④ as an animal strong

6. They are playing _____.

   ① basketball　② the basketball　③ a basketball　④ one basketball

7. _____ has many friends in the city.

   ① Lee　② Lees　③ The Lee　④ The Lees

8. It is _____ to go hiking.

   ① fun　② a fun　③ funs　④ the fun

9. He is _____.

   ① a honest man　② an honest man　③ a man honest　④ an man honest

10. Meats are sold by _____.

    ① a pound　② the pound　③ pound　④ pounds

11. We should do our best to help _____.

    ① poor　② the poor　③ a poor　④ this poor

12. I'd like to speak to _____ in charge.

    ① the person　② a person　③ person　④ persons

13. He used to play _____ when he was _____.

    ① basketball, a boy　② the basketball, a boy　③ basketball, boy　④ the basketball, the boy

14._____ 24 can be divided by 2, 3, 4, 6, 8, and 12.

① The number ② Number ③ A number ④ Bumbers

15._____ of this house has been removed by the movers.

① Furniture ② Furnitures ③ A furniture ④ The furniture

■ 試題解析

1. ② 母音前用an。

2. ① by the +計量單位。

3. ③ 特定人物。

4. ① kind of / sort ot + 單數名詞，且不接冠詞。

5. ③ as + adj. + as：和…一樣…。

6. ① 運動項目不加定冠詞。

7. ④　the +姓氏s =全家人。

8. ① fun「樂趣」為抽象名詞且不加定冠詞。

9. ② hoesnt的h不發音，所以第一個音是母音。

10.② meats：不同種類的肉；若是用meat則為物質名詞。

11.② the + adj. = 集合名詞。

12.① 特定對象；the person in charge：負責的人。

13.① 運動項目不加定冠詞，boy為普通名詞，單數時前需加不定冠詞。

14.① 特定數目。

15.④　雖furniture為不可數名詞，前本不該加定冠詞。但因指特定的furniture所
　　以選④。

筆記頁

子句，句子及基本句型
(Clauses, Sentences and Basic sentence patterns)

子句是句子的一部分，且有主詞和動詞，但因缺少完整的意思，故稱子句。

■ **本章重點**

● 對等子句

● 主要句子與從屬子句

● 句子的種類

● 句子的功用

● 附加問句

● 五大基本句型

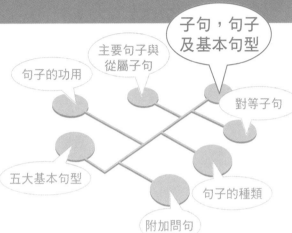

● **對等子句**：在句子裡，處於對等的文法關係的子句稱為對等子句，此類句子通常用對等連接詞，如：and、but、or、so、for、yet等連接。

▶ The girl grew up, and (she) became a beautiful lady.
這女孩長大變成一位漂亮的小姐。（若前後主詞相同時後者可省略）

▶ She is a nurse and her sister is a doctor.
她是位護士而她姊妹則是一位醫生。

▶ Study hard, or you will fail.
努力讀書，否則你會失敗。

● **主要句子與從屬子句**：在一個句子裡作為主體的子句稱主要子句。主要子句可以獨立而成一意義完整的句子。若句子的意思不能獨立且需依附在

主要子句才能完整表達意思者稱為附屬子句。從屬子句通常由附屬連接詞所引導。

▶I believe that the boy is innocent.
我相信那男孩是無辜的。

▶I know a man who always helps the poor.
我知道一位總是幫助窮人的男士。

▶I knew him when I was a child.
我還是孩子時就認識他。

1. 從屬子句的種類及功能

1 名詞子句：在句子裡當作名詞功用的子句稱之。可當句子中的主詞、動詞、介詞受詞、補語及同位語等。

▶That the earth is round is true.
地球是圓的，是真的。

▶I don't know where she was born.
我不知道她在哪出生。

▶Our attending the meeting depends on whether it is fine tomorrow.
我們出席會議與否，視明天天氣而定。

▶My opinion is that he is innocent.
我的意見是，他是無辜的。

▶The reason that they did not come here yesterday is quite clear.
昨天他們沒來的原因是再明顯也不過的了。

2 形容詞子句：在句子裡相當於形容詞作用的子句稱之。形容詞子句都由關係代名詞及關係副詞所引導。

▶The boy who is sleeping is my cousin.
睡覺中的孩子是我的表（堂）兄弟。

▶He told me the news which was not true.
她告訴我的消息是假的。

▶ This is the spot where I lost my watch.
　這是我丟掉手錶的地點。

3 副詞子句：在句子裡用來修飾動詞、形容詞或其他副詞的子句稱
　之。

　▶ You stay here until I come back.
　　你在這待到我回來。

　▶ The little girl is afraid when it thunders.
　　小女孩在打雷時很害怕。

　▶ He runs faster than I do.
　　他跑得比我快。

◆比較 I know where she lives.　我知道她住在哪。（名詞子句）
　　　I know the place where she lives.
　　　我知道她住的地方。（形容詞子句）
　　　I will go where she lives.　我會去她住的地方。（副詞子句）

● **句子的種類：**依結構，句子可分為簡單句、集合句、複合句及混合
　　　　　　　　句四種。

1. 簡單句（S + V），只有一個主要句子所形成，不含其他形式子句的句子稱之

　▶ Time is money.　時間是金錢。
　▶ Time and tide wait for no one.　歲月不待人。

> 小提醒
>
> (A)複合主詞是兩個或兩個以上的名詞連接而成而當作一個
> 　主詞；複合動詞是由數個動詞連結而成。若句子是複合
> 　主詞加複合動詞所組成，就結構而言，仍屬簡單句。
> 　The boys and girls sang and danced all night.
> 　男孩女孩們又唱又跳。

2. 集合句（S＋V＋and／but／or...＋S＋V），有兩個或兩個以上的主要子句連結而成的句子

▶ The sun came out and the grass dried.
　太陽升起小草枯萎。

▶ Wool is warm, but silk is beautiful.
　羊毛是溫暖的，但絲綢是美麗的。

▶ Hurry up, or you will be late.
　快點，否則你就要遲到了。

▶ Mary sang, Jack danced, and they both had a good time.
　Mary唱歌，Jack跳舞，他們兩人玩得很開心。

3. 複合句，由一個主要子句及一個或數個從屬子句所組成

▶ I don't know the place where she comes from.
　我不知道她出身的地方。

▶ Though she is poor, she is honest.
　她雖窮，但她誠實。

▶ When you meet a new word, write it down lest you should forget it.
　當你遇到了一個新字，把它寫下以免忘記。

◆比較 Being tired, I went to bed early.
　　　 累了，我提早上床睡覺。（簡單句）
　　　 ＝ I was tired, so I went to bed early.
　　　 我累了，所以我提早上床睡覺。（集合句）
　　　 ＝ As I was tired, I went to bed early.
　　　 我提早上床睡覺因為我累了。（複合句）

4. 混合句，在集合句中的任何一個或每一個對等子句中，另外含有從屬子句的句子

▶ Billy cried but Tom laughed because he is happy.
　Billy大哭可是Tom卻因快樂而笑。

▶ Mary told me that she had visited Edward, but she did not mention his illness.
　Mary告訴我她去看Edward，但是她沒告訴我他生病的事。

▶ I will help you only if when it is necessary, but you have to do your work yourself.

我會在必要時幫你，可是你一定要自己做自己的工作。

● **句子的功用：** 可分為敘述句、疑問句、祈使句及感嘆句。

1. 敘述句是用以說明事實的句子，句尾要用句點「．」；其公式為：S + V

▶ You will be sorry if you do so.

如果你如此做，你會後悔的。

▶ Except me, all my family went to the movies last night.

除了我之外，我家人昨晚都去看電影。

▶ There comes a knocking on the door.

有人敲門。

▶ Never had I seen such a beautiful girl.

我從沒見過如此漂亮的女孩。

> 🎧 小提醒
>
> 若句子是以here / there開始時，要用倒裝：
>
> ▶ Here comes the bride!
>
> 新娘來了！
>
> ▶ There goes our chance to win the game.
>
> 我們贏得比賽的機會飛了。

2. 疑問句是用以詢問事情的句子，其主詞要置於動詞或助動詞後，句尾要加問號「？」

▶ Is he an honest man or a liar?

他是老實人還是騙子？

▶ Do you have anything to do today?

你今天有任何事要做嗎？

▶ Does she object to your going abroad?

她反對你出國嗎？

▶ May I go now?

我能走了嗎？

▶ What is the man doing?

那個人在做什麼？

▶ Where is your father?

你父親在哪？

▶ Who visited you yesterday?

昨天誰來看你？

▶ What made you so angry?

什麼事讓你生氣？

🔊 小提醒

一般疑問句（不用疑問詞且用yes / no回答）

▶ Do you like the movies you saw last night?

你喜歡昨晚看的電影嗎？

Wh-問句（帶疑問詞不用yes / no回答）

▶ Where does he live? 他住在哪？

3. 祈使句用來表達命令、請求、勸告、禁止等，句尾用句點或驚嘆號「！」。肯定時用V原形 + ...或be動詞 + 形容詞；否定時用Don't / Never +V原形或Don't be + 形容詞

▶ Study hard. 用功讀書。

▶ Be quiet, please! 請安靜！

▶ Don't make a noise. 別製造噪音。

▶ Don't flatter me. 別拍我馬屁。

（以上主詞為第二人稱）

▶ Let us take a walk.　我們去散步。

▶ Don't let them wait too long.

= Let them not to wait too long.　別讓他們等太久。

（以上主詞為第一 / 第三人稱）

4. 感嘆句用來表達驚訝、高興、悲傷或讚美等句子，句尾用驚嘆號「！」

▶ What a good student he is!

= How good a student he is!

他真是個好學生！

● 附加問句

1. 基本原則：肯定的敘述用否定的附加問句，否定的敘述用肯定的附加問句

▶ Peter is very happy in his job, isn't he?

Peter在他工作上很快樂，不是嗎？

▶ Jack isn't happy in his job, is he?

Jack在他工作上不快樂，是吧？

2. 附加問句的動詞變化

敘述句	附加問句
be V	be V
V（一般）	do / does / did
動詞片語	第一個助動詞
have	have（助動詞）
	do（本動詞）
had to	did
had better	had

▶ He is a diligent worker, isn't he?
他是個勤勉的工作者，不是嗎？

▶ She works very hard, doesn't she?
她工作很努力，不是嗎？

▶ Your homework has been finished, hasn't it?
你的功課作完了，沒有嗎？

▶ You had better go if you want to be there on time, hadn't you?
如果你要準時到那，最好走吧，好嗎？

▶ You had better not stay here, had you?
你最好別待在這裡，好嗎？

▶ He had to help you, didn't he?
他一定得幫你，不是嗎？

3. 附加問句的主詞變化

敘述句	附加問句
there	there
these / those + n（複數）	they
this / that / Ving / to +V（原形）	it
非人稱的單數名詞	it
名詞	代名詞
代名詞	代名詞

▶ There is someone in the room, isn't there?
屋裡有人，不是嗎？

▶ These are good books, aren't they?
這些是好書，不是嗎？

▶ Studying English is not easy, is it?
讀英文不容易，不是嗎？

▶ Mary is charming, isn't she?
　 Mary很迷人，不是嗎？

4. 祈使命令的附加問句變化

敘述句	附加問句
Let's （提議）	shall we?
Let us （請求）	will you?
Let me （請求）	will you?
Let's not	all right / OK?
V（原形）	will you?

▶ Let's go, shall we?
　 我們走，好嗎？

▶ Let us go, will you?
　 讓我們走，好嗎？

▶ Let me try the machine next time, will you?
　 下次讓我試那機器，好嗎？

▶ Let's not tell him about the news, all right?
　 我們別告訴他那消息，好嗎？

▶ Pass me the salt, will you?
　 把鹽遞給我，好嗎？

▶ Have a glass of water, won't you?
　 喝杯水，好嗎？

● **五大基本句型：** 依動詞及物與否，所有句型應用都是由五種基本句型所衍生而成。

1. S + Vi（完全不及物動詞；本身意思完整不需受詞或補語）

▶ Flowers bloom.　花開。

▶Birds fly.　鳥飛。

由此基本句型所衍生的應用。

S + Vi + adv.

▶Flowers bloom beautifully.　花開得漂亮。
▶Birds fly high in the sky.　鳥高高地飛在天上。

There + Vi + 介詞片語

▶There is a lamp on the desk.　桌上有盞燈。

S + Vi + 介詞 + 受詞

▶He looks at me.　他看著我。
▶He insisted on seeing the new product first.
　他堅持先看到新產品。

S + Vi + to + V原形

▶He stopped to take a rest.　他停止去休息。
▶She will remember to mail the letter.　她將會記得寄信。

2. S + Vi + S / C（不完全不及物動詞；因動詞本身不能表達完整的意思，所以需要主詞補語）

▶I feel hungry.　我覺得餓。
▶The man is a doctor.　這人是醫生。
▶Lemons taste sour.　檸檬嚐起來酸。

本句型通常與be動詞（am、are、is、was、were），感官動詞（taste、smell、sound、look、feel）或感覺動詞（seem、appear）及如：become、come、go、get、grow、run、turn、fall、remain、continue、stay等動詞連用。

▶ They are good friends.
他們是好朋友。

▶ The cake looks delicious.
這蛋糕看起來很可口。

▶ It became so dark that one thought it might rain.
天變得如此的黑，以至於讓人覺得要下雨。

3. S + Vt + O（完全及物動詞；動詞後需受詞才能使句意完整）

▶ We learn English.　我們學英文。

▶ Thank you very much.　非常謝謝你。

▶ I shall have a good time there.　我將會在那玩得很快樂。

此句型後所接受詞可能會是名詞、代名詞、不定詞、動名詞、名詞片語或名詞子句。

▶ I finished my report last night.
我昨晚完成我的報告。

▶ The result of the exam disappointed me.
考試結果讓我失望。

▶ The rich should help the poor.
富人該幫窮人。

▶ My car needs repairing.
我的車需要修理。

🎧 小提醒

▶I hope to meet you again in the future.
我希望未來能再見到你。

▶I don't know what to do.
我不知要做什麼。

▶Do you know where John lives?
你知道John住在哪嗎？

4. S + Vt + I / O（間接受詞）+ D / O（直接受詞）（此句型中的完全及物動詞後需加兩個受詞意思才會完整）

▶Mary bought her mother a purse.　Mary給她媽媽買了個皮包。
▶Tell me what he said.　告訴我他說什麼。

🎧 小提醒

當間接受詞和直接受詞的位置對調時，應加適當的介系詞。

▶The sun gives us light and heat.
= The sun gives light and heat to us.
太陽給我們光和熱。

▶I will buy you a book.
= I will buy a book for you.
我將為你買本書。

▶He asked me a question.
= He asked a question of me.
他問我個問題。

▶Jack palyed his friends a joke.
= Jack played a joke on his friends.
Jack開他朋友們玩笑。

🔊 小提醒

(A) 動詞，如：pay、give、lend、send、show、offer、tell、sell、teach、write、bring、deliver與to連用。

(B) 動詞，如：buy、choose、make、leave、get、order與for連用。

(C) 動詞，如：ask與of連用。

(D) 動詞，如：play與on連用。

5. S + Vt + O + O / C（本句型的完全及物動詞除受詞外，還需加受詞補語意思才能完整）

▶ We chose the wise man our leader.
我們選這位智者當我們的領袖。

▶ I found the book interesting.
我發覺這本書有趣。

▶ John had his car repaired by the mechanic.
John要機械師修他的車。

🔊 小提醒

此句型中的受詞補語可以是名詞、形容詞、不定詞或分詞。

▶ We elected him our president.
我們選他當我們的總統。

▶ I found the test easy.
我覺得測驗簡單。

▶ He asked me not to go with her.
他要求我不要和她去。

▶ I heard somebody talking in the other room.
我聽到有人在另一間房間說話。

▶ I need to have my hair cut.
我需要剪頭髮。

see、hear、feel、keep、leave、find、catch、make、have及get等動詞若表示主動時用現在分詞，表示被動則用過去分詞。

■ **實用測驗**

1. Mary is going to have her hair _____.

   ① 1. do ② to do ③ did ④ done

2. I felt somebody _____ me.

   ① touch ② to touch ③ touched ④ had touched

3. He told us _____.

   ① not to go ② not go ③ to not go ④ not go to

4. The speaker found himself _____ all alone.

   ① leave ② to leave ③ leaving ④ left

5. Canned foods do not go _____ easily.

   ① spoil ② to spoil ③ spoiled ④ spoiling

6. She found her money _____.

   ① steal ② to steal ③ stole ④ stolen

7. He sat there _____ a book.

   ① read ② to read ③ reading ④ reads

8. It began to _____ dark.

   ① make ② let ③ have ④ grow

9. I didn't enjoy the movie because I _____.

   ① was boring ② bore ③ was bored ④ was born

10. I don't need a beauty queen in the office; a girl who looks _____ will do.

    ① presentable ② comfortable ③ convenient ④ essential

11. _____ is unknown to me.

    ① Where he is ② Where is he ③ He is where ④ Is he where

12. Smoking, _____ is bad habit, is nevertheless very popular among youngsters.

    ① which ② that ③ thought ④ it

13. He worked so hard _____ to go home.

    ① that forgot ② he forgets ③ that he forgets ④ that he forgot

14. I didn't come yesterday _____.

    ① because I am ill ② because of I was ill ③ because of illness ④ because I illed

15. My sister had her watch _____ last night.

    ① repair ② to repair ③ repaired ④ be repairing

■ 試題解析

1. ④ have + 事物 + p.p.。

2. ① feel + 受詞 +V原形。

3. ① tell + 人 + (not) to +V原形。

4. ④ find oneself + p.p.：發現自己在…狀況中。

5. ③ go = become，後加形容詞；過去分詞較現在分詞來得更恰當。

6. ④ find + 事物 + p.p.。

7. ③ 現在分詞當主詞補語。

8. ④ let, make及have都是使役動詞，其後加原形動詞；grow後加形容詞。

9. ③ 用過去分詞表示情緒感受。

10. ① 根據題義選①是最恰當的答案；beauty queen：美人。

11. ① 名詞子句當主詞。

12. ① 關係代名詞的形容詞子句。

13. ④ so + adj. / adv. + that + S + V；副詞子句。

14. ③ because of + 名詞；because + 子句。

15. ③ have + 事物 + p.p.：被動語態。

筆記頁

筆記頁

筆記頁

筆記頁

國家圖書館出版品預行編目資料

超簡單英文文法速成／李普生著.─初版.─臺
北市：書泉,2013.12
　　面：　公分
　ISBN 978-986-121-875-5（平裝）
　1.英語　2.語法
805.16　　　　　　　　　　102021597

3AG0

超簡單英文文法速成

作　　　者 ― 李普生(81.7)

發 行 人 ― 楊榮川

總 編 輯 ― 王翠華

主　　編 ― 朱曉蘋

執行編輯 ― 吳雨潔

封面設計 ― 吳佳臻

出 版 者 ― 書泉出版社

地　　　址：106台北市大安區和平東路二段339號4樓

電　　　話：(02)2705-5066　傳　　真：(02)2706-6100

網　　　址：http://www.wunan.com.tw

電子郵件：shuchuan@shuchuan.com.tw

劃撥帳號：01303853

戶　　　名：書泉出版社

總 經 銷：朝日文化

進退貨地址：新北市中和區橋安街15巷1號7樓

TEL：(02)2249-7714　　FAX：(02)2249-8715

法律顧問　林勝安律師事務所　林勝安律師

出版日期　2013年12月初版一刷

定　　　價　新臺幣380元